ONE CANDLE BURNING

By the same author

CATHERINE GAVIN

ONE CANDLE
BURNING

HarperCollins*Publishers*

HarperCollins*Publishers*
77–85 Fulham Palace Road,
Hammersmith, London w6 8jb

Published by HarperCollins*Publishers* 1996
1   3   5   7   9   8   6   4   2

A catalogue record for this book
is available from the British Library

ISBN 0 246 13589 1

Set in Palatino by
Rowland Phototypesetting Limited
Bury St Edmunds, Suffolk

Printed and bound in Great Britain by
Caledonian Book Manufacturing Ltd, Glasgow

To Rivers Scott

1

The mail coach came into Reims an hour late on the last night but one of 1799. The horses put between the shafts at Soissons had slowed down when the snow came on and the road turned into a slough of mud. The two men on the box had wound so many shawls and scarves round their shoulders that they were mere hillocks of cloth and worsted in the darkness, feebly lit by the side lamps. The coachman drove by a sense of touch alone; the other man's freezing fingers were stiff on the horse pistol he carried.

The mail coach seated ten, but the passengers were only four in number, for people were unwilling to travel in these troubled times, although the French Revolution was officially over and the country was now governed by a Consulate. Years of insecurity, suspicion and legalized murder could not be forgotten in a matter of weeks. Strangers meeting in public said as little as possible about themselves or their affairs. Two of the travellers in the coach were businessmen on their way home to Reims, but they had carried the details of their business in their heads and just enough money in their pockets to pay their travel expenses. There were bandits on the roads of France as much to be dreaded as the guillotine. The third man was not in uniform, but there was something decidedly military about his double-caped greatcoat and his top boots. Also he had a black patch over the left eye and a badly puckered cheek, which seemed to indicate a recent wound. More and more Frenchmen wore patches or slings or walked with sticks since the campaigns of Napoleon Bonaparte began.

He was accompanied by his wife, who was pale and slender, and dressed in deep mourning.

It was his words to her, following on a shout from the coachman, which broke the silence inside the vehicle.

'Look, Marie! Those are the lights of Reims!'

'Thank heaven!' said one of the other men, peering out of the snow-dabbled window. There were only feeble lights to be seen, but they marked the direction of streets and the existence of tenanted houses, so that the coachman whipped up his weary horses and blew a note on his post horn which saluted the sign of The Golden Lion and the end of their journey.

They were welcomed by an outburst of noise: the shouts of ostlers come for the horses, the demands of postal clerks come for the mail carried in the padlocked *fourgon*, and the clamour of the porters come for the passengers. There was somewhere, floating across the dark inn yard, the sound of male voices uplifted in song. The two businessmen, who expected to be met, jumped up at once, and one of them was fumbling for the latch when he remembered his manners and made way for the lady.

'Thank you,' she said, 'please go on, we must wait for our baggage. *Bon voyage, messieurs!*'

Sounds of activity on the roof indicated that an army valise, a lady's portmanteau and two heavy boxes were being hauled down an iron ladder to the ground, and the one-eyed man prepared to follow them.

'Wait, Charles, let me go first!' exclaimed his wife. 'Remember there are two steps down! Wait, they're bringing lights –'

He missed the first step, tripped on the second, and fell against his wife with his full weight. She might have been knocked into the snowy yard, but she had been half-expecting the stumble and was braced against it. As it was, she was sufficiently knocked off balance for her shoes to be full of snow before she got her left arm round her husband just as a man carrying a lamp shouted, 'Take your time!' A formula which she knew Charles Latour had come to hate since he was wounded in the storming of Jaffa.

2

'We're quite all right,' she said. 'Show us the way indoors. We have a reservation – Colonel and Madame Latour.'

'Enchanted, citizeness,' said the man, tilting the lamp to show an open door. 'We were afraid you had met with trouble on the road. This way, if you please.'

He ushered them into a lobby where a bright fire was burning, and a young porter came forward to take their wraps. The older man announced that he was Grignon, the innkeeper. 'Joseph,' he said to the servant, 'go and tell Marthe to hurry with the hot wine. Our guests are frozen.'

'Hot wine sounds wonderful,' said Madame Latour. She took off her bonnet and shook it clear of snow. The ends of her short fair hair were wet and limp against her cheeks. She murmured her appreciation as a pretty little maid offered steaming glasses of hot mulled wine.

'Marthe will show you to your bedroom and unpack for you –' said Grignon.

Colonel Latour cut in, 'No hurry. She may show us to the salon I reserved by letter – and bring wine for three people, good and hot.'

Monsieur Grignon bit his lip.

'I'm sorry to say the reservations have been cancelled,' he said. 'The officers of a regiment returning from Holland have requisitioned every room in The Golden Lion for tonight. I locked the bedroom reserved for you against them, but they're sleeping four to a chamber everywhere else in the inn. A thousand apologies, *mon colonel* . . .'

His apologies were drowned in the protests of Charles Latour, of which 'monstrous' and 'scandalous' were the least offensive. The innkeeper turned with relief to the lady.

'It really is awkward,' she said soothingly. 'We expect a guest this evening whom we would prefer to receive formally and not in our bedroom.'

'I quite understand, madame.'

The innkeeper, like everyone else in France, was divided between the revolutionary 'citizen' and the autocratic 'sir' and 'madame' which the Consulate had just brought back into

3

use. This girl, whose quiet authority was more impressive than her husband's bluster, was obviously to be called 'madame'.

'Does your friend dine with you?' he asked.

'My guest is a stranger,' said Latour. 'He is the commissioner of the Republic and he comes to see me on business.'

'I saw the late marquis,' said Grignon, 'in the year '80, when he last visited Vesle, and stopped here on his way going and coming. I saw you too, monsieur, and your elder brother, two lively lads as you were: do you remember your last visit to The Golden Lion, I wonder? You must have been . . .'

'Eight years old,' said Charles. 'I don't remember Reims, but I remember Vesle, and the villagers cheering poor Edouard as their future feudal lord. The feudal system ended in the Revolution, and my brother fell at Quiberon Bay.'

'So you inherited the title,' said Grignon.

Charles emptied the dregs of his wine on the stone floor, and shrugged. Marie gave a slight shake of her head as a warning that they had touched on a painful subject, and drew the attention of both men to her sodden shoes.

'Madame's feet are wet,' exclaimed the maid, who had hardly taken her eyes off the lady from Paris since her arrival.

'How'd you manage that, Marie?' asked her husband. 'You haven't been out in the snow.'

'I think I must have stepped into deep snow when we left the coach,' she said apologetically. 'I really would like to put on dry slippers before Monsieur Laguerre gets here. Which, if he is punctual, will be in a quarter of an hour from now.'

'Well, hurry up then; don't be all night about it!'

Her husband's sharp words were lost in Grignon's order to the porter to lend a hand to the waiters in the big dining room, and to the maid to show madame upstairs. He was inwardly reflecting that in spite of the bluster and the snubs, the Marquis de la Tour de Vesle relied on his wife: he didn't want to face Laguerre without her.

'This way, citizeness,' said Marthe, holding open a staircase door for the lady from Paris. 'If you'll please to give me your keys I'll unpack your bags for you. Joseph took them straight upstairs.'

The ancient Golden Lion had been built on two storeys, the upper of them being a corridor where all the doors stood open on bedrooms which gave ample proof that the inn had been requisitioned by the army. There were views of muddy over-coats, hats adorned with dingy feathers, sword belts and half-empty valises disengaging the acrid smell of sweat. The room at the far end of the corridor had indeed been locked against all-comers, but the key was still in the lock, presumably left by Joseph when he had carried up the Latours' baggage.

'No one can have been in here, the soldiers are all in the *salle*,' said the maid, anticipating Marie's complaints, 'and your bags are locked anyway. What a lot of luggage you have! Are you *émigrés*?'

'No, we are not,' said Marie.

She had no intention of explaining the Latours to a servant, and handed over the keys to her portmanteau with a word of thanks for the magnificent fire and the ewer full of hot water.

'*Le patron* insists on good fires,' said the girl. 'One thing we aren't short of is firewood. Not as short as we are of food tonight.'

'Short of *food*?'

'You hungry?' said Marthe. 'Don't worry. There's a beef-steak and rabbit pie locked up for you in the larder. The soldiers are getting rabbit pie as well as their own rations. Poor fellows, no wonder they're hungry after all that fighting in Holland. Are those the shoes you want, citizeness?'

'No, I'm sorry. I should have told you, they're right at the bottom of the portmanteau. Will you give me a pair of stock-ings from the top tray?'

She sat down to put the black silk stockings on, very con-scious of the maid's look of appraisal. *Silk* stockings: that was what Marthe had expected of a lady from Paris, who so far had been a disappointment. When her overcoat was off she was very plainly dressed in a black merino gown with a high

5

neck and long sleeves, no sash and no fillet round the fair hair, now, in the warm room, fluffing and almost curling against her cheeks. She failed to understand the tact which caused Marie to dress in mourning on her first visit to her father-in-law's estate. She thought the poor woman had caught cold on the journey and ought to be cheered up.

'Would you like another drink, or a drop of brandy?' she asked abruptly, and was surprised when the lady – the *citoyenne* – refused politely, and asked, 'How old are you, Marthe?'

'I'm fifteen.'

Marie Latour was twenty-five, and was now made aware for the first time that she was no longer a member of the younger generation. She had been amused by this young girl's familiarity, so unlike the demeanour of the servants in the inns along the road travelled last October from Fréjus to Paris. True, there had been very little service in those inns when everyone was out cheering and trying to see General Napoleon Bonaparte.

'Thanks for your help, Marthe, and for making the room so comfortable,' she said. 'I must go downstairs now.'

'If you give me your husband's keys I can unpack for him too,' volunteered the maid. 'I'll be coming up again to put a warming pan in your bed.'

She didn't mean to be forward or impertinent, Marie felt; she was just a cheery, confident little French girl of the post-Revolutionary days. Not like the nervous teenagers who had shared Marie's national service, sewing shirts for the army, but then their national workshop had been only ten minutes' walk from the great square where the blade of the guillotine rose and fell inexorably all day and every day.

She said with a smile, 'Thank you, but I think Colonel Latour prefers to keep his keys in his own pocket.'

'As you please,' said Marthe, and then, as a burst of melody came upstairs: 'They're singing again, so the wine is going round. Don't worry, *citoyenne*, they won't keep it up too late. The officers will have to get their men up early to take the road for Châlons.'

'Where are the men?'

'In the town barracks – officially.'

The girl's wink implied that some soldiers might take the risk of slipping out to see if Reims had kindlier beds to offer than a pallet in a barracks.

Marie smiled and said nothing while Marthe held the bedroom door open, and even dropped a curtsy.

An oil lamp had been lighted above a mirror in the corridor next to a staircase window. It showed the yard, which had been crowded less than an hour ago, and where a thin coating of ice now lay over the snow. The choral singing had ended, like the thump of wine flagons on the dining tables, and a single voice, a fine baritone, took up Chénier's *'Chant du Retour'* – 'The Return Song', which would, of course, please men on their way back from the wars.

The Directory had organized a celebration of Napoleon Bonaparte's series of victories over the Austrians in Italy, and in the eyes of Marie Latour, who had loved him in secret for years, the snowy inn yard became the great square of the Luxembourg. In her imagination she saw the dais, with the Directors and their ministers in flamboyant robes as the background to a small figure in shabby army blue.

She was too firm in the habit of self-command to sob or shed a tear. She became aware that the innkeeper was coming up to say something about Commissioner Laguerre's arrival and she allowed him to usher her down the narrow stair and into his business room. It held a locked desk, a letter file, a calendar, and a proclamation, nailed to the wall opposite the door, signed with the name near to Marie's heart: BONAPARTE.

It was a bright room, lighted by six wax candles and the flames of one of Grignon's roaring fires. There was a solid oak table, on which lay a huge iron key in a leather wallet, beside a jorum of hot wine. Her husband and a stranger sat on either side of the table with glasses in their hands.

Charles stood up when Marie entered and drew out a chair for her; the stranger remained seated. Not so long ago a commissioner of the Republic had inspired terror: Commissaire Laguerre was not an alarming figure in the vestiges of his official uniform. He had laid aside his cloak, and under his jacket he wore an embroidered vest without insignia and a tricolore sash. In his hat, which he did not remove, was the official tricolore cockade. His distinguishing feature was a birthmark at the corner of his upper lip, a splash of red which twisted his mouth into a permanent sneer.

'Madame Latour, may I present Monsieur Laguerre,' said Charles Latour, and the ugly mouth seemed to sneer at the formality.

'Sit down, citizeness,' said Laguerre, without raising his eyes from a sheaf of official papers. 'You are Marie Madeleine Latour, born Fontini, residing with your spouse, here present, at 17 Quai Voltaire, Paris?'

'My maiden name was not Fontini, but Fontaine,' said Marie. 'F-o-n-t-a-i-n-e.'

With a grunt which sounded like 'Those clerks!' Laguerre laid down the papers and gave her an appraising look. He took in the black dress, the absence of all ornament, the dark blue eyes, and the fair head shaken in a silent negative to Latour's offer of a glass of wine.

'You chose bad weather for your journey, citizens,' said Laguerre. 'What made you set out in December?'

'I was anxious to get on to Vesle,' said Charles Latour. 'More than two months had passed since I got the news, in Egypt, of my father's death.'

'You were wounded in Egypt, *mon colonel*?'

'Actually in Syria, at the siege of Jaffa, which was part of the campaign in Egypt.'

'Of which General Bonaparte made an unbelievable mess,' said Laguerre, and Marie said sharply, 'Very few of us who were with him in Egypt would agree with you!'

'You – you were in Egypt, citizeness? You were one of the devoted women who accompanied their husbands on a campaign doomed to disaster from the start? I hardly know whether to praise or pity you.'

'Madame Latour was in Egypt on active service,' said her husband. 'She worked in the Pharmaceutical Section of the French Institute. And we both owe a great deal to General Bonaparte, who brought us back to France with him when he returned last October.'

'Leaving his Egyptian army in the lurch. You're very loyal, Colonel Latour.'

'I was one of his ADCs from his Italian campaign onwards.'

Referring to the dossier: 'Yes, that is noted here,' said Laguerre. 'What is not noted is your wife's scientific prowess. Pray, citizeness,' turning to Marie, 'what did you *do* in the Pharmaceutical Section?'

'I was an assistant in Professor Royer's laboratory at Nasriya,' said Marie briefly.

'Doing what?'

'Preparing medicine for use in our Cairo hospital, and in Dr Larrey's Flying Ambulance Service.'

'Treating what?'

'Ophthalmia and syphilis were the most frequent complaints,' said Marie.

'I never heard of such a thing!' cried Laguerre. He was genuinely shocked. He had heard venereal disease spoken of by loose women, but never by an *aristo*, which was what he supposed she called herself. 'It was most unsuitable work for a woman.'

'So I've been told,' said Marie. 'Come, *Monsieur le Commissaire!* We haven't met to discuss army medicine but the restoration of my husband's property, forfeit to the Republic some years ago ... Is that the key of the château?'

Laguerre shook his head.

'I've been doing my best to explain to Citizen Latour,' he said, 'that his restored property is not a château as the term was understood before the Revolution – the residence of a so-called aristocrat. This is the key of the old Tour de Vesle, all that was left standing after the Duke of Brunswick's Prussian troopers invaded France in 1792, followed by your *émigré* father's devoted peasantry, eager to grab their own share of the Rights of Man. The Tower, which is just not quite a ruin, attracted no purchasers when it was put up for sale as National Property.'

'But it is habitable, we were assured,' said Marie, seeing that her husband was speechless.

'It is wind- and watertight,' said Laguerre. 'I don't suppose you'll want to inhabit it for long.'

'That is for us to decide,' said Marie, and Laguerre bowed.

'Monsieur the Faithful Aide-de-Camp,' he said to Charles, 'I'm afraid General Bonaparte did not give you a detailed picture of your family's inheritance when he sponsored your request for repossession.'

'He had a great many other things on his mind last November.'

'Ah yes, the famous *coup d'état*. But you were in attendance upon the general at St Cloud, no doubt?' said Laguerre.

'I was taken to hospital at Val-de-Grâce as soon as we returned to Paris.'

'By Bonaparte's orders?'

'By Dr Berthollet's orders, who attended me from the time I was wounded at Jaffa.'

'But we know all the details of the *coup d'état*,' said Marie. 'They've been made public for all the world to know. Look behind you, *Monsieur le Commissaire*.'

Laguerre looked casually over his shoulder at the proclamation, signed in printed capitals BONAPARTE, that Marie had seen as soon as she came in.

'Oh that!' said Laguerre. 'I have a copy in my own office and there's another in the town hall – the general's version of what happened at St Cloud when the people's elected representatives called him an outlaw, and his brother Lucien saved the day for him when he whistled up the soldiers to hunt the Deputies out of the Palace.'

'Is that *your* version of how General Bonaparte became First Consul of the French Republic?' said Marie. 'Do you imply that there were others who had a better right to the title?'

'My own choice would have been General Masséna,' said

Laguerre. 'He won a famous victory over the Russians in Switzerland. Don't you agree?' he asked Charles Latour.

'I admired the victory, when I heard of it some time after it was won,' said Charles. 'I knew General Masséna in Italy. But you must forgive me, *Monsieur le Commissaire*. I've been out of touch with national affairs too long, first in Egypt and then in hospital, to engage in any kind of political debate with you.'

Laguerre took the hint. He muttered something about not wishing to start an argument, and slung his cloak round his shoulders. Charles picked up the key to the Tour de Vesle and put it in his pocket.

'Thank you for your visit, monsieur,' he said formally.

'I wish you good luck at Vesle,' said Laguerre, adjusting his tricolore sash. 'I only hope you may not have left hospital too soon. There is no doctor at Vesle, in fact none nearer than Reims, and of course no priest. The schoolmaster died in a skirmish with the Prussian invaders and was not replaced. Your future tenants are a wild, lawless lot, and will probably resent your arrival. Let me know how you get on and if I can be of any assistance. Unfortunately the troop at my command has been reduced since the rise to power of the First Consul ... Citizen Latour, citizeness, *au revoir*.'

'What a horrible little man!' exclaimed Marie, as soon as the door of the innkeeper's private room closed behind Laguerre.

'Don't shout it out,' said her husband. 'He's in the lobby with Grignon and can probably hear every word you say.'

'I hope he does.'

'Now you're being silly. There's no point in antagonizing the *commissaire de la République*.'

'For how long? Only till Napoleon replaces all the *commissaires* in France by his own prefect system. This man must be expecting it, since he admitted himself his troop had been reduced.'

'Marie, I wish you wouldn't pretend to know as much about politics as you do about pharmacy. You took care to let Laguerre know all about your work for the army medical services, while I would rather have heard him talk more about the situation I shall find at Vesle . . .'

Marie bit her lip. 'Did I talk too much?' she asked.

'You always do. Those doctors spoiled you at Nasriya. They locked you up and made you think you were a brilliant scientist, and Bonaparte completed the job on the voyage home – '

'Don't, Charles! I'm sorry. I didn't mean to make you angry. I'll do everything I can to help you when we get to Vesle.'

'He didn't paint a very encouraging picture of the place, did he?' Nervous apprehension forced the words from Charles Latour. 'No doctor, and a hostile peasantry . . .'

'Do you think we should go back to Paris and wait until the spring? It's only a week since you left hospital . . . and you lost your balance badly when we left the coach this evening.'

'The step was slippery with freezing snow. That loss of balance nonsense is one of Dr Berthollet's fads. But he discharged me as *bon pour le service* when I left Val-de-Grâce. I'm not going back to Paris now.'

They stared at one another, the old invisible wall of misunderstanding rising again between them. Into the angry silence came the sound of the door opening, the pleasant odour of a rabbit pie with garlic and carrots, and the voice of Monsieur Grignon.

'*Madame la Marquise*, shall I serve dinner now?'

2

Silence enveloped the town of Reims for the first few hours of New Year's Eve, but in The Golden Lion the silence was broken early by the sounds of men preparing for departure. Bedrooms were vacated to the noises of doors banging and valises dragged to the top of the stairs, raucous greetings exchanged between men in high spirits because they were beginning the last day of a long hard journey.

The noise woke Colonel Charles Latour, who was accustomed to it. He dressed in the dark and slipped out through the lighted house to the crowded courtyard where soldier-servants were loading the officers' luggage onto baggage carts.

Marie was still asleep. Tired by two days of coach travel, and by the bitter little scene with her husband, like so many prompted by his jealousy in Paris and Egypt, she slept dreamlessly until the shaded light of a lamp shone on her eyes and the anxious voice of Marthe, the chambermaid, said, 'Are you still asleep? I didn't think you would be with all this row going on! I brought you some tea.'

Marie was dazzled by the lamplight. She murmured, 'Tea?' disbelievingly. Then her senses steadied. She remembered The Golden Lion – New Year's Eve, the day of Vesle – and she smiled.

'Thank you, Marthe,' she said, and raised herself on her elbow to take the cup. 'What time is it?'

'The soldiers are supposed to leave at seven,' said the girl, 'and they haven't left yet. The bakeries don't open till half-past seven, and you'll get coffee downstairs then. I think you'll like that better than tea, won't you?'

'Tea's very nice,' said Marie, gallantly attempting a second sip of the tepid, bitter brew. 'Marthe, I must get up.'

'There's no hurry. Citizen Laguerre told *le patron* last night it wasn't safe for you, and he was talking to Colonel Latour about it after he came downstairs.'

'Is my husband downstairs now?'

'He's outside with the soldiers.'

'I must hurry.'

When she swung her long legs out of bed Marie consulted her little Breguet watch on its stand on the dressing table. It registered twenty minutes past seven. It was not really cold in the bedroom, for there were hot cinders in the grate, but she felt for a shawl in her portmanteau. It was the same shawl she had worn in the first access of seasickness on the voyage to Egypt, aboard the flagship which Nelson had later sent to the bottom of Aboukir Bay with nearly the whole of Napoleon's invasion fleet.

Marthe had left the lamp, and by its light Marie drew the heavy curtains and looked out of the window. It commanded a view of the courtyard, now thronged with men and lit by torches, and she saw her husband, talking animatedly to a man wearing colonel's insignia. Charles's wounded cheek was hidden. In the flickering torchlight nothing was revealed but the great good looks which five years earlier had helped to urge her into an impetuous marriage. Even now the sight of him, so keen and interested, roused her pity. How pleased he is, she thought, to be back with troops again!

Monsieur Grignon was in his office when Marie went downstairs, setting the table for breakfast. It was his pride to have spread it with a fresh checked tablecloth instead of the damask of the evening before, and he noted Marie's appreciative glance. Poor girl, when would she breakfast on fresh rolls and eat off white china in a savage place like Vesle?

'Good morning, madame,' he said. 'I'll tell the colonel that you're ready, shall I?'

'I can wait,' said Marie. 'I think he's enjoying himself with the officers.'

'Better drink your coffee while it's hot,' said Grignon, pouring a cup full. 'The sergeants are bringing the men here from the barracks, and then the whole battalion will leave for Châlons.'

'And we must be on our way too,' said Marie.

She sat down on the chair Grignon had pulled out for her, added hot milk to her coffee and took the first restorative sip.

'Monsieur Grignon, tell me something. Are there any shops in Vesle?'

'There's a wine shop, a rough-and-ready sort of place, where they sell groceries from Épernay when anybody goes to fetch them –'

'Épernay?'

'The centre of the champagne trade, only five kilometres away.'

'I was going to ask if you could lend me a map of the district. Otherwise, no shops?'

'Other than the Tuesday market in the village square, no. But every Friday a cart leaves from Reims with fresh meat and bread and groceries, and sells them at the wine shop.'

Grignon hesitated. She looked so calm, sitting there drinking coffee and spreading butter and honey on a roll! He was afraid of saying too much, and upsetting her. But something must be said, and he took the plunge.

'The *commissaire de la République* suggested to me last night that you and your husband might consider postponing your journey until Friday and travelling to Vesle in the cart. That way you would have a bodyguard –'

'A bodyguard of butcher's boys?' She had flushed, and the innkeeper was not too distressed to note that it was becoming. 'I don't think the colonel – the marquis – would want to proceed to the home of his ancestors in a grocery cart!'

The man bowed in silence. He felt like saying, 'The marquis was fortunate not to proceed to the guillotine in a tumbril with his father and mother if they hadn't run away from France and he hadn't run away from home!' But he couldn't afford the luxury of saying that. In this troubled France, a day short of the new century, one never knew how things would turn out.

'Thank you, milady,' he said. 'I'll send my son to take your orders as soon as the soldiers have left. Excuse me now.'

She heard sounds outside the door which suggested that he had collided with Charles – as if Charles, with one of his miscalculations of distance, had stumbled against him, but mindful of his annoyance last night she said nothing about it when he came in. He was in high spirits, kissing her with lips cold from the frost out of doors, and then going to the window to look his last on the departing troops. They heard the stamp of feet and a strain of music, always popular, which was now heard everywhere that the First Consul appeared.

'They're the 4th Battalion of the 3rd Light Infantry,' said Charles Latour. 'I've been speaking to some of the officers.'

'I know, I saw you talking to the colonel. Come and have your coffee, you must be frozen.'

'The colonel's a very decent fellow. His name's Tavernier,' said Charles, sitting down. '... Brioches as well as rolls, splendid! Honey too ... I hope to fall in with Tavernier again.'

'How will you manage that? You'll be a long way from Chalon.'

'From *Châlons*?'

'We stopped at Chalon-sur-Saône when I went to Italy with Joséphine Bonaparte, and it's leagues from Reims.'

'Have you never heard of Châlons-sur-Marne, where the big army camp is? That Châlons isn't a day's march away.'

'Oh dear,' said Marie, 'the sooner I get hold of a map the better. I'm sorry,' she added, 'you know I wasn't properly educated.' This put her husband in a high good humour.

In which mood they finished breakfast, when the growing daylight reminded Marie that young Grignon would be coming for his orders.

'By the way,' replied Charles, falsely casual, 'I've been discussing our trip with Grignon.'

'And Laguerre has been discussing it with him. The idea!'

'Don't turn up your nose, Marie. There's a lot of sense in what Laguerre said.'

'What, about its being too dangerous for me?'

'Yes.'

'Grignon himself says there are no bandits on the roads in this area, and even if there were, the 4th Battalion of the 3rd Light Infantry will be on the road to protect us –'

'Get a map,' said Charles. 'They won't be on the same road. Marie, don't make it too hard for me! I hate leaving you behind. I wish to God I'd made you stay in Paris. But Napoleon said you ought to come to Vesle with me, so of course you took his words for gospel, you always do! Neither one of you thought what my feelings might be, but after all the Tower is *my* home, not yours –'

'Wait a minute,' she cut in. 'Too many people have become involved in this, and they're all talking at cross-purposes. Leave Napoleon out of it. This is between you and me, and *you* always said you wanted me to go to Vesle with you. Are you telling me now that you want to be alone when you meet your father's tenantry?'

'Not tenants now.'

'Well then, say alone when you visit the Tower for the first time?'

'Yes,' he said. 'Don't be angry. I would like to be alone then.'

'I can understand that.'

If she did, it was more than anyone else could say during the more than two hours over which the journey to Vesle was hotly debated in The Golden Lion. Young Robert Grignon, the son of *le patron*, while protesting his readiness to drive the citizens anywhere, contributed a few cautionary tales on the savagery of the Vesle natives. Servants who were shifting furniture to bring The Golden Lion back to its usual aspect put in their word, and about nine o'clock Marthe created a diversion by entering to say that she and Joseph had now prepared a private sitting room for the citizens if they proposed to remain in Reims. Possibly the pert girl took too much for granted, since Charles Latour presently announced his decision to go to Vesle at once, and alone, and to send Robert back next morning with a letter for Marie.

So she was smiling when the *carriole* drove off, loaded with the bedding and other household matters they had brought in their boxes. She pretended not to hear old Grignon's growl of, 'Bedding, perhaps, but will there be bedsteads?' She gratefully watched a sack of firewood being stacked with the other items 'just in case', and a provision of cold meat, bread and cheese for meals 'on the thumb'. Then Charles kissed her hand, climbed into the *carriole* and he and Robert were off.

After the hubbub of his departure, and the curiosity of the passers-by, staring at a one-eyed man, Charles Latour was glad when they were outside the town and past the junction of the road to Châlons-sur-Marne. The day was leaden under heavy clouds, but the little river Vesle, running alongside the highway for a short distance, had an encouraging sound. Robert Grignon told Charles the name of the singing water, and said it wound among the fields as far as the Tour de Vesle.

'The fields don't appear to be cultivated,' said Charles Latour, trying to look at the snow-covered landscape with a farmer's eye.

'This is the chalk country,' said Robert Grignon. 'The nearer we get to Épernay it's what's under the soil that matters most. My father deals with a man called Clicquot, who has the largest cellars of champagne in the district.'

'Presumably the vines grow on the surface?'

'Yes, we'll see them when we've gone a few more miles.'

Charles Latour reflected that he knew nothing about the *méthode champenoise* of wine-making, 'or much of anything but soldiering,' he said to himself. With that his thoughts went to Colonel Tavernier, now on the road to Châlons-sur-Marne, who hoped that Napoleon would give him what he called 'another crack at the Austrians.' If Charles Latour thought of Napoleon Bonaparte he thought of Marie Fontaine, as she had been when they first met, a girl of eighteen living in Paris and

18

working behind the counter in her uncle's pharmacy. Before he knew her, Sergeant Charles Latour of the National Guard had seen Marie and her uncle dining with Bonaparte (was he a captain then, or still a lieutenant?) and suspected that she was in love with him.

Bonaparte had become a general and married Joséphine de Beauharnais, but the suspicion still lingered and came to a head in Egypt. Once he had taxed Marie with it in self-defence, when she had come back unexpectedly to the rooms she occupied alone (not with him, oh no! not with her husband! Madame the great pharmacist lived in solitary grandeur) and found him, humiliatingly half-naked, in the arms of her little Arab maid. He had taunted her with Napoleon, and she had told him to get out . . .

Charles Latour, in the overloaded wagonette, bit his lips and looked sideways at the stolid face of his driver. Had he said anything, made any sort of jarring movement which had revealed the deep inner trouble which those memories always brought? There was no need for trouble, because Marie had forgiven him. Fully and freely, when he returned wounded, half-blinded from Jaffa, she had taken him back, helped him through the hospital days in Paris, supported him in his claim to Vesle –

What a blackguard he was to feel sometimes, oppressively, that Marie was entirely too good to be true!

He broke the silence by saying to young Grignon, 'Have you often been to Vesle?'

'Not very often, citizen. They're funny sort of folk in Vesle, and that's the truth. The kind of folk who got the Chalk people the name of being hard-headed and hard-hearted and they don't welcome strangers. Gee up, there!' with a crack of the whip. 'Last time I had a posting job there I took a man who wished he'd stayed in Reims.'

'Sounds alarming. What happened?'

'Well, it was like this, see? Some thin-skinned folk in Épernay – some of the champagne crowd – laid an information to Commissaire Laguerre about a crazy woman they said was loose in Vesle and insulting them when they drove by. Laguerre, he didn't want to get mixed up, but he asked Dr Tellier to go down and see into it, and maybe bring the woman back and clap her in the town asylum.'

'Pretty severe punishment. Had she been mad from birth, or what?'

'She went out of her mind when the grandson was killed, fighting with Bonaparte at Lodi Bridge.'

'Poor woman. I got a wound at Lodi Bridge myself.'

'Not your eye?'

'No, that was at Jaffa, more than two years later.'

'You've really been in the wars, haven't you, citizen? Do you think there'll be more war, now Bonaparte's the boss?'

'Bound to be. I suppose this man was his grandmother's sole support?'

'No, she lives with his sister – her granddaughter. Her name is Madame Collonge, though the whole village calls her Mémée. I thought she was a decent, quiet old woman, but she certainly can stir up trouble! Dr Tellier was mobbed when he went near her. Nearly every man in Vesle swore to have his guts if he laid a finger on Mémée, and they were all in the square armed with sticks and hoes and yelling like mad – '

'How did you get out of a mess like that?'

'Thanks to the blacksmith, Roger Marchais. He told me to drive the wagonette inside the smithy – I was afraid they were going to make it into a bonfire – and then, I don't know how, he persuaded Dr Tellier to say he was going back to Reims, and home we went with our tails between our legs ... Gee *up*, Hélène!'

While Robert gave all his attention to his team, Charles Latour digested the story of Mémée. Presently he asked the young man if that was why 'they' had said it wasn't safe for madame to accompany him to Vesle?

'I think so, yes,' was the honest answer. 'And saving your presence, citizen, I make bold to say you should wait a day or two before you go into the village. They don't like to be taken by surprise and if you were to turn up saying, "Hey there, I'm the marquis," there might be trouble. Seeing that your parents were – er –'

'Among the first to emigrate,' said Charles grimly. 'Well, I must go to the Tower and see what sort of state it's in. Then we'll see.'

Little more was said while they drove on to a crossroads where an almost illegible signpost indicated 'Vesle 2 km, Épernay 8 km' and 'Châlons-sur-Marne 10 km'. The third road, grass-grown and rutted, Robert Grignon said led to the Tour de Vesle. Try as he might, the lord of the land could remember nothing of his visit as a child to this barren landscape. They had seen rows of vines further back, but there was none here: there had once been a wood to act as screen for the Tower, but it had been cut down, presumably for firewood, and there had been a garden, but it had been devastated.

They saw the Tower long before they reached it, for it stood on rising ground. Four storeys high, with glazed windows on the first and second, and arrow slits on the third and fourth, it had a huge oaken door which looked ready to withstand an army of Prussian invaders, and above the door remained in crumbling stucco the coat of arms. Charles had never borne arms in that sense of the term; he had been too young before he ran away from home to throw in his lot with the Revolution, but of course he had seen them in the house in Versailles, which was now rubble, and he recognized the cockleshells which showed that one of his remote ancestors had gone on Crusade. He stood staring at the escutcheon with something like a lump rising in his throat, while Robert tactfully unloaded the wagonette. Then with an effort Charles turned the massive key in the lock and opened the door upon the past.

The past smelled of ashes, brandy and mouse droppings. Charles, with Robert Grignon at his back, stood in a large room where light filtered in through the dirty, barred window and down the wide chimney of the huge open fireplace. The walls, once covered with white paint, were now covered with graffiti extolling the Revolution and denouncing the royal family and the la Tours. There was only one piece of furniture in the room. Against the wall opposite the fireplace there stood the framework of a sofa or day bed, meant to hold cushions, on which a mattress, bursting at the seams, had at some time been flung. The top beam, made of oak, had been adorned with the carved escutcheon of the la Tour family. A knife held in a mischievous hand had hacked away all but one of the crusader's cockleshells.

'The place has been gutted,' said Charles, in a voice as hollow as the room.

'Except for this,' said Robert, kicking at the sofa, 'and they left it because it was too big to go into any house in the village.'

'It would have done for firewood. What's in here?'

He pushed at a door beside the fireplace, which opened on a stone-flagged room where the smell of mice was stronger than ever, and which a pump above a stone sink identified as the kitchen. Charles pulled the handle and a rusty trickle of water appeared. He eyed the fireplace over which hung an iron bar to hold pots and pans above the blaze. Primitive, he thought. No wonder my mother never came to Vesle. Not that I can imagine her cooking on any kind of stove, anywhere.

He remembered how, when he apologized to Marie for the antiquity of their kitchen in the rented apartment on the Quai Voltaire in Paris, she had laughed and told him that since her twelfth year she had cooked all the meals for her uncle and herself in pots slung on an iron bracket over a wood fire. She might be able to make a go of this contraption – if she were here.

Charles became aware, because of a draught on his cheek, that Robert had found the back door and beyond it a yard of sorts. He followed the boy outside, and found him gazing into a well surrounded by empty bottles and other rubbish.

Robert pointed out a rusty bucket wound up on a frayed rope. 'Will you risk a drink of well water, citizen?'

'Not I!' said Charles. 'That well must be cleaned, first thing.'

'Sounds as if you've made up your mind to stay,' Robert grinned.

'No,' Charles protested. 'I was thinking of Bonaparte in Syria. How we were under orders never to drink well water unless the well had been inspected and had the army's stamp on the lid.'

'He thought the water was dangerous?'

'He knew the Syrians were poisoning the wells.'

Robert Grignon dropped the subject of a campaign whose evil he could not contemplate. He said, 'Do you want to explore the rest of the Tower now, citizen? If you do I should blanket the horses and put on their nosebags.'

'You ought to have a nosebag for yourself,' said Charles. 'You know your way around Vesle. What I want you to do is go to the wine shop and make them give you a hot dinner; here's money to pay for it. You can bait your horses while you eat. Then come back here and by that time I may have made up my mind about what I'm going to do. You needn't tell the people at Vesle I'm here.'

He didn't want to be forced into playing the part of a Dr Tellier, hunted out of town! When he was alone he opened one of the packets of bread and cheese from The Golden Lion, and a flask of wine from which he filled the silver cup he had carried on campaign. The mattress on the sofa was an uncomfortable place of rest, and as soon as he had eaten Charles went up the narrow stair which wound from a corner of the room to the floor above. He did remember his father telling him it had been the principal bedroom, but there was no point in being sentimental about it; his father and mother had never slept at the Tower together. What he hoped to find in the extension room, the room above the kitchen, was some sort of sanitary installation or the possibility of one in the future. There was nothing, unless a chamber pot without a handle could be called that. It was standing on what appeared to be a coloured mat, on closer investigation proving to be the oil painting of a girl.

He knew the picture well, for the original had hung in

the grand salon of their Versailles house. 'Marie-Sabine de Polignac, 1763' said the inscription in gilt letters. It was his mother at eighteen, when she was engaged to his father. As a little boy he had loved the picture of a happy, pretty girl with dark eyes and light brown ringlets, in a pink satin dress with a tight bodice. This, the copy, had been disfigured by a brush laden with black paint, which had dashed a thick hussar moustache over the smiling mouth.

Charles felt himself trembling with rage. His impulse was to light a fire in the grate downstairs and destroy the travesty of his mother's picture. But that would leave traces, which would mean explanations, to whom he could not yet tell. The Marquis de la Tour de Vesle ran downstairs with the picture under his arm and out into the courtyard with the well.

He had seen already where the two wings of the Tower had been demolished but now he hurried beyond the yard to what appeared to be a stable smelling of dried manure, with stalls for three horses and space for one vehicle. He wrapped the picture in a jettisoned sack and thrust it deep in a hay rack. It wasn't a good place but would do for the time being. At least it got the thing out of the house.

Charles returned from the stable slowly, but his defective eyesight caused him to lose his balance as he passed the well. He fell heavily against the stone coping and his thigh was aching when he limped back into the house. He hauled the mattress off the sofa and sat down on the creaking slats. He felt very isolated in the silent Tower and wished young Grignon would come back.

He heard a cheerful whistle and the sound of wheels nearly an hour later. The boy was flushed, as if he had been drinking, but he looked very serious when he saw Charles Latour, and his first words were the hated, 'Are you all right?'

Ignoring this, Charles's greeting was, 'What news from the wine shop?'

'They're all in great form. Merrymaking for *le Jour de l'An*.'

Charles realized that he hadn't thought about New Year's Day since he heard the shouts of *Bonne Année* in the morning.

They were in the kitchen by this time, where Robert was taking two bottles out of his capacious pockets.

'I bought a litre of *vin rouge*,' he said. 'I'd have liked to buy some milk, but I thought they might wonder who it was for. I did get you some water from a clean well. I said I'd better mix my wine with water if I was going to drink it on the way back to Reims.'

'Very ingenious,' said Charles. 'Here are the clean glasses we brought with us – the wine I'll pay for – let's drink to the New Year.'

The *vin rouge* was rough and heady; it put new resolve in him. Confused as he was, Charles knew that he could come to no decision about the Tower until Marie had seen it.

'Robert,' he said, 'could you get a bed tonight at the wine shop?'

'Yes, I could.'

'You're sure of that?'

'I asked.'

'Oh, you did! You wouldn't mind joining in the merry-making, eh?'

'But what would you do, citizen?'

'Listen, Robert. Here's ten francs. You go back to Vesle. Say it's too late to start for Reims, have a good dinner and a good night's sleep, and be back here by eight o'clock tomorrow morning. Then either I'll go back with you or give you a letter for *madame la marquise*. Understood?'

'Ten francs is too much,' said the boy, to whom ten francs was a fortune. 'Besides, where would you sleep?'

'On the sofa.'

'On those wooden splints? Impossible.'

'In Italy General Bonaparte taught us how to bivouac. He rolled himself in his overcoat and lay on the ground beneath a cannon. I've done that many a time; I can do it again.'

When Robert drove away, the first shades of twilight were falling, and a rug from the wagonette had been spread over the naked slats of the sofa. At one end a lighted candle had been placed in an empty bottle and beside it a platter of food

25

and a glass of wine had been arranged. True to The Golden Lion's tradition, Robert had lit a fire in the empty grate, and the flames were keeping at bay the menacing shadows in the corners of the room.

The fire, the food and the improvised bed made a little island of comfort and civilization in the desolate place. The only thing lacking, thought her husband, was Marie. If she were here she would be spreading some of her soothing salve on the aching place where he had hurt himself on the coping of the well. As she had soothed his wounded cheek daily aboard the little ship in which they had travelled back to France with Napoleon. Following the emotional stresses of the day, the memory of the ship on the Mediterranean, in danger from the English, perhaps in danger from the French, swelled to prime importance in Latour's mind. He felt the lulling movement of the waves, and he slept.

He had told no one that he was going armed to Vesle, but when he was awakened by a loud knocking at the door Charles Latour felt for the army pistol in his right-hand pocket before he asked, 'Who's there?'

The candle had half burned down, the firewood too; the room was chilly as Charles crossed to the door and said again, 'Who's there?'

'Simon Marchais, the father of the Vesle blacksmith, your honour. Will you open the door?'

Against his better judgement, Charles drew the heavy bolt. A little old man stood outside, with white hair like a winter dandelion blowing round his forehead. He was turning his hat in his hands.

'I came to wish you a good New Year,' he said, 'and to tell you how pleased we all were to see lights in the Tower again.'

'How did you know it was I?' Charles managed to say, and the old man smiled.

'My son heard that you and her ladyship were expected at Reims,' he said, 'so when we saw the lights we guessed. Some of us will be up tomorrow to help you to get settled in. Good-night now, *Monsieur le Marquis*, and welcome home!'

As his footsteps died away Charles leaned against the door, still gripping the pistol in his pocket. The visitor from Vesle seemed like a dream, and the one spoken word he retained was the word 'lights'. He stared disbelieving at the solitary flame. One candle burning, and to the people of the Chalk, in their village, a lighted Tower!

3

There was very little 'merrymaking' for Marie Latour on New Year's Day. Ushered to the restored sitting room by the innkeeper himself, she noted its deficiencies in silence. The windows looked out on a dreary view of stables and other farm buildings. Indoors, against flowered wallpaper, were stiffly ranged a table and a sideboard, two easy and two upright chairs, and a small bookshelf containing copies of *Paul et Virginie* and *Manon Lescaut*, both of which she had read before.

To these novels was added a map of north-eastern France, depicted on cracked linen and marked with the thumbprints of two generations of postboys. The shores of the English Channel were indicated by sketches of dolphins and flying fish, and the distances between the Channel ports by a kilometrage that was highly imaginative. Grignon himself said it was not an accurate map. Soissons, for instance, was shown as practically a suburb of Reims while Marie knew by experience that nearly sixty kilometres separated the two towns.

It was the land round Vesle that interested her, however, and here the map-maker had been clear enough. The highway ran through Vesle to Épernay, with a side road from Épernay to Châlons-sur-Marne. Then from Châlons the road ran east to Verdun where the Duke of Brunswick's troopers had abandoned their invasion of France, and thence to the fortress of Metz, which Joséphine Bonaparte's first husband had been guillotined for his failure to reduce. There on the soiled linen was drawn a bloody hand, and Marie, with quickly drawn breath, realized that the Tour de Vesle was indeed a watch tower in the path of the invader. If invaders should come again to France – if the Austrians, who had scored so many successes while Napoleon was in Egypt, should be tempted to cross the Rhine – what a heavy responsibility would fall on the chatelains of Vesle! Would they be equal to it?

Marie sought in vain for the name of Valmy, which to a patriot had almost sacred associations. At Valmy a French contingent of untried recruits had engaged Brunswick's Prussians and put them to flight. It was the first victory of the Revolution, the first triumph of the young Republic, and it had been dearly bought. Among the French dead at Valmy was Michel Fontaine, Marie's beloved cousin who was to have succeeded his father in the pharmacy and whose place she had struggled to take. Valmy did not appear on the map because the place, which amounted to no more than a windmill, had not been heard of when the map was made, and the victory was insignificant compared to Napoleon's later roll of honour at Lodi Bridge, Arcole, Rivoli, the Pyramids and Mont Thabor.

Would there some day be a victory of Vesle?

Marthe broke in upon these military musings with the news that it had begun to snow again, which would delay Robert Grignon's progress if he set out for Reims that day, but had not delayed the group of local businessmen who were meeting for a New Year's luncheon in the dining room recently vacated by the officers.

'There'll be no singing with this lot, I promise you,' said Marthe. 'It's all dead earnest and good food with the Reims gentry. Joseph has been picking out some of the good things to make a luncheon tray for you. So cheer up! You know Citizen Latour will be doing himself well too.'

'I do know it and I'm very grateful,' said Marie. 'Why, here's Joseph now bringing – what's that? – turkey? And a glass of champagne?'

'From *le patron*, to wish you a happy New Year,' said Joseph, opening the bottle expertly. 'And one of our carters saw Robert on the road. He shouted out that everything was all right at Vesle.'

Marie thought this news was even better than champagne.

While she ate her luncheon Marie heard a shuffling of feet entering the nearby dining room, and voices, presumably those of Reims businessmen, wishing each other *Bonne Année*. She took the wish to herself. It could be a good New Year for the Latours if, as she had been trying to do for months, she put her husband's interests first, at Vesle and in Paris. That was what she had vowed to do before they left Egypt, but since they had returned to France the name of Napoleon Bonaparte had been on everybody's lips and in her heart.

I must forget him, she told herself for the thousandth time. But what if he *will not* be forgotten? What if he goes to war again? Then Charles will follow him. His constant repetition of Dr Berthollet's verdict that he was *bon pour le service* – fit for active service – showed how his mind was working, and his eagerness to be with Colonel Tavernier and his officers confirmed it. But his return to active service might mean his death.

Only General Bonaparte could refuse the services of a respected aide-de-camp. And Bonaparte was the last man to do that.

Marie toyed with the idea of appealing to Bonaparte herself. He had told her, in the sunlit garden of his home in Ajaccio, that he loved her, and she had confessed that she had long loved him. He had said he would divorce Joséphine, who had been unfaithful to him within weeks of their wedding, and with her lover had engaged in worse than shady dealings in the sale of army supplies. And then, if Marie would divorce Charles Latour, they two could be married ... She had sent him back to Joséphine. Could she now interfere further with his life, and his dealings with his staff?

One solution would be if Charles found such satisfaction in Vesle that the life of a landed proprietor would speedily come to mean more to him than military success had meant since his first days in the National Guard. His brother, who had been a soldier, an officer in the Flanders Regiment, had taken with enthusiasm to farming in Wiltshire after the emigration, and had made a great success of his farm until the day he was persuaded to join the *émigré* expedition to Quiberon, the *émigré* invasion of France in which his life was forfeit. Would the same sort of change of purpose and interest happen in the case of Charles? The thing was, not even to hint at the possibility; stubborn as he was, that would put him against the mere idea. And if he thought that Marie fancied herself as a success in the role of a farmer's wife, that would be fatal.

When Joseph came in to clear the table he found Marie with her hands clenched in the folds of her black dress and the *crème brûlée* which the cook had made as a special dessert for her quite untouched. He started to say how vexed Cook would be when Marie interrupted him with a sharp question about Robert Grignon. When, exactly, had the carter seen him on the highway? Ought he not to have reached The Golden Lion by this time? What did his father think?

'Ah, I see how it is,' said Joseph sympathetically. 'You're expecting a letter from Colonel Latour, and Robert is taking longer to bring it than you expected. But don't worry, Robert will turn up, he always does. Would you like a cup of coffee? A fashion magazine to amuse you? Or Marthe to keep you company? Or *anything* I can get you?'

'Nothing, thank you, Joseph. Please tell Cook my lunch was wonderful, I really couldn't eat it all.'

'Let me turn one of the big chairs round to the fire for you. A little sleep would do you good, *Madame la Marquise.*'

She nearly said, 'Don't call me that!' but the honorific was due to Charles, not to her, and so Marie only said, 'How kind you are!' as an easy chair was piled with cushions, the table cleared, and a fresh log placed on the fire. The ugly little room became a rosy cavern of warmth and silence, where Marie yielded to Joseph's suggestions and fell asleep.

At first the dream images were of her husband, stumbling half-blind through a thicket of doubt, and then that gave place to a more potent image: Bonaparte leading his troops in battle, holding the Tricolore high as he stormed over the pontoon bridge at Arcole, Bonaparte with his arms around her in the garden at Ajaccio, covering her face with kisses, telling her she was the girl he should have married years ago 'when we were young.'

'*Corragio, Napoleone!*' she had said to him when they parted. In the dream she heard him say, 'Courage, Marie!' which nobody had ever said except Professor Royer, her chief in Cairo, when something went wrong in the laboratory; and in her dream she wept.

If a man who cared for her could have looked in at the window from the darkening courtyard and studied the slim figure in the black dress flung down among the cushions in the big chair, with her tangled fair hair and tear-stained cheeks, would he have thought of her as a girl mourning for lost love? Or as a little castaway adrift on the always troubled sea of political France?

When Marie awoke it was pitch-dark outside, but the room was full of light from a lamp held by Monsieur Grignon, who was ushering in his son and saying, 'Good news from Vesle, madame! Here's the letter you've been looking for!'

'Please give it to me.'

Robert Grignon bowed, and handed over Latour's letter, its cover crumpled and warm from his inside pocket. Marie read.

My dear wife,

The Tour de Vesle is bad but not too bad, and I would like you to see it. I've asked Robert Grignon to drive you down tomorrow morning, with the rest of the stuff we brought from Paris, and some more eatables. I had a wonderful welcome from the villagers and you will too, so be quick, and don't forget a frying-pan.

Your Charles.

Marie was sitting erect in the deep chair and her dark blue eyes were fixed appealingly on young Grignon.

'Is my husband really all right?'

'Certainly he is, madame. He told me he had a good night's rest on an old sofa.'

'Where were you?'

'He sent me off to sleep at the wine shop.'

'He says here he had a wonderful welcome from the villagers. Did you see any of that?'

'I saw it all, madame. Ten men from Vesle went up to the Tower this morning and started cleaning out the well. The blacksmith, Roger Marchais, was in the lead. He's an old mate of mine, so I thought I'd better stay and lend a hand, and when the well was in working order the marquis was talking about a bonfire.'

'A *bonfire*?'

'There's a good deal of rubbish lying about – or was.'

'But if you had left earlier you could have taken me back yesterday.'

'With great respect, madame, the marquis was against that. "I don't want the marchioness on the high road after dark," he said to me.'

'And quite right too,' said his father, coming forward. 'Madame, you'll be all the better for another night in a comfortable bed, and this boy of mine needs a good rest too.'

'Of course he does,' said Marie remorsefully. 'Tell me, are the shops still open?'

'Open for another hour, madame.'

'Then, if you please, could you send one of your servants out to buy me a frying-pan?'

Next morning Robert had two fresh horses between the shafts of the wagonette, and as he gave them an admonitory touch of the whip he thought how strange it was that he should be driving an *aristo* again so soon. The young man was a typical product of the French Revolution, believing that the monarchy, ended on the guillotine, and the aristocracy, were the collective enemies of the People. Citizen Le Bon, Laguerre's predecessor, had set an example of brutality in office which had brought shame to the name of Reims. Robert would hardly have thought it possible that he could be chattering and laughing with a female *aristo* like the Marquise de la Tour, and yet he found himself enjoying her company and admiring her good looks.

His father had called her 'the poor little thing', but to a boy of twenty she was not a poor little thing – not with that bright hair and those blue eyes. She was not 'little'; Marie was a tall girl, nearly as tall as her swaggering husband, and she was far more interested in the sights and sounds of the countryside than her husband had been. Above all she was interested in the people of Vesle, and Robert found himself giving brief sketches of all those who had gone to help out at the Tower that morning.

It was the story of Citizeness Collonge, called Mémée, which touched her most, and Robert could have sworn there were tears in Marie's eyes when he told about the poor old grandmother still grieving for the young soldier who fell at Lodi Bridge.

'I hope her granddaughter is good to her,' was all Marie said.

'Good enough according to her lights,' was Robert's equally dry comment, but as they jogged on in silence he made up his mind to add something which was no business of his and which he would never have mentioned to Marie's husband.

He cleared his throat more than once before he began: 'It's generally known in Reims, madame, that the First Consul, Napoleon Bonaparte, sponsored the marquis's claim for repossession of the Tower and estate of Vesle –'

'How is it generally known? Those transactions are supposed to be confidential.'

'Citizen Anatole Laguerre didn't make a secret of it.'

'Ah! Monsieur Laguerre! Of course not. Well?'

'I venture to suggest, madame, that you should not refer to General Bonaparte as a friend of the family – or even as your husband's commanding officer.'

'I take your meaning, Robert, and I appreciate your advice.

34

But General Bonaparte is not an easy man to relegate to the fields of silence.'

'I suppose not, madame.'

An awkward silence might have fallen then, but the Tour de Vesle appeared at that moment on the skyline, and Marie had a score of questions to ask, and her driver to answer. He did so with only half his attention, for he was listening to a sound of singing coming from not far away: the voices of men and women, not unmusical, uplifted in one of the revolutionary songs.

'What on earth can that be?' said Marie.

'Some of the villagers, still celebrating the New Year,' said Robert.

'Do let's go and find out.'

He wasn't sure it was the wisest thing to do, and he only hoped her husband was there, but he turned his horses down a track hardly fit to be called a path, and brought them out on a natural lawn graced by a little fountain set among the dead leaves of wild flowers and ferns. The 'lawn' was divided, just south of the spring which fed the fountain, by a hedge of shrubs or bushes, and a number of young men and women were trimming the hedge and pulling dead leaves and other rubbish from its base. They did not acknowledge the arrivals, which offended Robert Grignon's sense of propriety, for he called out in the tones of the mayor of Reims announcing a distinguished guest at a civic dinner: '*Chapeaux bas! Voici Madame la Marquise de la Tour!*'

The whole company turned at once to greet Marie with an irregular handclap to which one old man with white hair added an uncertain hurrah. Before she could speak there was the sound of running feet, and through a gap in the hedge burst the new Marquis de la Tour, so that the villagers, while officially execrating the very name of Versailles, watched breathlessly to see how the son of one of the late Queen's ladies of the palace would greet his wife.

The new marquis gave them all a lesson in etiquette. He slowed his pace to a walk when he was a few yards short of

Marie, halted, and bowed from the waist. It had already been decided that he was a fine-looking young man, with his crisp dark hair, his height and his broad shoulders, even with the pitiful addition of a black patch over his left eye. And she, in her mourning dress, was a sweet creature, though her husband's bow and touch of his lips to her hand were criticized by some of the men. 'Maybe that's the way the gentry does things,' muttered one strapping rustic, 'but if that pretty girl was mine, I'd ha' given her a smacking great kiss.'

He was surprised, and so were they all, when Marie replied to their welcome by spreading her skirts and dropping almost to the ground in the curtsy just coming into fashion again at the First Consul's Court of the Tuileries.

'Do please carry on,' they heard her say. The voice was not loud but very clearly articulated. 'We greatly appreciate your help.'

This was something they had not expected, this spontaneous, friendly greeting, this acceptance of their friendship! This, from an *aristo*, one who, the commissioners of the Republic enjoyed telling them, was sworn to grind the faces of the poor! There was an incoherent murmur of gratification and all looked towards the white-haired old man, whose name was Marchais, and who seemed to be a natural leader among them.

'We thank you, madame,' he said. 'The marquis has consented to attend a *vin d'honneur* in Vesle at about six o'clock. We hope your ladyship will do us the honour to accompany the marquis, and let us drink your health along with his.'

'I shall be delighted, monsieur.'

There was no lingering on the greensward after that. Robert Grignon took the lead among the men in looking round for his horses, and those who had none set off at a round pace for the village. A group of matrons emerged from the direction of the Tower to show its new mistress all they had done in preparation for her arrival. Young mothers went calling for their children, and children not so young were shouting for their relatives. The noisiest of these was a woman of about

Marie's own age, of gypsy good looks and flamboyant dress, who came out of a barn with straw on her skirts and a piercing cry of 'Mémée! Grand'mère!' The older woman so referred to told her not to make so much noise.

She looked completely sane, this so-called madwoman, who could not bear noise, or to hear the name of Bonaparte. She was a tall, strongly built countrywoman, walking with a free stride as, after murmuring with her granddaughter, she came towards Marie, bent her knee in a country bob and said, 'Welcome, citizeness. But why are you dressed in black? A bride should wear white at her wedding party.'

'I am wearing black because my husband's father has died,' said Marie resourcefully.

'I thought you might be wearing black for France.'

'The good days will soon be coming back to France,' said Marie.

'Are you sure?'

'Positive!' Marie's smile brought an answering smile to the old woman's face.

'I see you and Madame Collonge are making friends,' said old Marchais, coming up to them. 'I'm afraid I must part you now. Alice, my daughter-in-law, would like madame to see what preparations have been made at the Tower.'

'We'll meet again at the *vin d'honneur*, Madame Collonge,' said Marie, taking Marchais by the arm.

'But,' said the old woman, 'before we are really friends you must call me Mémée.'

4

As Marie held out her hand to the blacksmith's wife she heard
Charles say from the top of the stairs behind her, 'Is there
somebody in the back room, Madame Alice?'

'Only my sister-in-law, monsieur. She's hanging up
madame's dresses in the *armoire*.'

'I didn't know there was an *armoire* in that room,' said
Marie.

It was quite a good-sized cupboard, as she realized when
Alice stepped aside to let her see: almost another little room
in itself, with a mirror and a nest of drawers against the back
wall, and on a bar a familiar row of dresses from among which
scrambled a big girl whose own attire consisted of a shawl
fastened across her breast with a horseshoe brooch, a striped
wincey petticoat, knitted stockings and a pair of clogs.

'This is my sister-in-law, Germaine Marchais,' said Alice,
as the country girl stood silent in embarrassment.

'Bonjour, Germaine,' smiled Marie. 'Thank you for
unpacking my things. Did you happen to see a white lace
fichu among them? I'd like to wear it to the party.'

Germaine smiled for the first time.

'The people will like that too, it's beautiful, madame. Here
it is.'

From the top drawer she drew a delicate web of lace which
did indeed embellish Marie's black dress, and drew a smile
from Charles Latour. His silence had not been lost upon his
wife, who could not know that the *armoire* had held the
wretched caricature of his mother's portrait. I should have
burned it before now, he thought desperately. I didn't know
the place would be swarming with peasants.

'Well, what do you think of it?' he asked Marie, when the two other women had gone down to the kitchen for hot water. 'Not big enough, is it?'

'The Tower is more than big enough,' she said cheerfully, 'and this room is big enough for a single bedstead with the cockleshells from your family crest carved in the headboard, and some other furniture. Only ... where are you going to sleep?'

They both stood with their eyes fixed on the crusader's cockleshells, not looking at each other, Marie thinking that the New Year would mean a new beginning of their lives together, and wondering what Charles would reply. But when he spoke it was to say that two beds had been brought back to Vesle, though not by whom; that the second had been placed in the room upstairs, and 'that's where I shall sleep tonight,' he said with finality. 'It'll be wonderful after that collapsing old sofa downstairs.'

'Poor dear, were you reduced to that?' she said, and traced the outline of the family crest with one forefinger. In the first forgiveness of his infidelity, her first sorrow for his disabling wound, Marie Latour, in Egypt, had taken her husband to her bed and her arms. She was too thoroughly a Frenchwoman to shun the marriage relationship because of a single slip by her husband. But if he meant to keep apart from her – it would be a relief. Following that scene of pardon and charity in her room at Nasriya there had been another scene in a Corsican garden when Napoleon Bonaparte, the only man she truly loved, had told her of his early dream that he might marry her ... After that avowal another man's embrace would be impossible. The clatter of clogs on the staircase brought the awkward scene to an end.

'Here's your hot water, *Madame la Marquise!*' said Germaine, entering in a hurry, followed by Alice. 'And please, my brother says we'd better start. Grignon's all ready. But may I have a word with you before we go?'

'If it's not private, may I hear it too?' said Charles. The blacksmith had given him a hint of what he would hear: that his sister, Germaine Marchais, would like to enter service at the Tour de Vesle, as a *bonne à tout faire*, maid of all work, including cooking. Would Their Graces give her a trial?

'How old are you, Germaine? How much experience have you had?' said Marie.

'I'm nineteen, madame. I was in good service for three years near Épernay, when I looked after the younger Madame Clicquot when her first child was born. I also worked in the dairy at milking time, and then in making butter and cheese –'

'Come back tomorrow and let us talk it over,' said Marie. 'You see, Germaine, there's neither cows nor babies here.'

While Marie washed her hands and face the two Marchais women, after enquiring if they could do anything more for her, clattered downstairs, and when she followed them she found the big room empty. The fire had been allowed to die down, but the room was warm, and already looked familiar to the new mistress. Charles had gone to the top of the house, and she heard him whistling as he made his way down two flights of stairs. If he was feeling cheerful, so much the better! But he looked grave enough as he took her overcoat from the sofa and shook it open for her to put on.

'You weren't very enthusiastic about our would-be servant,' he said, as she slid her arms into the sleeves.

'I wanted to find out what you thought.'

'Oh, I'm quite agreeable. But that woman who worked for us at the Quai Voltaire – you jumped at her, when the concierge's wife brought her up to the apartment. Of course she was special, wasn't she? Her husband fell at Valmy?'

Anyone who had been bereaved by the battle of Valmy was sure of Marie's sympathy. Her cousin Michel, brought up with her like a brother, had fallen in that action which, even more than the early victories of Napoleon, was sacred to French patriots. It was the first battle (Charles Latour called it a skirmish) which French troops had won after their defeats by the far more powerful forces arrayed against the Revolution. Teasing Marie about her sensitivity to Valmy was one of Latour's oblique ways of criticizing her.

She bit her lip, but replied equably, 'Armande had a home of her own in a tenement round the corner. Her lodging was no problem. Where would Germaine sleep if she came to work here?'

'In the bedroom off the kitchen. You saw the door, didn't you?'

'I thought it was a pantry.'

'If you're determined to go to this affair at Vesle tonight, you can investigate it tomorrow. Two maids used to sleep there, according to old Marchais.'

'Yes, and that's another thing. I wanted to know how you felt about employing another Marchais. I wondered if you felt the Marchais family were running the Tour de Vesle.'

'Don't be a fool, Marie, of course they're not. I owe a debt of gratitude to the old man. It was he who gave me the wonderful welcome. I wrote to you about it.'

'How?'

With his eyes on a solitary candle left burning on the table, Charles told how the blacksmith's father had walked all the way to the Tower to welcome him and express his pleasure at seeing the ancestral home of the la Tours 'all lighted up'. 'All lighted up, Marie!' he repeated. 'Illuminated, on the strength of one candle burning!'

'It was a nice idea.' Marie hardly knew what she said. It was so rare for her husband to display emotion that she was amazed at his broken words and shaken voice. But she was happier than she had been since they left Paris. She was encouraged to think that Charles might take to his diminished estate, and might play a useful part in the founding of a new France. She rejoiced in her husband's ascent of Robert Grignon's wagonette, without a stumble or any loss of balance, as they set off for the *vin d'honneur*; she was even glad to feel his strong shoulder against her own.

Young Grignon wrapped shawls and rugs around Marie and then she listened passively to his discussion with Charles about the time he should drive them back home: he would

41

like, himself, to be back in Reims by midnight – would nine o'clock be about right? She was surprised at the suggestion that the *vin d'honneur* would last so long, but they would not hurry away from the village. She would be happy to drive on and on under the stars, which were very bright in the wintry sky, and in their reflection in the Vesle river which ran singing by the side of the road.

Vesle village was shaped like an L, in two streets of small houses, most with a garden before the door, and all with a lamp or 'one candle burning' in the front window. The villagers were gathering outside what Grignon indicated with his whip was the wine shop, with benches fastened round a leafless tree growing at the apex of the L.

'That was called the Tree of Justice,' said Charles. 'My father told me his ancestors used it as a place to deal the high justice, the middle and the low, among their tenants.'

'In feudal times,' said Grignon drily. He had been listening. 'It is a *peuplier*, the people's tree, and there was a travelling guillotine beneath it for a few months in '93. Citizen Laguerre's predecessors kept it busy.'

Marie shivered. A child of the Revolution, to her the sound of the tumbrils carrying the victims to the stationary guillotines in Paris still came back in dreams. She was grateful for Charles's whisper as he helped her to descend.

'Too bad the poplar tree has shed its leaves. Now the villagers can't see the autumn bronze which saves your hair from being merely flaxen.'

Marie smiled as his fingers tightened on her hand. Years ago, at the very beginning of Latour's courtship, he had declared that her hair had the two colours, light and dark, of a poplar growing beside the Seine. But then her feet touched ground, and people were coming up to look at them, and lead them into the wine shop, which had been scrubbed vigorously and furnished with extra tables and chairs.

'You have a fine large room here,' said Marie to the man who introduced himself as the wine shop keeper, and told her his name was Maurice.

42

'Lucky we have, tonight,' he replied. 'Before my brother and I took it over, this was the village school. But the schoolmaster was killed when the Germans invaded, and he never was replaced.'

Marie was silent. She accepted a glass of wine and a piece of cold bacon laid upon a slice of buttered country bread, and noticed that the blacksmith seemed about to make a speech. As he got to his feet there was an interruption: two young men carrying fiddles, and a third eclipsed by a cello, entered to a burst of hand-clapping and took their places on a raised platform at the far end.

'The musicians are very welcome,' said Roger Marchais in his impressive way. 'And we shall all enjoy dancing after supper, but something even more enjoyable must come first. Fill your glasses, my fellow citizens, and let us drink together to Monsieur le Marquis de la Tour de Vesle and his lady, whom we are all happy to welcome among us.'

There was a burst of applause and the toast was drunk, and Marie's eyes filled with tears. She felt they had come home and were among true friends. She slipped her hand into her husband's, and side by side they bowed their thanks. She looked from one to another of the faces which a few hours ago had been strange but were now familiar – old Marchais and young Grignon, buxom Alice and smiling Germaine – and watched their growing interest and pleasure as Charles spoke.

She dared not look at him, for she could tell he was nervous, but his voice was steady and distinct, with a resonance which obviously impressed his hearers. He began by saying that he and 'madame la marquise' were glad to be at Vesle, the home of his ancestors, which had been severely tried in the war years now over, and to mark the occasion they wished to make a present to the whole community.

This present would consist of a flock of sheep, eighty ewes and a ram. He had arranged with Farmer Hédiard, whom they no doubt knew by reputation as a successful farmer at Épernay, to select two healthy ewes for each of the forty families in the village, and deliver them with a shepherd at the end of the present week. The shepherd would be boarded at the Tower, and would see the new flock through the lambing season, which would shortly be upon them. Until that was over the ewes would be housed in one of the barns still standing at the Tower. After that, the owners would no doubt wish to have their animals on their own premises, and they would find him ready to supply wood for building sheep pens from a supply of timber he had seen in one of his stables. He hoped this gift would be a source of profit to his former tenants – perhaps a source of food as the flock increased – confirming them in their well-deserved liberty and independence.

The young man's confidence increased as he went on, and he finished to a burst of applause in which shouts of *'Bravo!'* and *'Merci!'* and *'Vivent monsieur et madame!'* almost drowned the clapping of hard and toilworn hands. Charles was flushed with the pleasure of success and Marie's whisper of 'Wonderful, darling!' Then there was a great scraping as chairs and tables were dragged across the wooden floor to make more space and Simon Marchais, the master of ceremonies, ordered the musicians to strike up a country dance.

'Will you honour me by walking a quadrille with me, *Madame la Marquise*?' he said to Marie, with a bow.

'Very willingly, monsieur,' and she gave him her hand.

It was some time before the set could be formed, for so many dancers surrounded Charles, with questions about the breed of the sheep to be expected, the time of their arrival and – from the inevitable critic – how the two ewes per family were to be allocated without favouritism. The two owners of the wine shop were busy filling glasses and tumblers, while their wives passed wooden platters of bread and sliced beef, bread and cold ham, and bread and cheese. At last Charles was free to lead out Madame Alice and the quadrille began.

'You'll have to lead me. I'm not much good at this,' said Marie to her partner.

'Didn't you dance in Paris?'

'Very often. But not square dances. Polkas, mazurkas, and of course the waltz.'

'Ah! Our young folks are crazy to learn the waltz. Could you and monsieur give us a demonstration of it, after the quadrille?'

'I dare say we could.'

Charles as a shepherd, me as a dancing teacher, thought Marie. Vesle is turning us into new people. Meantime they had both caught the rhythm of the quadrille and were dancing energetically, though Charles jumped at the idea of the slower tempo of a waltz.

When the fiddles, after two false starts, began a simple melody imported from Milan and often heard in Paris, he took Marie in his arms and whispered, 'Not very like Frascati's, is it?'

Marie giggled. The hot shabby wine shop and the crowd of gaping villagers indeed bore no resemblance to the smart salon where she and her lover had waltzed so often with elegant men and women all around them. But she said, 'I like it,' and she spoke the truth.

'Was I really all right?' Charles whispered, with his lips close to her ear, and she knew he was still anxious about his speech.

'They all thought you were wonderful, and I did too. I told you so, didn't I?' And she rested her cheek against his own, which caused two stout matrons seated near the orchestra to exchange meaningful glances.

'They're a handsome couple,' said one.

'They're in love all right,' said the other.

'She's a very sweet girl. Quite different from the dowager. You never saw her, did you? She only came here once, and thought not one of us was good enough to look at her.'

Neither Marie nor Charles heard the criticism, but Marie caught the smiles and significant glances, and guessed they were being praised. Unconsciously she tightened her clasp on her partner's shoulder.

'Your speech was a great success,' she said. 'You spoke far better than General Bonaparte, the only time I ever heard him speak in public.'

'Good heavens, Marie! When was that?'

'When the Directors welcomed him at the Luxembourg after he came back from the Italian campaign.'

'He never speaks well to civilians. He's wonderful with troops.'

He held her a little away from him and studied her face.

'Better than Bonaparte, eh? That certainly is a compliment, coming from you.'

The dance had brought them into the sight of a new group of spectators, and with a pang of fear Marie recognized the crazed Mémée, who hated to hear of battles since her grandson's death in action. Could she have overheard the name of Bonaparte and the inference that they knew him well? Marie shivered. She felt herself back in the worst days of the Revolution, when a careless word could lead the speaker to imprisonment or death.

Bonaparte had put an end to the Revolution, but he had his enemies, sane and insane. His very name had power to change a village wine shop, where she had been enjoying the firelight and good fellowship, into a sinister place of shadows and unspoken dread.

The *vin d'honneur*, and the various emotions of the day, had tired Marie into a heavy sleep, from which she woke to find herself alone in a strange bed in an unfamiliar room. At first she fancied herself back at The Golden Lion, because she was aware of a delightful aroma of coffee. She was content to lie still and enjoy it, until the sound of half-familiar voices, and of wooden shoes upon the stairs, told her who had made the coffee, and she was ready with a smile and a pleasant greeting when Germaine Marchais pushed the bedroom door ajar and said softly, 'Do I disturb, madame?'

'No, I was awake. Come in, Germaine. How did you get here?'

'My brother drove me over. I hadn't seen anything in the kitchen for breakfast . . .'

'So you brought coffee – and milk too, I see. Bless you, Germaine,' said Marie, sitting up in bed and holding out her hands for a wooden tray with a yellow bowl full of *café au lait*. 'Did you make some coffee for my husband too?'

'Of course, madame. He's having it downstairs. I lit the fire, so he's quite comfortable.'

'I'm sure he is. And how is everyone at Vesle this morning?'

'Terribly excited about the sheep, of course. My two nephews and half a dozen other boys set off for the crossroads when it was hardly light, hoping to meet the shepherd and the ewes.'

'I don't think they'll be here today. Aren't there some pens to be built first?'

'My brother was talking to monsieur about that.'

'You're all so busy, it's high time I got up. Your coffee was wonderful, Germaine, but we need so many things – how does one go about shopping in Vesle?'

'There's a market twice a week, Tuesdays and Fridays, when the coach comes in from Reims. The market stalls are set out round the poplar tree, or, if it's wet, in the wine shop. Oh but, madame, it's too far for you to walk to Vesle and back!'

'Not as far as I used to walk in Paris. Don't worry, we'll work something out. Now here's the empty bowl; when you go downstairs tell monsieur I'll join him in five minutes.'

'Five minutes! Oh, madame!'

It was nearer ten minutes than five before Marie was dressed in the rough frieze skirt and bodice she had worn on cold winter mornings in Dr Berthollet's laboratory, and left her bedroom. Germaine had spoken the truth when she said monsieur was comfortable. She had set out his breakfast – with two coffee pots and two cups on a little table drawn up to a roaring fire – before which he was stretched out in an easy chair which he promptly yielded to his wife.

'Did you sleep well, darling?' he asked.

'Like a log. Where's Roger Marchais? And Germaine?'

'He's poking about in the barns, and she's in the kitchen. Have some more coffee?'

'I see there's a baker in Vesle as well as an open-air market,' said Marie, eyeing the fresh bread and butter on the table. 'What did you think when she turned up this morning so early?'

'I thought she was making damned sure of the job,' said Charles. 'You'll have to hire her now, Marie!'

'When she's seen the bedroom off the kitchen.'

'Oh, don't worry about that, it'll seem like a palace to her. Those peasants – '

He left the sentence unfinished, warned by Marie's frown that she would not approve of one of his mother's favourite axioms: 'Those peasants live like their animals.'

'I'm sure Madame Alice keeps a very tidy house,' said Marie stiffly, and then, breaking into a smile, 'Oh, Charles, isn't it nice to be in a house of our own again?'

'You've been very good about the whole thing, dear.'

'I'm very happy about it, truly I am.'

'Here comes Marchais, ready to talk about those infernal sheep.'

But when the blacksmith pushed open the front door, and ducked his head in an awkward acknowledgement of Marie's presence, he said nothing about sheep, but only that he had 'lit the bonfire as monsieur directed.'

'Right! I'll be with you in a minute.' And Charles, telling his wife to firm things up with Germaine, snatched up his overcoat and hurried out. Marie was left wondering why he had ordered a bonfire to be lit.

She was happier about her husband than she had been the day before. In his hurry to join Marchais he had moved carefully and quickly among the many tables and chairs which had been muddled into the salon, without once stumbling or losing his balance, which made her hope that the wretched side effects of losing an eye were wearing off permanently: she took her coat from the back of the chair where she had laid it the night before and slung it round her shoulders before she opened the door.

The two men were out of sight, but a thick column of smoke was evidence that a fire had indeed been lit.

She sniffed the frosty air. There was a curious odour about, as if painted wood had been used to light the fire, but the good country smells predominated, and the scent of the pines, which formed a ring around the Tower. Marie drew a few long breaths. It was a day to go exploring, but her new duties kept her indoors, and with a quick glance at the contents of the purse in the pocket of her coat she turned back towards the kitchen.

In a couple of days life at the Tour de Vesle was organized and running smoothly. Germaine was delighted with the kitchen bedroom, where Marie installed her only after the bed, unoccupied for so long, had been heated for twenty-four hours by a copper warming pan. A feather mattress and a *duvet* had been found and arranged on a pile of sweet-smelling hay in the barn which Farmer Hédiard's shepherd, a Breton named Yves, was to share with the ewes. Yves was a sober widower, about forty years old, who hardly made any audible conversation during the meals which he ate in the kitchen with Germaine.

The blacksmith's sister was a good plain cook and a tidy servant. If she had a fault it was that her big strong body was not yet fully co-ordinated, so that her sweeping and dusting were very noisy, and her clogs made a tremendous clatter on the stairs. 'That great lump!' was Charles's amiable name for her, and Marie thankfully saw that there was no danger of a flirtation ending in folly, like his seduction of her little maid in Cairo.

Once it had been thoroughly cleaned and aired with generous fires in every hearth, the château began to feel less like a semi-ruin, more like a home. Marie and Germaine planned new curtains and carpets to keep out the draughts.

Charles spent a good deal of time with Yves and Roger

Marchais, whom he commissioned to rent a pony carriage and an animal gentle enough for Marie to drive, thus giving her freedom to go in and out of the village. He met her delight in this arrangement with many kisses and loving words. He was in excellent spirits in those first days, and Marie never knew that his mood reflected his relief that his mother's vandalized picture had been consumed in the fire that Roger had laid.

There was a great deal of coming and going between the village and the Tower. Men came to carry away the timber made available by Charles to construct their own rough sheep pens, and of course to overlook the animals. Knowing the contentiousness of his fellow countrymen, and their willingness to quarrel over every point at issue, this was one part of his bounty which worried Charles Latour: the village jealousies and arguments likely to be stirred up by the allocation of the sheep. Once again, old Marchais proved helpful by suggesting that the two ewes per family be chosen by the shepherd himself when the pens were ready, and this was accepted by the villagers with overt heartburnings. Old Marchais gave much of the credit of this to Marie. She was as active in the meadow where the sheep were turned out to graze as she had been on the dance floor, and she encouraged the young married women who brought their excited children out to see the sheep to come in to the big room at the Tower for a cup of coffee (milk for the children) before they faced the three miles back to Vesle. She made them understand that to have the shepherd allocate the animals was the fairest way for everybody, and she encouraged each of them to tell her personal story of the problems of living in a community with no church, no doctor, no school and no postal service. She was a good listener, and the laboratory had taught her patience.

When market day came on Friday, Charles drove her to Vesle in the pony carriage, and she found many of her new friends behind the stalls arranged round the poplar tree where the ancestral la Tours had dispensed 'the high justice, the middle and the low'. They greeted her with a chorus of

'*Bonjour, madame!*' '*Comment ça va, madame?*' '*Madame a bonne mine!*' to which she replied in kind. Charles was still, and always, *Monsieur le Marquis*, but the women had dropped the *marquise*, and Marie was glad to be 'madame' without the title.

She was interested to see Mémée at a stall and bought from her a quantity of root vegetables. Mémée was standing up when Marie caught sight of her, holding a bunch of carrots in one hand and a bunch of kale in the other, and both as if they were bouquets of roses.

'*Bonjour, madame!*' Her voice was ringing, her tanned face wore a smile, and her coat was scrupulously neat.

Why, she's as sane as I am, thought Marie, pressing forward to shake hands. Why did that horrible Laguerre try to put her into an asylum?

But Citizen Laguerre's day was over. When Charles and Marie went to buy beef at the wine shop, and incidentally to have lunch there, the brothers handed Marie a letter from Professor Guiart, her old teacher, brought by the coach, and a copy of the *Moniteur* forwarded from The Golden Lion. While the men talked about 'the everlasting sheep', Marie had time to glance at the headlines on the front page of the *Moniteur* before stuffing the official newspaper and the letter into her reticule.

The headline read: 'Innovations by the Consulate!' and continued, 'The First Consul revises the financial systems and reforms the structure of local government!'

'Any war news in the paper?' Charles asked, as soon as they were alone and driving home.

'Thank heaven, there was not!' said Marie emphatically. 'At least not on the front page. The news is all about financial and local government reforms. Did you expect a declaration of war?'

'Considering that every Power in Europe is in arms against us, I wouldn't have been surprised. Cheer up, Marie, don't look so downhearted! It's got to come some day, and Bonaparte knows it . . . No, don't give me the paper now,' as she began to fumble in her reticule, 'I want to read the news

51

carefully and then we can discuss it. You've got some reading matter of your own, haven't you? Wasn't that a letter from old Guiart I saw you pocketing?'

It was, of course, and the light tone of sarcasm revealed what the Marquis de la Tour de Vesle thought of all the pharmacists, young and old, who had engrossed his wife's attention for so long. When she read Professor Guiart's letter in the privacy of her bedroom, Marie admitted he would have cause for irritation.

Guiart wrote to say that Louis Rocroi, the young chemist whom he had sponsored as the tenant of Marie's house and pharmacy on the rue St-Honoré, was in financial difficulties, and his father-in-law refused to help him with the rent. He was compelled to ask for employment with the Service de Santé, the Army Medical Corps, where his health had already been undermined. Professor Guiart was prepared to renew his offer to rent the shop and even the house to use as an annex to his own – the living room and bedrooms would be useful as storerooms, and he could place an assistant, not living on the premises, in the little laboratory where Marie's uncle had done so much creative work.

As a matter of form he was compelled to ask if Marie would consider taking over the whole concern herself. Certainly her qualifications were equal to it, especially after her experience in Egypt, but perhaps now that she was safely housed in her husband's estates she was ready to exchange the discipline of a laboratory for the pleasures of country life and – dare he express the hope? – in due course a family. In a shower of compliments her old teacher brought his letter to an end.

While she read this epistle the deep blush of her girlhood turned Marie's pale cheeks to red and the fingers of her free hand slowly clenched. What! Sell Prosper Fontaine's shop and workplace, even to the man who had always been his friendly rival? Or risk a permanent breach with Charles by taking all the charges of an apothecary on herself? Leave her new friends at Vesle to fend for themselves under the jurisdiction proposed by Napoleon? If only *he* was here, she thought, and tears came to her eyes. He would tell me what to do, and his advice would be wise and good.

It was still light enough in the yard for Charles's tall figure to be visible to Marie as he strode towards an early supper and discussion of the *Moniteur*. He was walking briskly, with a military snap in his step, and carrying his three-cornered hat in his hand. Marie smiled as she noticed his obvious good spirits, then gasped as he lost his balance. Instead of going through the gate, he stumbled up against it, and the elbow injured at Lodi Bridge hit against the woodwork with a crack quite audible to Marie at her open window. She heard him swear, and had to restrain herself from running headlong downstairs to comfort him. 'Oh, poor Charles! Poor darling!' she said aloud, and only the awareness that he resented any reference to his disability kept her from hurrying to his side. She watched him come slowly but steadily up the garden path, and he had scarcely entered the house before she heard him shouting to Germaine to bring the brandy. Well, perhaps brandy was better than sympathy any day.

When she went downstairs he was in the easy chair, sipping the golden liquid and looking quite composed, holding out the newspaper as soon as she asked for it, and even teasing her about not believing in the First Consul's reforms until she read them for herself. But he did not continue on the subject of Bonaparte, asking instead if she would like a dog.

'Oh Charles! Oh I would!'

'Hédiard sent a collie pup over with Yves this morning. He's the whelp from his best collie bitch and he thinks he'd be useful with the sheep if he's half as good as his mother, but I said it would depend on what madame said, she wasn't used to dogs –'

'Because my Uncle Prosper didn't want a dog in the shop, so I never had a pet, not even a cat to keep down the mice ... But a collie – here in the country where there's plenty of room – oh Charles, do let us keep him!'

'We'd be none the worse for a watchdog. But upon my

word, there's a lot of the child still in you, Marie!' He drew her head to his shoulder and kissed her.

'Can I see him now, Charles?'

'Can't you wait till tomorrow morning? I'm too tired to go trailing back to the stable tonight. He's all right with Yves ... and Germaine says dinner will be ready in twenty minutes.' And Marie, remembering the stumble and the hurt elbow, murmured something about being sorry, which Charles pretended not to hear.

Dinner was brought: a comfortable country dish of steak pudding with slices of carrot, potatoes and turnips swimming in a luscious, onion-flavoured gravy, and the young owners of the Tower did it full justice. They heard Yves come in, and his words of approval; heard Germaine ask if he wanted to take the dog's dinner over to the stable now, and exchanged smiles when they heard him say yes.

'When I was given my first puppy I always wanted it to be fed first.'

Marie asked if it had been a collie pup.

'No, it was a spaniel and very sentimental.'

Marie laughed, but she kept the talk on dogs as a way to keep off any reference to Guiart's letter, and presently Germaine was clearing the table, and Charles was telling her to get up a bottle of the good burgundy from the cellar and pour a full tumbler of it for Yves and another for herself.

'Monsieur is generous,' said the girl. 'May I bring the bottle to you here? There's not a lot of the best burgundy left.'

'Yes, you do that,' said Charles. 'And then don't disturb us for an hour. Madame and I have business to discuss.'

'Parfaitement, Monsieur le Marquis.'

She dropped a curtsy and went out. Almost before the door closed Marie was asking if she could see the *Moniteur* now.

'Here you are.'

The first bold head in the leading column read, 'Establishment of the Banque de France', and Marie gasped. 'Oh, is it about banking?' she asked. 'I'll never understand it. You know I've no head for figures!'

'Only because your education was neglected. You're smart enough at figures when it comes to pharmacy. And this is quite simple. Napoleon means to do away with the assignats – the paper money which was quite valueless – and substitute a sound currency supported by a sound bank, and a reliable Finance Minister. There'll be no chance of the speculation Barras and Tallien made their fortunes at – and an income tax of twenty per cent which everyone must pay.'

'And who collects it? Men like Anatole Laguerre?'

'No, the tax collectors will be a body of men called *receveurs*, with special qualifications both in arithmetic and honesty.'

'Laguerre and the other *commissaires* won't like that.'

'There won't be any *commissaires*. Napoleon means to replace them by a corps called *préfets* in the great districts and *sous-préfets* in the small, all appointed from Paris, and the mayors will have more power in the towns. And the one who will have the most power, whether *préfet*, *sous-préfet* or mayor, will be the man who appoints them all – Napoleon Bonaparte.'

5

The new system of finance and local government made little or no difference to the villagers of Vesle. There were a few arguments in the wine shop, usually stopped short of fisticuffs by one or other of the brothers, and the sheep continued to be the preferred topic of conversation. Lambing began in the barn, and the lambs were soon a decoration as they frisked in the big meadow in front of the Tower, before being distributed to their new owners. The collie pup assumed a responsibility more serious than his name, for Yves, unbidden, had taken to calling him Toto.

He and Germaine fell out over the name, and there were raised voices in the kitchen at meal times instead of the heavy silences which had begun to make Marie uneasy. Charles reported that the shepherd, at first so willing to do any odd job, was talking about getting back to his regular work at the Hédiard farm.

Marie felt that the one job too many had been her husband's request that the big Breton dig over the kitchen garden which had been neglected for years, and which Charles proposed to plant with new vegetables. She herself, having made progress on the house, was now thinking of a garden. There was an ideal spot near the river, at the edge of the pasture where she had met the villagers on the day she arrived at the Tower. There a rivulet ran through a little dell where wild flowers grew, and there was a sweet scent of violets and primroses. She took Germaine to see it, and the two girls gathered wood anemones to fill the vases on the dining table at the Tower.

'All that moss is growing harder,' said Germaine. 'It needs turning over, to let the air in.'

'Do you think so? I'm almost afraid to ask Yves, he was so snappish about the *potager*.'

'It isn't much of a job,' said Germaine. 'I could do it myself in a couple of hours, every bit as well as that lazy Breton.'

'But it isn't your work, is it?'

'I like working out of doors.'

Charles Latour's advice, given in a whisper, was: 'Let her do it. That great lump could swing a mattock as well as any man.'

'Oh, not a mattock!' Marie exclaimed. 'That would be far too heavy. I used a hoe in Uncle Prosper's garden.'

'Did you indeed? Well, let me see what I can find in the tool shed.'

The tool shed yielded up a hoe, a spade, and a variety of trowels, while Charles contributed some good advice. The moss was loosened round the little basin which the spring had hollowed out on its way to join the Vesle beyond the little curtain of bushes and shrubs which defined the limit of the meadow, and alongside which a track ran down to the crossroads.

Germaine apparently regarded the garden of the spring as part of her work. Every morning, after the kitchen was put straight and milking time was over, she came to join Marie by the rivulet and help her to start a wild strawberry patch by transferring the green plants from the woodlands to the damp, reclaimed earth beside the spring. 'Plenty of raspberry canes in the thicket,' said Germaine. 'We won't have to buy fruit in the village come the month of June.'

Marie enjoyed the companionship, and found herself daily listening for the clump of heavy sabots along the track. She had lived so long surrounded by her fellow workers in the laboratories of Paris and Cairo that she did feel lost in the solitude of her new estate, and enjoyed Germaine's gossip of *la ferme Hédiard*. The new routines kept her from brooding over Guiart's letter and the future of her own pharmacy in the rue St-Honoré.

The *Moniteur* informed Marie that the First Consul and

Madame Bonaparte had given up their temporary lodging in the Luxembourg to take up residence in the Tuileries.

So now his home was in a palace where the King of France had lived! Napoleon was further away from her than ever.

February was almost over when an emissary arrived from the Hédiard farm in the person of the farmer's son, a shock-headed youth of fifteen. He bore an urgent message from his father for the shepherd's immediate return. Lambing there, which was later, had begun in earnest, and the assistants hastily summoned were lost without Yves. The Breton himself was obviously anxious, when he came with young Hédiard at his heels, to take formal leave of *madame la marquise* and her maid.

'I'm sorry to be off in such a hurry,' he said, when Marie scrambled up from the damp turf and put her hand in his. 'But your flock is in good heart, and *monsieur le marquis* has a good grasp of the elementary rules. I'll try to get over to Vesle one afternoon next week and see that all's well in the sheep pens at the cottages.'

'That would be very kind, Yves,' said Marie. 'You've done so much already, we'll be for ever in your debt.'

The man touched his forehead in a rough salute. 'Monsieur gave me a very handsome present when I said goodbye. If all the *aristos* were like you two there wouldn't have been a French Revolution.'

'It had to be,' said Marie. 'Well, good luck to you, Yves, and come back soon. Goodbye, *jeune homme*,' to the farmer's son.

'Goodbye, Germaine,' said Yves. 'You're doing a great job here.'

'*Au 'voir*,' said the girl, with averted face. '*Bonne chance*.'

The two women were silent until the man and the boy had gone.

Then Marie said: 'You weren't very gracious to Yves, Germaine. You used to be good friends.'

'I wished him good luck, didn't I? After he was rude to you

58

and me? Calling you a good *aristo*, and telling me I'd done well what that big lazy Breton wouldn't do himself?'

'That's twice I've heard you say "lazy Breton", Germaine. I don't like your use of the adjective, as if to be lazy were a speciality of Brittany. My own family came from there and I'm sure they were hard-working enough.'

'You a Breton? Oh, forgive me, madame! We all thought you were Parisienne – and had studied pharmacy.'

'Quite true. But my grandfather, Michel Fontaine, walked from a Breton farm to study pharmacy in Paris, where he opened his own business on the rue St-Honoré, and his son, my Uncle Prosper, followed him.'

'The poor man who was guillotined?'

'You talk too much, Germaine. Come on, pack up the trowels, we've done enough for one day. Let's go and find monsieur and make him come back to the Tower too. I'm sure we should all be the better for a cup of coffee.'

Next morning was the time for confidences beside the spring, when Germaine admitted with tears that the 'friendship' between Yves and herself had advanced to the point where he had proposed marriage and she had said no.

'I did like him, madame, and I know he's a good man,' she said, 'but I thought he was too old for me – old enough to be my father. And Alice was against it.'

'It wasn't your sister-in-law he wanted to marry,' said Marie. 'But if your own heart was against it you were right to say no.'

I wish someone had said something sensible to me before I married Charles, she thought. But her first concern was to comfort Germaine, and she succeeded so well that the routine of the Tour de Vesle was restored to tranquillity within a few days.

Yves did not pay his proposed visit to the village, sending a letter to Simon Marchais saying the lambing season was keeping him close to the Hédiard farm and recommending a villager named Albert Porrier as a promising substitute.

Germaine seemed disappointed, and apt to say, '*Voici Monsieur Yves!*' every time they heard footsteps on the track beyond the spring.

She didn't say so when they heard hoof-beats one fine morning in May, but she clambered to the high ground above the spring to see who the horseman might be, and called down to Marie that it was a stranger ... 'wearing uniform ... very handsome ... oh madame, it's a French officer ... and he's coming here.'

'Then you come down – carefully, that turf is slippery – and let's find out what he wants,' said Marie coolly. She knew her husband was not far away, for she could hear him whistling in the meadow, and she knew he could cope with any strange French officer who came along. Besides – *was* the man a stranger? He had halted on the far side of the thicket, dismounted, and was tethering his horse by the reins to an elder tree. Marie advanced cautiously towards a gap in the thicket, through which she could see the face, not handsome certainly, but humorous and cheerful as always, of her old friend Junot.

He had been a sergeant when he saved Napoleon's life at Toulon; he was a general in Napoleon's army now, and he wore the red and white sash of an ADC in a bow above his right elbow.

'Andoche!' cried Marie, and was caught into a bear hug which almost stifled her next words: 'Where did you come from?'

'From Reims. We've been kicking out a fellow called Anatole Laguerre and installing his successor, and the innkeeper told us how to find you and Latour. Marie, it's so good to see you – and you look wonderful!'

'Who's *we*? Who's *us*?' she asked urgently.

He released her and snapped to attention.

'A bodyguard of cavalry and their commanding officer, General Murat. And His Excellency the First Consul, General Napoleon Bonaparte.'

'Napoleon? Napoleon in Vesle?'

'Yes, my dear. This side trip was his idea. We're on our way to Army Forward at Châlons-sur-Marne via Épernay, and Napoleon said, "Let's see if the new marquis and his lady can give us a bite to eat at noon to help us on our way." It's not too much to ask, is it, Marie? Bread and cheese and a glass of wine will be fine.'

'Come now, Andoche, you're not on campaign. We can do better than that, can't we, Germaine?' said Marie to her maid, who was standing behind her, fascinated by the glittering apparition of the officer who was not a stranger. 'I can't undertake to feed a bodyguard, but there's a wine shop in the village –'

'The men have rations in their haversacks. We're not going into Vesle. They'll wait at the crossroads until we're ready to start for Châlons.'

'Oh, but Charles must hear all this! He'll be so interested about Châlons . . . and the general's visit to Army Forward . . .'

'Where *is* the old fellow? Why isn't he here, helping you with – what's that you're making, a water garden?'

'He's busy with more important jobs all day long. Actually he's in the big meadow across the river. You can get to it across the stone bridge you must have passed as you came up the track. Why don't you go and find him, and then he can bring you back to the Tower, where there's stabling and fodder for your horse?'

'Food for man and beast, eh? I can see you're an excellent chatelaine, Marie,' said Junot. He repeated her instructions on how to find her husband, saluted, and went off in the direction she indicated, while the two young women began picking up the rest of the paraphernalia strewn around the spring.

'Did I hear aright?' asked Germaine. 'That gentleman spoke too quickly for me. But I did think I heard that we'll have four guests for luncheon, and one of them the First Consul.'

'Quite correct, and I bet you're thankful that I bought a pair of spring chickens in yesterday's market.'

'Am I to roast them both?'

'Yes, and serve them with creamed potatoes and a salad.

61

Yesterday's vegetable soup to begin with, and the Brie cheese after the chicken. You're sure you have a clean apron?'

'Certain. Alice sent two back yesterday.'

They were walking quickly and were nearly at the Tower. Marie was trying to control her own excitement by picturing Charles's jealousy when he saw Junot wearing the ADC's sash. His own, wrapped like a precious object, was laid in a separate drawer of his bureau.

She was startled to hear Germaine say, 'I can't believe I'm going to wait on the First Consul.'

'Yes, well, don't say too much about it down in Vesle. General Bonaparte likes discreet persons about him. Too many people invent stories about things he's supposed to have said, and never did.'

'I'll be discreet, madame.'

'Here we are, and the stable clock says half-past ten. Not too bad, but we've a lot to do.'

There were fires to be lit in the big room, where a mahogany bureau held a freshly starched and ironed damask tablecloth and six matching napkins with the family initials, L de V, embroidered in heavy silk thread. They were repeated on the handles of the heavy table silver which Marie took from a canteen set on a side table and Germaine distributed at the places for her master and mistress and their four guests.

'*Monsieur le marquis* will sit in his usual place, madame, opposite yourself?'

'Not today, Germaine. My correspondents in Paris tell me that when the First Consul accepts an invitation to a meal he assumes the position of master of the house.'

'Very good, madame.' It was said, and she could only hope that Charles's inherent good breeding would be stronger than his jealousy. If Napoleon Bonaparte honoured the Tour de Vesle with his presence, the owner might gracefully accept to be superseded at his own table! But there was Germaine obviously awaiting the answer to a question which had somehow passed unheard.

'What did you say, Germaine?'

'I asked you – forgive the liberty – what you were going to wear, madame.'

'A dress I bought last year in Milan, Germaine. It's hanging up in my closet. Pink.'

'Then may I help to dress you, madame? There isn't very much time left . . .'

'And you'll need it all to put on your best black and your pretty apron. I can manage by myself, thank you.' And with one quick look around the table, Marie was off, running up the stairs two at a time, bursting into her bedroom to change just as the first sound of horse harnesses were heard from the yard.

When she heard the voice of Bonaparte – that voice more often heard uttering words of command than compliments, barking out orders to 'advance', 'retreat', or 'take the enemy on the flank' than in the liquid charm of the Italian which was his first language – Marie instinctively folded both her hands upon her heart. There *he* was, the man who had told her he loved her, who had held her in his arms in the garden of his Corsican home, and who at the same time had accepted his destiny at her hands. Both were married: no marriage was possible for them, and his mistress she would never be. Never! She picked up the towel which lay across the china basin and drew it hastily over her eyes. No tears now! *'Corraggio, Napoleone!'* she had said to him in the Corsican garden . . . *'Courage, Marie!'* Would he say as much to her?

The men were all talking at once, challenging, interrupting, so that Marie picked up only a word here and there. But she heard enough to know that it was soldiers' talk; of the Austrian enemy who had invaded Italy again; of the French camp at Châlons-sur-Marne, and the French reinforcements that might arrive from Egypt – and at the name of Egypt, where Napoleon had left his expeditionary force under the command of General Kléber when he returned in secrecy to France and his public destiny; at the name of Egypt, the little group of men in uniform standing round the fire seemed to break up,

63

or change position, so that she and Napoleon were facing one another.

She knew that in actual fact he was the shortest man there, and yet by some gift of personality he seemed to be the tallest. His extraordinary eyes, neither blue nor grey, but flashing as he took in every detail of the lovely girl before him, from the fair hair with the golden fillet round it to the pink dress with the décolleté bodice and the voluminous skirt which she picked up in both hands to execute a sweeping curtsy which caused the First Consul to exhale the words, on something like a sigh of relief: *'Ecco! La bella contadina!'*

As if on cue, the men around him kissed Marie's hand and told her she was beautiful. They were all tall and handsome: General Murat, very recently married to Napoleon's sister Caroline, the groom who had made himself into the very picture of a dashing cavalry officer; General Duroc, his only intimate friend; General Junot, the best-tempered; and – of course – Marie's own husband, Charles de la Tour de Vesle, the tallest and best-looking of them all. He kissed her hand as the others did, and then he put one arm round her shoulders, drew her close to him and kissed her on both cheeks.

'Marie, *ma chère*,' he called her.

They all sat down and there was much talk of the wars, and also of Vesle and the estate that the First Consul himself had helped restore to Charles.

In the kitchen Germaine heard Napoleon's voice and, eager to show her willingness, appeared in record time in the doorway, grasping a big silver tureen by its two handles and saying, *'Madame est servie!'*

'Merci, Germaine,' said Marie, and to the whole company: 'The First Consul will preside at table ... Your Excellency, may I beg you to be seated?'

Germaine had set the tureen at Marie's place and whisked out the carved armchair at Napoleon's, who linked his arm through Charles's and said, with an affability unusual on his set face, that he would accept the place of honour 'provided I may share it with you, Marquis,' and moved away with him to the far end of the table. Marie invited General Duroc, the oldest man present, to sit beside her, and Murat and Junot, good friends, took the two remaining places. Marie served the soup, but her attention was caught by two parcels wrapped in gift paper and set between the carving fork and knife.

'What can this be?' she wondered and Napoleon, who had been watching her, replied that there were two trifling gifts from the Bonapartes – 'a fan from Joséphine and a book from me.'

'A fan! The fashion page of the *Moniteur* says they're all the rage in Paris now,' said Marie. She had unwrapped the costly trifle, and had spread the swanskin fan out to its full extent, admiring the copy of a Watteau painting done in pastel colours.

'My wife has a dozen of those things,' said Murat, and looked offended when Marie said she hadn't seen Madame Caroline since she had been in Egypt.

'I didn't know you knew her at all,' he said.

'We met for a few minutes at Joséphine's, the same evening that Dr Berthollet recommended my going to Cairo as a pharmacist,' she said, and Junot gave her a wink which was meant to say, 'Well done!'

But it was what Napoleon said that mattered, when he laid down his spoon with a word of praise for the soup which he called *minestrone*. 'My mother met you that night too,' he said. 'She was very impressed. You must call on her when you go back to Paris.'

'Thank you, sir, but I don't expect to be going to Paris very soon. There's so much to be done down here.'

'Come now, you mustn't turn into a country mouse completely! Take a look at that book I brought you if you want to see all Paris has to offer. It was compiled by a clever fellow, Robert Chevalier, and I find it very inspiring. I want to make Paris the most beautiful city in the world.'

'I'm sure you will, if all I hear about your estate at Malmaison is true,' said Marie.

Napoleon's lip curled as he said: '*Joséphine's* estate at

Malmaison, my dear! Another good reason for your return to Paris – to pay a visit to Malmaison.'

'With Charles?'

'I have other plans for Charles,' said Napoleon.

'Very welcome plans,' said the younger man, but his eyes were anxious when Marie met his gaze. 'He wants me to go to war again, and I'm a soldier, I must go,' was what his expression foretold.

'You don't ask Andoche about *his* plans,' said Murat, with a grin at General Junot, who had been eating his dinner placidly, and seemed to be lost in his own thoughts. Marie, who had a fair, if unwelcome, idea of what those plans might be, but was glad to change the subject, asked innocently, 'Are you going to be married too, Andoche?'

Through the laughter and applause which rose she heard Junot say almost defiantly, 'Yes, I am,' and General Duroc break his silence to ask if she could guess the name of the charming bride.

'At a guess, I would say Mademoiselle Laure Permon.' She smiled sweetly, but if asked why she would have said, 'Because the Permon girl's been chasing him for months.' She said aloud: 'I've thought so ever since he escorted her to our wedding party,' and saw Napoleon bite his lip and Charles smile.

The next moment one of Junot's moist kisses was pressed on her hand, and he whispered, 'Thank you, dear Marie. She's a wonderful girl . . . and she admires you very much.'

Marie smiled graciously, but in truth there was no love lost between Laure Permon and herself – on Marie's side because Laure had committed the crime of making fun of Napoleon. As a penniless second lieutenant he had appeared at the house one day in heavy riding boots entirely too big for his scrawny legs, and Laure and her sister had thought it amusing to call him Puss-in-Boots. The little wretches! Puss-in-Boots, indeed! She glanced down the table at Napoleon. He was finishing his cheese, and though the heavy bunches of hair round his jaws were called 'dog's ears' and the fringe hanging down to his eyes was also not especially feline, he did look very like a sleek well-fed cat at that moment.

Marie was delighted when she saw the success of her meal, and how nicely the dining-room table had been made to look. The silver was gleaming, the smell of coffee was appetizing, and the splendid St-Honoré cake, which now miraculously appeared, thanks to Madame Alice's art, set in a wreath of pink rosebuds, might have graced the wedding breakfast of any of the happy couples whose healths were being drunk. Charles raised his glass to his wife. She saw that he was pleased with her, and she was glad.

But what mattered to Marie was General Bonaparte's approval, and she wrinkled her forehead in puzzlement when he said: 'Are you celebrating Christmas or Easter, Madame Marie?'

She began to say it was too late to celebrate either day when she saw on what the soldier's keen eyes were fixed – the stub of a red candle, fixed in a tin candlestick opposite her husband's place at table.

Then Marie changed the subject from the Feasts of the Church, which since the Revolution were forbidden by law to be celebrated in France, and began to tell Napoleon the truth. It was a habit which these two people, Napoleon Bonaparte and Marie Fontaine (as he had known her when she was a girl), had formed at the start of their friendship. Less than half a year earlier, in the garden of his old home in Corsica, they had confessed to falling short of the truth in their young days when they failed to declare their love for one another. Nothing had come of that belated confession, for both were married to other people, but as she told the poignant little story of the candle, Marie felt that Napoleon was drawing the truth from her word by word, and that only the truth would do.

Marie's story was a very simple one, but told with feeling and with her eyes as steady on Napoleon's as his were on hers. Junot and Murat exchanged covert smiles at their commander's total absorption in the story and the narrator, while

Charles feigned complete boredom. Marie told how, on his solitary first night at Vesle, her husband had lain down on the old sofa with only the one red candle for light, and had been awakened by a knock at the door. He had opened it on an old man, the father of the blacksmith in Vesle. He said the villagers had all been glad to see a flicker of light in the old Tower and know that some of the family had come home. He, Marchais, had come to offer their welcome and say that some of them would come next day to help get the place in order. 'I shall never forget what Charles said when I arrived,' said Marie. 'The good people seem to base all their hopes for the future on just that – one candle burning.' So the stub of the candle had acquired the status of a family heirloom, even more significant than the crusader's cockleshells in the family crest.

'Beautifully told, Marie,' said Napoleon, and his officers applauded softly. Charles remarked that the general was indulgent to a lady's idea of romance.

'Don't disparage a story so much to your own credit,' said Napoleon. 'Congratulations, Charles, you've made a first-rate beginning. You've won the respect of your villagers, which is more than I can say of some men of your age who are stuck in the feudal system like their fathers. Marie, my dear, you do well to cherish your red candle. One candle burning, only one, but on a winter night it has shone in Vesle brighter than any victory illuminations.'

He smiled at both husband and wife, but it was to Charles that he next spoke.

'*Monsieur le Marquis de Vesle!*' he began. 'Have you heard if madame your mother intends returning to France in the near future?'

'I shouldn't think it's very likely, sir,' said Charles. 'I think since my father died she has found sympathetic friends in London. She has bought a house out on the west road, her man of business writes to me, and I don't believe she knows you have given gracious permission for one hundred and fifty thousand *émigrés* to return to France. She wants Marie and me to go to England and stay with *her*!'

68

'Out of the question at the present time.'

'I know, sir.'

Napoleon looked at Marie.

'Would I be outrageously rude if I asked for twenty minutes' private conversation with madame?' he said. 'I have come charged with every sort of message to her, not the least from my wife –'

'And from her old professor of chemistry, no doubt.'

'Why do you say that?'

'She had a letter from him earlier this week, and where Professor Royer is, there will you be also.' It was with Professor Royer that Marie had worked in Egypt.

There was the beginning of a scowl on Napoleon's brow but it smoothed away as he said pleasantly, 'Ah, yes, I hadn't forgotten that I was her sponsor when he began to teach her, and she did me credit, as you did in the field of artillery, my dear fellow! Where shall we go, Marie? I'd like to see all of this lovely place after eating such a marvellous meal.'

'I'll take you to see my water garden. Germaine has been helping me to make it,' said Marie, whereupon Germaine, gratified by a smile from Napoleon, created a diversion by asking if her mistress wanted to wear a hat.

'I'm not wearing a hat, my good girl, your Vesle weather is too fine,' Napoleon said, and Marie smiled. No, his head was bare, without even the tricorne hat and the tricolore cockade she knew so well. No sword, not even the little 'Roman' sword which members of the Convention had worn with their classical draperies, not even a pistol holstered in his belt. She offered her arm, and they walked away to where the little spring dashed down the hillside among primroses and violets.

'This might be a Corsican wood in spring.'

'You miss it, don't you?'

'Not all the time. Since you were there with me – yes.'

Marie looked up at the sky. It was deeply, darkly blue, without a trace, so early in the afternoon, of the rosy tints of sunset, and yet on Napoleon's face there was a kind of afterglow, like Marie's in her own blushing days. He said nothing to account for it, either of embarrassment or of excitement, his voice was as level as ever when he praised the cascade and the flowers it hid.

'Charles seems to be on edge though, doesn't he?'

'He's been like that ever since he lost the sight of one eye at Jaffa.'

'And does that worry you too? Do you care so much?'

'Only when I hear you talking about taking him to Châlons-sur-Marne – with the Austrians waiting on the other side of the river.'

'That would be very poor strategy.'

'My husband is content to leave all questions of strategy to Your Excellency. I confess to being on edge myself. You said you had a message from Joséphine for me. Am I not to know what it is?'

'Certainly you are. I was too absorbed in the charm of being alone with you to remember what I set out to do. But here goes! Did you ever hear the legend of the Little Red Man?'

She had been going to say no uncompromisingly when she remembered her Uncle Prosper when he first took her to look at the outside of the Palace of the Tuileries, telling her about the apparition which appeared in a red mist, foretelling mischief to the royal occupants.

'Has he been around again?' she said, as flippantly as she could. 'Has Joséphine seen him? Have you?'

'I found a letter from him on my table,' he declared. 'And Joséphine sees him in her rooms, in the gardens, everywhere. The only person who has seen him oftener is her daughter, Hortense –'

'Who is nearly as superstitious as her mother.'

'That's why we need you at the Tuileries, Marie – to blow away our superstitions with the breeze of your cool common sense.'

'I doubted you when you said you had a letter from the Red Man. Ghosts, or phantoms, don't write letters, Napoleon. You know that very well. Besides, it was the Bourbons the

Red Man delivered his awful warnings to, not the Bonapartes.'

'That's the devil of it,' the man said miserably. 'Since I took her to live at the Tuileries my poor wife has identified completely with the Bourbon monarchy – specifically with Marie Antoinette.'

Marie's pretty mouth puckered in an urchin's whistle of dismay. 'What do you want me to do?' she said.

'I want you to accept Joséphine's invitation to come to dine and sleep at the Tuileries tomorrow night. Then you can make up your mind if you're willing to become one of Joséphine's ladies of the palace.'

'Ladies of the palace? You mean – like a queen?'

Napoleon said sulkily, 'She thinks it's due to my position.'

'So the move to the Tuileries was Joséphine's own idea. Now that does surprise me. Here I've been thinking she was sorry to leave her own house in the rue des Victoires. She was so proud of it and she made it very beautiful. You wouldn't consider taking her back there to live, away from the Tuileries and all its – associations?'

'You don't seem to realize that it's not her house, it's my house, destined for Eugène de Beauharnais and his wife, when he marries. Nor to realize what sort of reptile I would look if I took Joséphine back to live in a house bought for her by Barras when he was her lover. You knew all about *that*, of course! I paid Monsieur Barras 50,000 francs for the lease plus the so-called "improvements", and now I'm poorer, but I have a clear conscience!'

'You're wonderful!'

'Shall we walk on?'

They walked on to where the slide of water splashed down among the flowers, and Napoleon asked if it had a name.

'La petite Vesle, according to Germaine.'

'Will you give me a flower to remember it by?'

'Of course. What will you have? An anemone? Or an evening primrose?'

'Nothing to do with evening, if you please! We're at high noon! And I've always liked the violets best.'

71

She slipped her arm out of his and dropped on her knees beside the spring. She gathered half a dozen of the little purple flowers, stood up again and began to thread them in his buttonhole.

'I don't know if you're meant to wear flowers with uniform . . .'

'If you give them to me they're more precious than gold. Oh, Marie . . .'

She was in Napoleon's arms again and could prove that he was only just as tall as she was. The whole of his body was taut against her and his mouth was on a level with her own. And then, through the sensation of delicious rest, came a sudden uproar, a crashing through the leaves of the copse where Junot had come that morning, and a woman's voice, screaming, distorted by mania.

'Woe to the Man of Blood!'

It was Mémée, the madwoman, seeking revenge for her grandson killed in battle. She had already fired one shot from the army pistol she carried and which might have been the boy's. When Marie saw this she gave Napoleon a violent push which sent him reeling to the green grass of the water garden, at the same time as his thin nervous hand was groping in his breeches pocket for the classic Corsican weapon of attack or defence, the stiletto.

As the slender blade slid out, Marie heard her own voice, terrified and strident: 'Oh, don't hurt her! Please don't strike her! Can't you see she's mad!'

'By God!' exclaimed Napoleon. 'I should say she *is* mad if she thinks you can turn a country stroll into attempted murder. What brought you fellows here?' he said, turning to Duroc and Murat, who had arrived breathless a few seconds after Mémée. Murat had tied her hands behind her with a length of binder twine.

'We heard shots, sir,' said Duroc.

'You all heard shots, or just you two?'

'All, Your Excellency.'

'Then don't enlarge on the subject to Latour. I'll tell him

72

myself that Marie, as she did at Arcole, has saved my life. Who's this you've brought with you?'

'This' was Mémée's wild granddaughter, whose arm was strongly held in the grasp of Simon Marchais, and who was admonished by Napoleon himself on the need to keep Mémée in a comfortable home under lock and key if necessary if she didn't want to see the woman carted off to a lunatic asylum. Marie knew the strength this threat had in Vesle and tried to explain it to Napoleon, but his only reply was to kiss her hand and say thank you, before Junot brought the horses up and the episode was over.

'Good heavens, Marie, what have you been doing to yourself?' Her husband's ill-natured query told Marie that the skirt of the pink dress was stained with the green of grass and water-weed from her impulsive tumble to her knees beside the spring. 'I saw Napoleon bore similar traces of his pastoral expedition.'

'Thank God he's not bearing traces of blood.'

'You must take some responsibility for that, for making a pet of that crazy woman. Inviting her here, talking to her as if she were sane, entitled to take any liberties with our guests. Just as General Bonaparte takes a liberty with my wife –'

He was hoping to 'get a rise out of Marie', as he called it. He enjoyed seeing her in a temper, swearing that Napoleon never 'took liberties' with her, in his own vulgar phrase. He saw her blush, with the bright blush of her girlhood, but she never spoke a word. Exasperated, but still rather fancying himself in the role of domestic tyrant, Charles asked her what had been the message from Joséphine which had made her husband drag Marie unceremoniously from the luncheon table.

'Oh, it wasn't anything exciting. He'd mentioned it already. About our visiting La Malmaison. But there was something more serious: an invitation to me to visit the Tuileries tomorrow, when Joséphine will ask me to be part of the establishment, as one of the ladies in attendance on herself.'

73

'Is she going to play Marie Antoinette in Paris as well as in the suburbs?'

'Not to the extent of having her head chopped off, I fancy.'

'Well, why don't you go along and hear what she has to say?'

'But you? What would you do? Would you come to Paris with me?'

'I've promised to follow Bonaparte to Châlons-sur-Marne.'

Husband and wife stood in silence until the sounds of their guests departing died away. '*Mon Dieu*, what a day! I hope they aren't punishing Mémée too severely!' Marie gasped, and Charles told her to shut up.

'Don't waste your sympathy on that madwoman,' he said. 'Save it for some more worthy object – like yourself.'

'Why myself?'

'For an eminent scientist, thought to be clever, you're really stupid, aren't you, my dear? If Bonaparte describes this episode to his Chief of Police, who orders an investigation, plenty of witnesses will be found to tell how you petted that woman – always patronized her stall in the market – had her here at Vesle half a dozen times –'

'Oh stop, Charles!' cried Marie. 'Don't think you can scare me by invoking Monsieur Fouché! Remember I was taken before Monsieur Fouquier-Tinville, who condemned the Queen to the guillotine! Who did the same for my Uncle Prosper, and sent me to prison ...'

'As Fouché sent half a dozen citizens to prison, whom he said were involved in the December conspiracy to kill the First Consul,' Charles retorted. 'My God, Marie, don't you realize what this could mean? This insane old woman threatens Bonaparte with a pistol – on *my* land and after he had dined at my table – it is *I* who will be held responsible!'

'And *your wife* took the pistol away from her,' said Marie.

'But the responsibility for the deed is mine,' said Charles, 'because in law I am responsible for you.'

This time she didn't answer back but stood digesting his

words with a sullen look on her face until Charles seized her by the upper arm, and, like a *sergent de ville* arresting a street rioter, marched her off towards the house.

The distinguished guests had gone and Germaine was washing dishes in the kitchen. She broke off when she heard Charles and Marie enter, and came into the big room with a curtsy, saying she hoped everything had been satisfactory.

'Very much so, Germaine, thank you,' said her master kindly. 'By the way, one of our guests, General Duroc, will be here tomorrow morning early. Please have coffee ready for all three of us at six o'clock.'

'Very good, sir.'

'Why Duroc?' asked Marie, and Germaine looked at her strangely.

'Let's go to bed, *chérie*, and I'll tell you all about it,' said Charles. 'I was present when Duroc got his instructions from the First Consul, when he returned from his talk with you.'

He took her affectionately by the hand and led her towards the staircase. Ignoring Germaine, who was asking helplessly if there was nothing she could do for madame, Marie waited until Charles had closed her bedroom door behind them, and taken off his cravat of Malines lace, now rumpled and grubby, before she repeated, 'Why Duroc? What "instructions" did he get from General Bonaparte?'

'You really must get accustomed to calling him "the First Consul", my dear! Or do you persist in thinking of him as "Napoleon"? Very well then. Napoleon told General Duroc that he wanted him to escort you to Paris tomorrow, take you home first, and then deliver you to Madame Joséphine at the Tuileries at four o'clock precisely.'

'Oh Charles, I always thought if I had to go back there that you'd be going with me.'

'I'm going in the opposite direction. I told you.'

'You mean you're going to war.'

'Why are you shivering? Don't pretend you care! Tell me what you thought might take you back to Paris. Was it Guiart's letter?'

'Monsieur Guiart is uneasy ... about the future of my pharmacy. I should have sorted it out by now.'

'Ah, the pharmacy, the sacred Pharmacie Fontaine! Has that fellow Rocroi turned out to be a loser?'

'I don't know.'

Her voice was so forlorn that her husband dropped his jeering tone. 'Get undressed,' he said. 'I'm staying with you tonight.'

Mechanically, without a word of protest, Marie began to unhook the bodice of her dress, and as the hair he had loved to stroke (and describe its colour as 'like poplar leaves in autumn') fell into waves on her bare shoulders, Charles Latour bit his lip.

He said, 'You've asked me several questions tonight, Marie. Permit me to ask you just one. What did Napoleon mean when he called you a something *contadina* – I can't remember exactly, he was speaking in Italian.'

Marie smiled. 'You mean "*la bella contadina*"? It's not difficult. It means "the pretty country girl". But Napoleon didn't mean me. He meant my dress.'

'Your *dress*?'

'Yes, the pink cotton I was wearing. That's what he called it the first time he saw me wear it in Milan.'

'More than I did. *When* did you wear it in Milan?'

'When I went to ask his advice – about having Monsieur Guiart to teach me pharmacy.'

'I might have known it,' the man said. 'Napoleon and Guiart – together or apart, they're formidable rivals. But remember, madame, that you're *my wife*, and that I don't permit any rivals in my bed.'

In a sudden movement he lifted the girl off her feet, pulled the sheets aside and laid her down. Marie lay there inert and passive. She had the strangest delusion that the solitary lighted candle – lit earlier by Germaine – had blazed up into a coruscation of sparks, punctuating the rhythm of her husband's unsubtle approach.

She had long known him to be a hasty and selfish lover,

76

but in the past there had been a tenderness, which had disappeared during their time in Egypt. She thought it had been consumed in the guilt he felt – or feigned to feel – when she came upon him *in flagrante* with her maid, a mere child in years, and ordered him to leave her. Within weeks she had forgiven him when his wound at the siege of Jaffa cost him the sight of one eye. There had still been tenderness in their reconciliation, at least until they were Napoleon's guests in his family home in Corsica on the way to France; there had even, sometimes, been a hint of the passion of their early married life in the Quai Voltaire. But this – assault, it was all she could call it – was more like punishment than passion, and when she understood the words he was muttering into her tangled hair, Marie Latour also understood the jealous reason for her punishment.

'*Bella contadina! Bella contadina!*'

He thought *she* was Napoleon's 'pretty country girl'; he hadn't believed her when she said the words referred to her pink dress.

But Marie knew some potent words of her own. Just as her husband's body trembled in the throes of climax and the flame of the candle steadied to a golden point of light she spoke them aloud: 'One candle burning! One candle burning!' And heard him reply, like a man roused from an evil dream, 'You should sleep now, Marie.'

'We ought both to be asleep,' said Marie. 'General Duroc is sure to be punctual. Where did *he* mean to sleep, by the way?'

Her husband did not answer. He rolled onto his side, and in what seemed to be an instant fell into a heavy, snoring sleep which inevitably kept Marie awake until she, too, dozed off and found oblivion at last.

It was still dark, and the candle had burned low, when she heard the sound of wheels and voices, and realized that Duroc, wherever he had passed the night, was back in the old Tower, where her little Breguet watch on its velvet stand told her it was now a quarter past five.

When she heard Germaine's voice in the room below and a man's voice replying, Marie slid cautiously out of bed. The last light of the guttering candle showed her Charles asleep with his mouth open, defenceless, with dark stubble coming out on his cheeks and jaws. She snatched up the velvet robe, which Germaine had laid across a chair, and let herself out of the bedroom before she put it on.

As she had expected, she saw General Duroc and Germaine, the former seated in one of the chairs at the dinner table, from which he sprang up to make his bow to her, and Germaine emerging from the lamplit kitchen with a coffee pot in her hand.

'Good morning, General,' said Marie. 'I hope you slept well?'

'Very well, I thank you, madame. This very efficient young person' – with a gesture towards Germaine – 'insisted on taking me to her brother's house, where a glorious feather bed was put at my disposal, and I slept like a child. Then the good man insisted on my borrowing his gig to drive you to Soissons, where we'll take the coach for Paris; it'll get us there on time.'

'To Soissons – that's the plan, is it?' said Marie.

'Yes, didn't Latour tell you?'

'But what'll happen to the horse and gig when we set off to Paris?' asked Marie.

She was not surprised when Germaine stepped forward and said proudly, 'I'll drive the gig back here in the afternoon and home to Vesle in the evening. It'll be quite simple, and I'll be here to look after *monsieur le marquis*.'

'But the marquis is going to Châlons-sur-Marne,' said Marie, and like an actor coming in on cue at the sound of his name, the Marquis de la Tour de Vesle appeared at the head of the stairs. He ran down quickly and offered a word of welcome to Duroc.

'How's the great man today?' he said breezily. 'Quite got over his little scare of yesterday, I hope?'

'His Excellency the First Consul does not scare easily, as of

78

course you know,' said Duroc gravely. 'He made no reference to yesterday's episode except to tell us, before we parted, that we were not to mention it in Paris. He and the other two got beds locally, which he said this morning was a great improvement on sleeping under a cannon, wrapped in his army cloak.'

'I'm glad he hasn't lost his sense of humour,' Charles said. 'Marie, my dear, we must all be on our way. Won't you pour us some *café au lait*?'

It was wonderful to be driving in the spring morning, away from the old Tower and the clash of personalities at the breakfast table. Charles had kissed Marie goodbye, and wished her luck in Paris. She had wished him luck in Châlons, and they had both put on a convincing performance for General Duroc's benefit. Duroc handled the reins with assurance, and within ten minutes they had left the estate of Vesle behind them.

It was still too dark to recognize any landmarks even if Marie had known where to look for them; and besides, her attention was fully taken up by Germaine's whimpering, still on the theme of not being allowed to do anything for madame.

'Let me come on to Paris with you, pray do! You will need a maid at your apartment, won't you?'

It was said in a whisper, half stifled by the woollen shawl the girl had wound round her face.

'But I'm not going to stay at the apartment, Germaine, I'm going to the Tuileries.'

'To the palace! Oh, how wonderful! Shall I ever see it? I've never been to Paris, madame.'

'Well, we'll have to do something about that one of these days, but not today. And now, please be quiet, I want to speak to General Duroc ... *Mon général!*' She succeeded in distracting his attention from the horses. 'Shall we have time to go to the Tuileries via the rue St-Honoré?'

'That depends on how much time you spend at the Quai Voltaire, madame.'

79

'Not long – I only have to change my dress.'

'For some ladies that would mean half a day.'

Marie was glad that she had made him laugh. She had seen the day before that General Duroc was out of spirits, and had wondered if he disapproved of the visit to Châlons. She could think of nothing more to say which would amuse him, and all three passengers in the blacksmith's gig were silent, except for Germaine's sniffs, while a watery dawn broke over the forest through which they were passing, and the kilometres rolled up behind them on the road to Soissons.

The market square was full of people gathered round the stalls and benches on which a tempting assortment of foodstuffs was laid out.

A coach without horses was standing outside the inn with its shafts lying on the ground, the entire equipage being observed very closely by half a dozen soldiers with glasses in their hands, who were passing a bottle of wine from one to the other.

'Hussars,' said General Duroc without fervour. 'I wonder where their officer is.'

'Inside the inn, perhaps?'

'It's possible, though I didn't see any sign of a hussar officer in the restaurant. He should be out here, ready to preserve law and order. The people of Soissons are quite agitated already.'

'Oh why, *mon général*?'

He told her, lowering his voice, and giving a backward look at Germaine.

'There's been an outrage by the Hot Feet.'

'Where? And how?'

'Oh, the usual, at a farm five miles outside the town. Don't be alarmed.'

'I'm not alarmed, only surprised to hear they're operating so far north. It was near Lyon that I first heard of them.'

'When was that?'

'When Madame Bonaparte was on her way to join the general in Italy. I was her companion on the trip.'

'You're a far-travelled young lady. Italy first, and then Egypt.'

'I've been very lucky. One soon learns to put up with bandits.'

Bandits was a mild word for the Hot Feet. They were always ready to attack stray travellers on lonely roads, but they preferred to terrorize the inhabitants of isolated farms, burning their naked feet at the kitchen fire to make them tell where their savings were hidden. This was 'the usual', which had earned them the name of Hot Feet.

Germaine, who had been listening, began to cry quietly.

'Don't cry, Germaine, we're in no danger,' said Marie, and turned in her place to pat the girl's hand.

'Not here, madame,' whispered the girl. 'Not now!'

'The hussars have got their officer, I see,' said Duroc, to create a diversion, 'and by good luck it's a man I know.'

'I know him too,' said Marie. 'His name is Garnier; he's a friend of my husband.'

'Would you mind if I went to talk to him for a few minutes?'

'Not if you let me come along with you.'

'Come on then.'

It was easier said than done, for the gig stood high and the wheel was in the way, but Marie gave herself into Duroc's arms and he lifted her clear of the vehicle and set her on the ground. She shook her skirts straight, and after a reassuring wave of the hand to Germaine, slipped it through Duroc's arm. They set out together across the square.

The group of hussars beside the coach had been augmented by a tall, good-looking young fellow, and pushed out of the way by grooms from the inn, leading out four horses. Within seconds there was a rush of about twenty persons who had been lounging on the inn verandah, and who obviously thought, when they saw the horses put in, that their journey to Paris was about to begin.

'We had better make sure of our own seats, hadn't we?' said General Duroc.

'Oh please, let us speak to Captain Garnier first,' begged Marie.

Captain Garnier was making his way towards them. He had called his men to attention at the sight of the general, whom they all saluted smartly, and who said, in the formula required by military etiquette: 'Madame la Marquise de la Tour de Vesle, may I have the honour of presenting Captain Garnier?'

They said, 'Delighted,' simultaneously, and the young man said, '*Madame la Marquise*, what a wonderful surprise! I thought you were miles away, at Vesle.'

'We came from Vesle this morning,' said Marie.

'At the request of the First Consul,' said Duroc, 'I have the pleasure of escorting madame to the Tuileries.'

'Very good,' said the young officer, 'but I could wish you hadn't chosen a day when the Hot Feet were active.'

'That's just what's worrying me,' said Marie. 'Do you see a gig with a young woman passenger in it – look, there, on the far side of the square? That's a friend of mine, Mademoiselle Germaine. Her brother is one of my husband's tenants, the blacksmith of Vesle. He lent us his gig, and she's supposed to drive it back. My husband couldn't do it because he has to join – er – General Bonaparte at Châlons-sur-Marne –'

'My men and I are bound for Châlons, madame.'

'Then – she's so scared of the bandits – couldn't your men be Germaine's bodyguard, *mon capitaine*?'

'Well, I don't know,' Captain Garnier hesitated. 'My orders were "Proceed without delay". Would there be any objection to a stopover in Vesle?' He appealed to General Duroc.

'I should think it would be regarded as a work of necessity and mercy,' said the latter with a smile, and Marie, concealing her surprise at biblical words spoken in these anticlerical times, chimed in with, 'You would have had a much longer stopover at Vesle if my husband had been there to offer you the hospitality of the Tower! Besides, the village is on the direct route to Évreux and Châlons – you needn't be hindered more than five minutes at the smithy.'

'That's a consideration, certainly,' said Garnier. 'Very well, madame, we will do as you ask.'

'Oh thank you, thank you –' Marie began, when he interrupted her to say, 'My men and I must have our *soupe* first – I've arranged it with the innkeeper.'

'Of course,' said Duroc, 'and my ladies and I must have a bite and sup before we go our separate ways. Shall we meet at the coach in three-quarters of an hour? Right? Then I'll go tell Mademoiselle Germaine of her good fortune, and get my belongings from the gig.'

The young captain excused himself and went to give orders to his sergeant while Marie watched General Duroc's return to their vehicle, and there arose about her a clatter as the hussars piled their empty glasses on the edge of the verandah. The innkeeper sent a servant out to collect them, and told the intending passengers that the coach would leave at midday precisely. Captain Garnier, returning, repeated the information for Marie's benefit and made sure she understood it.

'May I escort you to the restaurant now, madame,' he asked, 'or would you rather wait for General Duroc?'

'I'll wait,' she said. 'I'm not very hungry. Hearing the Hot Feet were out took away my appetite! Oh, *mon capitaine*, have you heard – do you know if they did much damage at the farm – I don't know what it's called . . . ?'

'It's called Ferme la Folie,' said Garnier. 'No, they didn't do any damage to the buildings, or the livestock . . . but the people – that's a different story. The farmer's feet were badly burned, because they held him up to a stove with an iron grate. His son, a kid of seventeen, was badly beaten when he refused to tell them where the money was. And his mother (the farmer's mother, I mean) was the worst off of anyone. Those brutes burned her legs right up to the knee as well as her feet. The doctor says she'll be lame for a couple of months.'

'Oh, poor old lady! But they managed to get a doctor to her?'

'Indeed. Let's hope there will soon be an end to such crimes. The First Consul has sworn to smash banditry in France before he is a year older.'

'He'll do it too,' said Marie.

'You believe in him, don't you?'

'Don't *you*?'

'He's all right. If he manages it, he'll score a bigger vote than ever in his next referendum.'

'Here's General Duroc.'

Duroc it was, striding through the crowd in the square, not so much leading Germaine as dragging her by a grasp of iron on her wrist. Marie took a few quick steps forward to meet them.

'Here she is, madame!' exclaimed Duroc. 'Your – er – your friend has graciously consented to accept the arrangements you made on her behalf!'

'Your arrangements!' Germaine blurted out. 'I thought – I didn't know what to think. I was worried – I'm still quite worried – about what my brother and my father would say when they saw me coming home with a band of soldiers, all strangers to us at Vesle . . .'

'Don't be silly, Germaine,' said Marie. 'Your brother and your father are two very sensible men, who'll be grateful to Captain Garnier and his men for taking care of you, instead of leaving you to the tender mercies of the Hot Feet!' at which a little shriek escaped from Germaine.

General Duroc said hastily, 'I think this good woman has something to say to us.' He indicated the innkeeper's wife, an impressive figure in her Sunday best, who had been hovering near their little group.

She stepped forward now, and with a curtsy said, 'If *madame la marquise* and the other lady would follow me . . .' She indicated a door at the back of the balcony. It opened on a bedroom without a bed, which had been arranged with tables, chairs and mirrors as a retiring-room for ladies. It was presided over by a chambermaid ready to pour warm water from a garden *arrosoir* and hand soap and towels to two women who might have been farmers' wives, half-stunned by such unusual attentions.

Marie smiled agreeably. She welcomed the presence of their fellow guests, which she saw would be a check on Germaine's panic about the Hot Feet.

Garnier was still expressing his opinions very freely, even in a crowded dining room, when the two girls completed their hasty toilettes and joined the officers at table. The men stood up politely and pulled out two chairs opposite the *banquette* on which they had been seated, but there was hardly a pause in their conversation, and Marie, as she accepted a bowl of hearty vegetable soup from a waiter, realized that the young hussar was trying to pick Duroc's brains. How, he wanted to know, did Napoleon mean to tempt the Austrians into another challenge to battle? The too-familiar 'Napoleon' was bad enough, but it was soon replaced by the nickname which Marie despised as being particularly unsuited to a commanding general, though it had its origin among the troops: 'the little Corporal'.

Marie knew that she was frowning, and knew that General Duroc saw the frown and sympathized. He cut the young man short with a summons to the waiter, asking him to bring the duckling, which was the next item on the menu. 'The soup is very good,' he said, 'but we all need something solid for such an afternoon as we have before us. May I pour the ladies some wine?'

'The wine is excellent,' said Marie, nodding over her glass to the innkeeper's wife, who had taken up her station behind the two girls and was agitating them by a babble of apologies for the hurried meal and the movement of the people around them, all working themselves into a frenzy over items of baggage they thought they had forgotten and hunting for keys which had certainly been mislaid. Germaine had kept her fingers through the handles of the small leather valise she held on her lap and even Marie's eyes were fixed on a bag set between her left leg and a leg of the table.

The landlady's recommendation of her own cream cheese

fell on deaf ears, and it was almost a relief when a stentorian voice began to call, *'En voiture! En voiture! Pour Paris! Pour Paris!'* and there was a concerted rush towards the door.

Captain Garnier, young and agile, slipped ahead of the throng and called to a trooper who was standing at the foot of the step with his arm round the newel post, and urged Germaine forward.

'Now, mademoiselle,' he said briskly, 'here's your driver. My sergeant, Guillaume, he's a good whip, and he'll have you safe at home in not much more time than an hour.'

'Too fast!' said General Duroc.

'Oh, let's see them start!' cried Marie.

She heard Duroc's warning about the time, Captain Garnier's assurance that their seats would be held for them, gave Germaine a spontaneous hug and told her to thank her brother and give *monsieur le marquis* her love, and while the girl was lifted into the gig wished her *'Bon voyage . . . bonne chance et au revoir!'*

Their places had certainly been kept for them. Two of the inn stable boys began waving and calling as soon as Marie and Duroc entered the coach, and made their way against the press of passengers until they had given up their seats to the general and the girl. Marie was breathless when she was settled by the window, and thankful for Duroc's protective arm round her shoulders. Half deafened by the uproar of farewells she was nevertheless aware that she must join in them, and she waved goodbye to the innkeeper and his family, who had assumed the aspect of old friends. By her side she heard Duroc muttering that the coachman's estimated time of arrival in Paris was half an hour later than the timetable said.

'Then I'll be late for Madame Bonaparte,' Marie said.

'I'm sure she'll understand that it's not your fault. You and she are great friends, aren't you?'

'We were in the Carmes prison together. And after that we shared a home until her marriage.'

'And your own, eh? Do you know her daughter, Mademoiselle de Beauharnais?'

'Of course, she was one of the family until she went to Madame Campan's school. I loved Hortense, she was a dear little girl.'

She fancied that this reply gave great satisfaction to General Duroc, for his face was creased in a broad smile. But his next words had nothing to do with Joséphine and her daughter but with Marie's comfort. She must be tired, she ought to try to doze, and presently Marie was aware that an army cloak was being wrapped around her and that she was drifting peacefully into sleep.

At the same time she was quite aware of her surroundings; of the buzz of conversation, dying away now to the merest thread of sound; of the bright panorama of fields and woods moving beyond the glass of the window with a little river running through the fields which she thought must be the Vesle. It made her think that she was on her way home – but since when had she thought of the Tour de Vesle as home? And she burrowed more deeply into the cocoon of sleep to banish the impression, which must be wrong.

When she awoke, to the sound of angry voices, she saw that the stream was still flowing outside the window but now it was broader, deeper, darker and within her line of vision, flanked by tall houses and spanned by more than one arched stone bridge. It was the Seine, and the girl baptized Marie Fontaine was back in Paris, her birthplace and her home as Vesle could never be. General Duroc, as she raised her head from his shoulder, saw tears in her eyes.

'Curse those quarrelsome fellows!' he said. 'They woke you up.'

'Oh, I had a very good sleep, thanks to you,' Marie rejoined. 'What were they quarrelling about?'

'One of them was smoking a vile cigar,' said Duroc, 'and refused when the others asked him, for his wife's sake, to put it out. The row stopped short of fisticuffs, I'm glad to say.'

'Not much room for a fist fight in a coach,' said Marie with a laugh. 'I thought it might be something political.'

'Political rows are out of fashion now,' said Duroc.

The coach turned a corner and was negotiating the first works by which Paris was to have a noble street named for one of Napoleon's Italian victories, the rue de Rivoli. And there at the end of it could be seen the massive bulk of the palace of the Tuileries.

'Madame – Marie – are you remembering the night when the mob attacked the palace and General Bonaparte dispersed them with what he called a whiff of grapeshot?' said Duroc.

'Fire from the cannon my husband fetched from the artillery park at Les Sablons,' said Marie.

'Was Latour in that? I thought Murat was the hero of the hour. He was very much the hero of the story when he told it a few nights ago at Soissons.'

'In that same inn?'

'Yes, we stopped there for dinner on our way to Reims. And Bonaparte set the record straight, when he told how you did first aid among the wounded. "She was the real heroine," he said, and asked us all to drink your health, which we did, with what the English call a cheer.'

'That was very kind of him,' said Marie. 'He makes too much of what anyone else could have done better than me, who had had my training.'

'You're too modest, madame.'

But Duroc saw that she kept her eyes on the palace as long as it was in sight.

'Well, my dear, here we are in Paris, in good time for Madame Bonaparte.'

'I'm glad.'

'So am I. Because there's something I would like you to say to her, if you will.'

'Anything you want, General Duroc.'

He patted her hand, but said no more, nor was there much opportunity for confidences as the coachman drew up his horses with a flourish in the courtyard of the central coaching office. Marie was glad to see a line of cabs waiting beyond the gates. She knew that they were at some distance from the apartment where she had lived with Charles, and she was aware that Duroc, who had got out of the coach slowly and stiffly, was limping as he walked. He had been seated in a cramped and awkward way so that she could be comfortable while she slept.

With guilt in her heart she said: 'You're lame, *mon général*! Is your old wound giving you trouble?'

'Yes, the hip wound I got at Jaffa, but don't worry about it, your husband was worse off than I was, losing the sight of one eye! But he has a wife to take care of him, lucky man – Do be careful!'

. Marie, in one jump, left the courtyard for the crowded street and annexed a cab. Seeing that one of his passengers was limping, the driver helped him into the vehicle, placed the bags at his feet, gave an arm to Marie and heard her say: '*Dix-sept Quai Voltaire.*'

'You said that so decisively,' said Duroc, who had been listening, 'I think you're glad to be back.'

'Oh I am, I am!' said Marie passionately, and for all her concern at Duroc's condition the feeling of joy persisted in her heart. As soon as the cab began to move she had started to pick up the landmarks: they were driving through what had been, in the days of the Revolution, the Second Section, and by craning her neck Marie could see the corner of the rue St-Honoré where her uncle's pharmacy had stood, which was now her own – yes, and the problem of her unsatisfactory tenant would have to be settled as soon as possible!

6

As the cab approached the far end of the Pont Royal, Duroc could not fail to notice that Marie's attention was far less securely fixed on the Tuileries than it had been earlier, and, being in a sentimental mood himself, suspected that she might have yielded to some tender recollections of her courting days not so very long ago. He was not far wrong: the sight of the horse chestnuts which edged the river bank, reminded Marie of Charles Latour's praise of the *blonde cendré* shades of her own hair, like the leaves of autumn poplars. Poor Charles – his praises hadn't lasted long! And then Marie's attention was again distracted by the prosaic sight of the great painted doorway of 17 Quai Voltaire – the paint faded by winter weather – and leaning against it the slack figure of the concierge, Monsieur Bélard, in his favourite pose of policing all the traffic and all the passers-by on the Quai Voltaire.

'Monsieur Bélard! Monsieur Bélard!'

'*Ah, Madame la Marquise! Soyez la bienvenue!* We heard you were coming back to town.' The man pulled open the door of the cab and extended a powerful arm to help Marie to the kerb. 'We are very glad to see you, looking so well.'

'Thank you kindly. But how in the world did you know I was to be in Paris?'

'A friend of *monsieur le marquis*, General Desaix, stopped on his way to the palace to let us know that we might expect you with this gentleman –'

'General Duroc,' said Marie, and Bélard acknowledged the presentation with a bow and a *'pour vous servir, mon général,'* which made Duroc smile.

'Come then, let us go upstairs,' said Marie. 'How's Madame Bélard?'

'Very well, thank you. She's in your flat with Madame Armande. When we heard you were coming I went round to Madame Armande's lodging and told her she must come back and make the flat nice for her young lady, which she was glad to do.'

'That was very kind of you and of Armande too,' said Marie. 'Shall we go upstairs?'

'Be careful, madame, don't trip on this awkward step,' said Bélard. He opened a kind of trap door in one half of the wooden doorway, and Marie gathered her skirts in one hand while Duroc watched with interest. As a young officer he had seen a similar device in many of the great houses of the faubourg St-Germain, a device used for coquetting in the showing off of a slim ankle and a slender waist. But Marie was not a coquette. She stepped indoors nimbly and gave all her attention to a woman hurrying across the cobbled yard. This was Madame Bélard, who bade her welcome and asked what she could do to help madame.

'You and Armande seem to have done most of it already,' said Marie calmly, and as if she heard her name the maid came thumping down the stone steps of a public staircase and greeted her mistress with the unconventional cry of: 'Oh, it's so good to have you back!'

'Look out my best blue dress, Armande, and a pair of white gloves and the little fur hat.' Marie lowered her voice to a domestic murmur about 'a bottle of the best Chambertin and the crystal glasses.'

'I have a letter for you, madame,' said Madame Bélard, producing it from her apron pocket. 'Madame Beauchet left it this morning, and I'm afraid it's bad news. Her husband is dead.'

'Dead? Oh, poor Marie-Josèphe! I'll try to go to see her tomorrow. What happened?'

'He had bronchitis which turned to pneumonia, and he passed away last week. I don't think they ever had enough to eat. And I suppose she's still worried about the Marquise de La Fayette?'

'Who's still in Holland, I believe.'

When the two women had gone downstairs, Duroc said, 'I couldn't help hearing that there has been a bereavement. I hope not in your own family?'

'No – oh, no! A dear friend has lost her husband. She and I were next-door neighbours when she was the personal maid of the Marquise de La Fayette and she used to play with the children and me in their garden.'

'You will miss him.' And General Duroc gave up a few minutes to wondering what Latour thought of the friendship between his wife and a servant. Probably that it degraded his precious marquisate!

By way of changing the subject, he said, 'What an attractive apartment this is!'

'Oh, thank you! We like it! We've rented it ever since we were married, so we like to think this is where it all began, though Charles feels we should look for somewhere better – but now, of course, we've got Vesle.'

'A beautiful and historic place.'

'Yes. General Duroc, would you excuse me for ten minutes? I really must get dressed, and you have something to say to me before we set out for the palace.'

'You're the first lady I ever heard say she could dress for a palace in ten minutes!'

'I can try.'

General Duroc was restless or nervous, or both. He took a few paces up and down the salon, put another log on the fire and examined the label on the wine bottle which Armande had brought in before she disappeared into the next room with her mistress. Only when he heard the sound of laughter and men's voices on the landing did he sink into his armchair. He was out of it again in a moment when two men in uniform came in.

'*Mon vieux, Duroc!*'

'*Latour! Comment va?*'

'I do well, but where's my wife?'

'Here I am!' Marie was in the room, not only dressed in ten minutes, but elegant in a high-waisted gown of blue shot silk with a shoulder pelisse, a reticule of blue morocco, and in one hand a pair of white kid gloves. 'I thought you were going to Châlons?'

Her husband kissed her palms and her wrists, and stood back while she welcomed General Desaix, whom she had known in Egypt. He was famous in the French army as a very able soldier and as, personally, the most untidy, even slovenly of men.

'Well!' said her husband. 'The plan is to kick Alvintzi and his Austrians out of Lombardy, and as for me, I'm to have one night in Paris and report tomorrow to the 4th Artillery at Fort Vincennes.'

'That'll be like old times, won't it?'

'As far as the regiment goes, yes, but Bonaparte has introduced new artillery tactics, which will take some getting used to. He's back here too.'

'You'll be all right by the time of the muster at Lyon,' said Desaix, and Marie's query, 'Are you going to Lyon?' received no reply.

General Duroc's proposal that the marquis should escort his wife to the Tuileries met with another snub.

'The First Consul is sending a *calèche* for both of you,' said Charles. 'We'd better do as he says.'

Marie said quickly that they ought to start without delay.

Down in the street she crossed to the river side of the Quai Voltaire and spoke pleasantly to two elderly stall keepers, who had arranged, the one flowers, the other books, for sale on top of the Seine wall.

'No sign of a *calèche* here yet,' said Duroc, and Marie admitted that they *were* early. 'But so much the better,' she said. 'You'll have time to tell me whatever it was you mentioned in the coach.'

Duroc looked as if he would rather face a cavalry charge. 'Promise not to laugh,' he said miserably. 'But you did tell me that you shared a home with Madame Bonaparte before her second marriage and knew Hortense de Beauharnais.'

'General Duroc,' said Marie, 'tell me if I've guessed correctly. Is it Hortense de Beauharnais you're interested in?'

The man's flushed face was all the reply she needed. But he was determined to tell the whole story and answered that he had never met Hortense – Ma'mselle Hortense – until last October, when she left school and came to live at the Tuileries with her mother. For him, Duroc, it was the *coup de foudre* ... and in November he asked her to marry him.

'And she? What did she say?' asked Marie, breathless.

'She didn't say much, but she let me feel that she was not indifferent to me. Her parents – her mother and her stepfather – were the ones who did the talking. They expressed their opposition to the match, and forbade it out of hand.'

'Her stepfather? You mean General Bonaparte?'

'Himself.'

'But he's *fond* of you, we all know that! He's always praising you . . .' protested Marie.

'But he says I'm too old for her. I'm only three years older than he is.'

'Which makes you thirty-five.'

'*She* doesn't think I'm too old. Madame Marie, all I ask you is to put in a good word for me with Madame Bonaparte. She's the one who matters. Napoleon listens to her. He'll withdraw his own candidate if she says so . . .'

'*Is* there another candidate? Have you a rival, General? Whom?'

'Napoleon's younger brother, Louis Bonaparte.'

The *calèche*, which drew up at that moment, and the driver's verbose excuses for being five minutes late, saved Marie from replying. General Duroc helped her in, and waited to get in himself until she had adjusted the tiny circle of fur which on a windy day did duty for a hat. He was glad her husband had not come down the *Quai* to see them start and to exercise his talent for sarcasm on the ramshackle vehicle, sent over from the palace stables, as suitable for a marchioness. They set off with a terrific rattle of wheels and creaking of leather, but Marie had no comment to make, either on the *calèche* or on Duroc's romantic story. In silence they crossed the Pont Royal and began to traverse the parade ground called the Carrousel.

Marie's thoughts had gone back to the day when General Bonaparte had used what was called 'a whiff of grapeshot' to clear the streets around the Tuileries of the rebel troops who had challenged the Convention, the rulers of France since the Revolution. She, the bride of a few weeks, had volunteered to administer first aid and nursing care to Napoleon's men. He had met her on the Carrousel to say 'Welcome!' and to thank her. At which point, aware of her husband's disapproval but quite carried away by her admiration for a man she thought of as tomorrow's leader, she had kissed Napoleon's hand as if he were a royal personage.

She was dimly aware that General Duroc was standing up in the *calèche* and pointing, while the flimsy vehicle rocked from side to side.

'Sit down, *mon général*! You'll have us over!'

'Look there, madame! That girl in green!'

It was Hortense de Beauharnais.

Hortense grown up, with a leghorn hat, a dress and cloak of pale green brocade, who was approaching the entrance to the Tuileries.

'I see her, General! Hurry and you'll catch her up!'

'I can't! I can't appear to be chasing her! It would make a very bad impression!'

'On whom? The sentries?'

Marie did not think she spoke aloud, but the next moment she could do nothing more than glare at the retreating form of the soldier who had talked of the *coup de foudre* Hortense de Beauharnais had given him, but who was willing to repay it by the kind of decisive retreat which Charles Latour would have taken in his and Marie's own courting days. She shrugged, and told the driver to go on quickly to the great

95

door of the Tuileries where four sentries in scarlet tunics were pacing up and down.

The entrance hall of the palace had changed since Marie was there last. It had been whitewashed, and the symbolic design of the red cap of liberty painted on the walls had disappeared in the tide of white. In the upper galleries a series of busts from classical and modern days provided the greatest soldier of the age with a background of heroes.

Marie had expected to see the usual crowd of soldiers swarming in the military offices of the Tuileries. She was not prepared for the individual who now approached her and enquired her name. A tall, stately person with a bare head, he wore an odd mixture of army uniform and civilian evening dress, with around his neck a chain of gold links from which hung a circlet of solid gold with an unfamiliar design. He carried a book bound in vellum, in which he appeared to verify Marie's name, for he said with a low bow: 'Madame Bonaparte expects you, *Madame la Marquise*. Please to step this way.'

He ceremoniously opened one half of a mahogany door with the panels outlined in gilt, and ushered Marie into a salon furnished in yellow and brown satin, with vases of spring flowers set on marble console tables.

Marie heard the click of the door closing, and looked around her uncertainly. She had expected to see Joséphine immediately, not to be confronted with this luxurious silence! Then she saw a partly opened door on the other side of the salon, which gave a glimpse of furniture covered in violet-blue silk. More flowers here, their perfume extracted by the warmth of wax candles massed in crystal chandeliers.

It's like the palace of the Sleeping Beauty, thought Marie, and beneath her breath she whispered, 'Joséphine! Joséphine!' as if she could call the woman to her side. There was no reply, and yet it seemed as if there was the sound of an indrawn breath from a third room – visible, as the second had been, through a partly open door.

Marie went boldly forward. The third room was dark, for

thick curtains were drawn across the windows, and a satin bedspread, striped blue and white, was drawn across a heavy mahogany bed. The sleeper lay on a chaise longue padded in white satin. A book lay where it had fallen from her hand, and by the light of a shaded lamp on a side table Marie saw that it was Joséphine.

The wife of the First Consul lay as Marie had often seen her lie in prison, or in the home they shared in the rue de l'Université. But then it had been cold; now her rooms were hot, and there was a faint film of perspiration on Joséphine's forehead. Her white muslin dress was crumpled, revealing much of her beautiful breast beneath a heart-shaped brooch of dark red garnets which Marie had never seen before. A love token from Bonaparte? She looked around the room for an answer, and met the eyes of a woman with her finger to her lips. It was Agathe Riblé, Joséphine's personal maid, still in her mistress's service in the Tuileries.

Possibly Marie, in her impulsive way, might have broken through the injunction to silence if she had not seen that it didn't only apply to herself. A girl in a green dress, entering the bedroom on her heels, was included in Agathe's finger-to-lips gesture: Hortense de Beauharnais. Agathe pointed to what appeared to be a bathroom and made a stabbing gesture with one hand which indicated that Hortense was to take Marie in that direction. The girl slipped one arm round Marie's waist and drew her away. Marie paused only for a last look at the beautiful, pampered and relaxed figure of Joséphine.

'How well your mother looks!' were Marie's first words after the exchange of hugs and kisses was over.

'Yes, though she's always complaining that the Tuileries doesn't suit her. She doesn't like it here.'

'Doesn't like the Tuileries?'

'Don't let's stand chatting in the bathroom, come into my own room, Marie dear.'

Hortense's room was furnished in blue and white, like her mother's. She wheeled up an easy chair for Marie, another for herself, kicked off her shoes and produced a box of chocolates.

'What distresses my mama, dear, is the thought that these were Queen Marie Antoinette's rooms before she was guillotined. She thinks the Queen must resent her being here and will make her pay for it.'

'Oh, what rubbish!'

'And now that my – the First Consul – has taken to seeing the Little Red Man around every corner, he's not much good at curing her delusions.'

'Ah!' Marie smiled. 'He told us about the Little Red Man when he came to Vesle.'

'He told us what a lovely home you have. Oh, Marie, you can't think how I envy you. That gorgeous-looking husband – with a title – and a splendid home to be mistress of . . . do you really know how lucky you are?'

'Oh yes, I think so. But, darling, you could have a fine house, and probably a title too, if you chose to accept General Duroc.'

'How did you . . . ? Oh, I suppose he told you when he brought you up to Paris.'

'He did, and very nicely too. I liked him very much.'

'Maman says he's too old for me.'

'That doesn't mean a thing. She's probably out of spirits, or out of humour, or both at once, since you say she doesn't like the Tuileries. Is there one special thing she doesn't like?'

'Yes, the way the people come in from the public gardens and crowd up to her windows while she's dressing. She says she has no privacy.'

'Ah well, that isn't to be tolerated. Can't the First Consul arrange for a patrol of sentries along the front of the building? Where are his rooms, by the way?'

'Up that staircase.'

Hortense smiled at Marie's look of amazement at that unusual adjunct to the bath, the bidet and other bathroom equipment, the polished oak staircase which rose to the second storey of the palace.

She said: 'Maman has learned not to disturb His Excellency with trivialities. He's much more grandly housed on the next

98

floor than we are down here, and as his windows don't face the gardens he knows nothing about the intruders. He keeps himself to himself upstairs and when he wants feminine society he rings a bell and comes downstairs to bask in our admiration.'

Alone with Hortense in her pretty little boudoir, Marie wondered how to introduce the subject of General Duroc again. She sought in vain for the right words, however, and found nothing better to say than an awkward, 'Who was that man?'

'What man?'

'That man in black with a gold chain round his neck, and a book with a lot of names in it, who met me at the door and let me into the suite . . . ?'

'Oh, he's the intendant of the palace. He's responsible for all the day-to-day arrangements, including the visitors' list. A new appointment by the First Consul. They had an intendant at Versailles, so of course we had to have one here.'

Marie was chilled by the sarcasm in her voice, and Hortense went on: 'Maman and her husband are working on some appointments to make her more important. She's his wife, so she must have ladies-in-waiting, women of the bedchamber, I don't know what all. When I saw you here today I thought you'd come to say you'd be one of them – I know she wants you.'

'I don't think I've the right background for a lady-in-waiting. You know what I was, a pharmacist's niece, working behind the counter of his shop, and sewing army shirts in a national workshop –'

'And one of the *savants* of Egypt before you were a marchioness. Don't underrate yourself, Marie! You can hold your own with any of the women who jumped at the chance to get closer to the Bonapartes!'

'And who are they? That's the kind of news that never gets to Vesle . . .'

'Well, there's Madame de Montesson, who was the morganatic wife of the Duc d'Orléans –'

'The regicide!'

'I told you they weren't in your class, my dear. Her claim to fame is that men wear silk stockings and buckled shoes in her salon. And then there's Madame Récamier, a banker's wife, whose reputation was built on the portrait David painted of her. But those women are another reason why my mother isn't happy here.'

'She *is* very pretty.'

'Oh pah! But you – I've heard Maman say to the First Consul that Marie has an honest heart, she's a girl of solid worth, and he agreed with her.'

'That makes me sound like a suet pudding.'

The tinkle of a bell ringing in the upper regions started them both. '*C'est Bonaparte!*' exclaimed Hortense, and she and Marie stood up instinctively at the sound of rapid footsteps on the stairs.

Joséphine must have been woken by the bell, for they heard her voice and Napoleon's reply, and then he was in the boudoir by their sides. It was the first time Marie had ever seen him out of army uniform. His velvet suit, a tail-coat and knee-breeches was the consular uniform devised by himself, the colour being what was called 'rose carnation', and Marie wondered if, when he saw himself in a mirror, the First Consul ever thought of the Little Red Man.

Napoleon Bonaparte was only two inches taller than the little woman who crept into Hortense's boudoir in his wake. He was paler than he had appeared to be at Vesle, and his hair was free of powder. He had ceased to wear the 'Titus' haircut he had adopted in Milan, and the lank black locks straggled over the brow that his phrenologist called 'noble'. Joséphine, shimmering in a dressing-sacque embroidered in diamanté, her lips and hands trembling, now appeared to be afraid of him.

'Weren't you glad to see Marie?' asked Joséphine of her daughter, and Napoleon answered for her that they were all glad to see Marie in such good looks. 'Did Duroc take good care of you, my dear?' he asked the girl.

'The best care,' she replied.

'I was sorry you had to find the Hot Feet in your path,' said Napoleon.

'I never even saw them,' said Marie.

'You never told me about the Hot Feet!' said Joséphine, and Napoleon replied that he had been thinking about nothing but the Hot Feet since the day before. He thought the only thing to do was burn them out of their hiding places in the forests. Otherwise they would soon be attacking citizens in the streets of Paris. He had discussed the danger with Eugène and Eugène agreed with him.

Tears, which Joséphine was prone to shed easily, appeared in her hazel eyes. She knew that her husband's discussions usually led to action, and was afraid her son, Eugène de Beauharnais, had been selected as the leader of an attack by fire upon the brigands.

'There's no cause for alarm,' Napoleon said sharply. 'It would be a perfectly routine operation, and not my first priority, madame!' Then, changing the subject: 'Aren't you going to offer some refreshments to these young ladies? Isn't your maid available? Take Hortense into your bedroom for a little *goûter* and leave Marie to me. I have a question to ask her.'

Now for it, thought Marie, while the scent of hot chocolate crept in from the room next door. Now for a cross-examination on why I don't want to be a lady-in-waiting at the Court of the Tuileries – for it is a court, another Versailles, with its ruler and its intendant, and even its pretty princess, who doesn't mean to stoop to poor old Duroc! But first she was ready with a question of her own.

'Sir, what *is* your first priority, if it isn't the Hot Feet?'

He was visibly taken aback. 'Why – I thought you knew. I thought I told you at Vesle. It's Alvintzi and his Austrians in Italy. I have to win back Italy for the second time.'

'By way of Fort Vincennes and Lyon?'

'And Geneva.'

'You're going into Italy through Switzerland?'

'The French were doing great things in Switzerland while

I was still in Egypt. General Masséna drove the Russians out of Zurich.'

'The Russians?'

'Come on, Marie, polish up your geography. Didn't you know perfidious Albion had brought the Czar and his ministers into the latest coalition against France?'

'I knew about Masséna, certainly. And when you decide to invade England that will be the end of their presumption.'

'I hope so. But now let me ask you something. What are you going to do now?'

'Now?'

'Immediately. When Colonel Latour leaves Paris. When the army moves into Italy.'

'Stay on in Paris and work at Val-de-Grâce, perhaps. But I've a feeling Charles would like me to go back to Vesle.'

'No!'

It was so explosively said that the faint hum of voices from the next room stopped at once, and Napoleon lowered his own voice before he said, 'I won't allow it.'

She stared at him nonplussed, and he saw he must explain.

'Do you think I'm going to let you go back to that lonely place, where one of the tenants is a madwoman who prowls the fields with a loaded pistol, and a dangerous bunch of brigands is terrorizing a district not many miles away? Never!'

'It's my husband's ancestral home and I've got to keep an eye on it.'

'Let him keep an eye on it himself. Look here, Marie, Latour is coming to take you back in about half an hour. Let me ask him if he wants compassionate leave to look after Vesle, and if he says yes I'll let him go.'

'You'd break his heart.'

'Nonsense.'

'It's true. I know how much it means to him to be in command of artillery again. More than Vesle and more than me.'

'More than you? What a fool!'

'Your Excellency forgets that I have a home on the other side of the river. I can very well stay on in the Quai Voltaire.'

'It wouldn't be suitable.'

'Why not?'

'With your husband at the front you couldn't live alone.'

'I've done it before, during the first Italian campaign.'

'Marie!' said Napoleon, and took two steps towards her. 'Why won't you let yourself be guided by me? If you would only accept the position of a lady-in-waiting, your home would be here at the Tuileries. You'd be protected, guarded in every way, honoured and admired.'

'Yes!' said Marie. 'And I'd be one of the women Hortense told me about today, who are said to have taken that job for the sake of getting closer to the Bonapartes. I don't want –' Her words ended in a sob.

The First Consul flung his arms round Marie and kissed her tears away.

'My darling,' he said, 'you can never be too close to me.'

7

Marie sat in the empty yellow salon, into which Hortense had led her, more wretched than she had been at any time since Napoleon, in his own Corsican garden, had told her he was in love with her – that she was 'the girl he ought to have married'. At that time, she knew, he had discovered Joséphine's infidelity. Then she, Marie, had persuaded Napoleon, for the sake of his own career, not to divorce his erring wife. So far her conscience was clear. The reward of Napoleon's unblemished record was that he had become First Consul of France.

She knew that Napoleon had taken a mistress in Cairo. The seductive Madame Fourès, called Bellilotte, had been his revenge on Joséphine. But Marie was proud that he and she had never stooped to the enjoyment of an illicit love. Now, on their first meeting, that very afternoon, they had been in each other's arms in what seemed to Marie like the essence of clandestineness, with his wife dismissed to the next room and Marie's husband outside, making his way towards the Tuileries!

At that moment Marie was ready to go back to Vesle.

By the time her husband arrived she had thought of an alternative scheme for herself which she had not perfected when Joséphine, affable as ever when she had a handsome young man in tow, left him in the yellow salon.

'The First Consul will be with you in a moment, *Monsieur le Marquis,*' Joséphine said formally. 'I know he wants to ask you about madame your mother.'

'She's very well, I thank you,' said Charles, concealing his surprise. Marie too, when they were alone, admitted her surprise at Bonaparte's interest in an *émigrée*.

When Bonaparte himself appeared in the yellow salon, giving Joséphine her dismissal by a summary jerk of the chin, he opened the subject at once.

'Ha, Latour!' he said. 'You tell me your mother doesn't plan on coming back to France?'

'She feels the law against *émigrés* would prevent her.'

'The new code, now in preparation, gives different interpretations of the law. In the meantime, my dear Latour, will you tell Madame la Princesse de Polignac et de Vesle that I should personally welcome her back to her native land?'

'Thank you, sir. Er, may I tell you that my mother does not use the title of Polignac, which was her father's? Only her husband's.'

'Very good. *Madame, mes hommages.*'

And with a bow to Marie, Napoleon left the room.

'I should like to see my mother's face,' said Charles, 'when she hears of a personal welcome from the man she calls "the Corsican usurper".'

'Are you going to tell her?' asked Marie.

'Not I. But she'll have to know if her name is to be taken off the *émigré* list. No, that's a job for the attorney. I'll write to him.'

'The name of the Princesse de Polignac,' said Marie, 'would look well among the ladies-in-waiting.'

'I take it you have refused.'

'Certainly.'

'Good girl.'

'I could see you didn't want me to do it.'

'It's not your kind of thing. But I would like to know what you do want to do.'

Marie took a few restless turns about the room, studied her reflection in the mirror and proposed that they should go for a stroll in the palace garden. 'It'll be dark in half an hour,' she said, 'and I've hardly been out of doors all day.'

'Well, for half an hour, then. I can't stay away too long. The general may want me again.'

Marie observed that by issuing orders for the next day the

First Consul had again become 'General Bonaparte' to his officers. She led the way from the luxurious suite.

The wind, blowing when she first crossed the Carrousel, had dropped to a breeze. It was a beautiful spring evening, fragrant with rhododendrons in masses. There was already lamplight in some of the windows of the Quai Voltaire.

'Isn't it peaceful now?' said Marie, with a shiver. She had remembered that her husband was to go to war on the morrow. Perhaps he was thinking the same, for he put his hand through her arm and pressed it to his side, though what he said was as banal as ever.

'I came down to see you start, after you rushed out of the apartment, but you were gone. That *calèche* can't have kept you waiting.'

'The driver was only a few minutes late. I wish General Duroc had been equally enthusiastic,' said Marie.

'What d'you mean?'

'I mean he told me he was in love with Hortense de Beauharnais, but when he saw her in the Carrousel he didn't hurry to join her. In fact he went the other way.'

'Very interesting, but tell me about yourself,' persisted Charles.

'Well! I told you Professor Guiart had written to me?'

'About the pharmacy?'

'Yes. About the man who was renting it, and is ready to give it up.'

'What's he going to do?'

'Guiart may take him into his own labo.'

'Not the Army Medical?'

'His health broke down in that before. So . . . I was thinking I might live there myself while you were away, and keep the pharmacy going.'

'Live in the rue St-Honoré all alone? I won't hear of it!'

'No, not all alone. I'd have a friend to live with me.' And while Charles listened with increasing impatience she told him that Marie-Josèphe Beauchet, who had been widowed,

106

would be the ideal housekeeper and companion at the Pharmacie Fontaine, and might even be taught to sell cosmetics and perfumes over the counter 'as I did before we met, darling,' Marie concluded. She saw in her husband's eyes that she had reminded him of the pretty vivacious girl he had come courting while Paris underwent the final horrors of the Revolution. And she knew that while he might protest he would not refuse her plan.

'Why can't the Beauchet woman keep you company in the Quai Voltaire?' was all Charles could suggest.

'Because there's only one bedroom in the flat. I can't ask Madame Beauchet to sleep on the sofa.'

'There's better accommodation at the Pharmacie Fontaine?'

'Three bedrooms,' said Marie proudly.

'Oh. That does make a difference. But it will take a bit of thinking over. Meantime, let's get on back to the palace. I've been away too long already.'

'Charles! Please wait just five minutes more! There's something I want to ask you. About the marriage of Hortense de Beauharnais.'

'You said she had refused Duroc.'

'Yes, but that's not the worst of it. Her mother wants her to marry Louis Bonaparte.'

'Napoleon's brother?'

'His next-to-youngest brother and current favourite.'

'So is Napoleon promoting the match?'

'Presumably.'

'What has that to do with me?'

'I want you to tell me if you know what was being said about Monsieur Louis in Milan last year.'

'There was some gossip, I believe. Did you hear it?'

'My Italian friends were full of it. They knew he was being treated in the Spedale Santa Caterina . . . for syphilis.'

'Marie,' said Charles, feigning shock and outrage, 'don't talk about such things! It's a disease no girl should be aware of, much less discuss . . .'

'You forget,' said Marie, 'I must have filled twenty of Dr

Berthollet's prescriptions for *sirop de cusenier* for French troops who contracted that disease in the souks of Cairo.'

'That damned Institute!' swore her husband, who had always resented his wife's membership of the group of *savants* whom Napoleon took to Egypt.

'Never mind that,' said Marie. 'The real meaning of all this is that Louis Bonaparte is not a fit husband for any girl. How Napoleon can even think of him for his stepdaughter, Hortense, passes my understanding.'

8

There was a crowd outside the Tuileries next morning, 6 May 1800. Hundreds of troops were drawn up by divisions, hundreds of civilians were assembled on the outskirts of the Carrousel to see them set off. It was the first time the Parisians had had a chance to cheer General Bonaparte on the way to what would undoubtedly be one of his spectacular victories.

The assembly had gathered on the Champ-de-Mars but the Commander-in-Chief was to join it at the Tuileries. It had been a long cold wait since seven o'clock of a spring morning, but the arrival of the regiments had been a great diversion, and after that came the arrival of the notabilities. Older men were glad to recognize Carnot, Minister for War under the Directory, but not under the Consulate, and Murat, with his flamboyant good looks, was always recognizable and sure of a cheer.

The trouble was that not all of the new men, the Bonaparte promotion, were immediately identifiable. The *Moniteur* gave their names in its official columns, but it could not paint their pictures, and many putative heroes remained anonymous. One whose good looks and bandaged eye interested the women in the crowd was Colonel Charles Latour, who was using his one eye to look for his wife. He found her after some minutes, standing next to a woman in mourning, and looking pleased with herself. Presumably because she had found a housekeeper for the Pharmacie Fontaine.

Marie was warmly wrapped in a green overcoat with a shoulder cape, several winters old but still comfortable, and she had not been waiting long, for Charles had warned her about the start of the proceedings on the Champ-de-Mars.

Now, like most of the women, she was studying Joséphine, who had appeared in the window of the only room of her suite not liable to interruptions from the gardens.

She was wearing a magnificent sable cloak, in which Marie thought she recognized an item 'acquired' from the Queen's wardrobe by Jean Tallien after Versailles was plundered, of which she herself had had and declined the first offer from his wife, Teresa. Joséphine was smart to move in quickly, thought Marie, remembering that Hortense had told her, on the previous evening, that Napoleon had forbidden his wife to see any more of Teresa Tallien, once her closest friend, because she was a disreputable woman. She had divorced Tallien and was living with the banker Ouvrard.

Joséphine was seated in an easy chair which had been brought on to the balcony – so that she can be above us all thought Marie – between her daughter, Hortense, and Madame Récamier, who as usual was dressed all in white, a perpetual bride. Madame Beauchet was asking a question about the group.

'Marie, do you know who the old lady is, next to La Récamier? She looks like a foreigner. A Greek, maybe?'

'I don't know what a Greek's supposed to look like. I never saw one,' admitted Marie. 'But you're right – if you can call a Corsican a foreigner. That's Napoleon's mother, Madame Mère Bonaparte. Very striking, isn't she?'

Striking was the word for Letizia Bonaparte, then barely fifty. She had a natural air of authority which went well with her savage style of beauty and a figure which, like her son's, had the energy of a steel spring. She was bored on the balcony and kept looking impatiently into the room behind her.

But the man she was looking for came from another direction, out of the great door of the Tuileries, a small man wearing a black tricorne hat and a grey coat over army uniform. Round his waist he wore a tricolore sash. When a groom led forward a superb white horse he sprang so lightly to the saddle that he was greeted by an outbreak of cheering which he stopped with one gesture of his hand.

'Soldiers!' said Napoleon Bonaparte, and every man in that great company felt that he spoke to him alone. 'We must proceed by forced marches if we are to drive the enemy from the fertile fields of Lombardy, which for the second time he has profaned. Follow me!'

A military band struck up the *Marseillaise*.

The crowd of spectators dispersed very slowly, Joséphine and Hortense departing, on Napoleon's orders, to find the carriage which should take them to luncheon at Very's with one of his consular colleagues, Citizen Cambacérès. Napoleon's mother sat alone in the balcony with her hands for once relaxed in her lap, as if she had released her grip on the shoulders of the man in the grey overcoat when he rode away to lead a forced march to – where?

The first halt on the march was not far off. They made their way to Fort Vincennes through streets lined with cheering citizens and there they were stood down to partake of their first *soupe*. Vincennes was an army post where Charles Latour had been inducted into the 4th Cavalry when the first expedition against the Austrians was in prospect. It was much more than an army post – once a fortress, a strong place in the defence of Paris, and subsequently the site of courts martial for high-ranking officers or important civilians accused of political offences. The great hall was where the troops lined up, *gamelle* in hand, to draw their rations.

'*La soupe*' was the name given to every army meal from breakfast through midday to supper, but at Vincennes that day it was served well before twelve noon, for Napoleon knew his men would be hungry after two long, cold waits at the Champ-de-Mars and the Tuileries. One of the secrets of his popularity was that he never left to a subaltern the task of tasting the *soupe* or asked the opinion of any enlisted man who happened to be standing by, but did so himself. '*La soupe est bonne, mon général*', would be the reply; and at Vincennes the soup was good, for at Napoleon's instructions General Berthier, the Chief of Staff, had ordered the army cooks to prepare an Italian minestrone full of fresh vegetables and shredded beef and sprinkled with grated cheese, which, served with a hunk of bread and a mug of wine, was a most acceptable meal.

A ten-minute break was permitted before the march was resumed. After a night's bivouac in the open air the sight of half a dozen field kitchens was very welcome, and the mugs which had held wine were filled with *la soupe*, which in the morning took the form of coffee. Then, not without curses from those stiff from so many hours in the saddle, it was off and away to Châlons-sur-Marne, an important army camp where there were veterinarians, blacksmiths and farrier-sergeants, and the welfare of the horses was the first consideration.

At Châlons, Charles Latour fell in again with Colonel Tavernier whose acquaintance he had made in Reims, and who deferred to him as one of Napoleon's ADCs. Latour was pleased and flattered by the deference and invited Tavernier to lunch with him in the ADCs' mess, to which the other man responded by a similar invitation to 'one of the best restaurants in Lyon', which was to be their next major halt, if they could get leave to move about the city.

Lyon had a dubious reputation. Napoleon had had an enthusiastic welcome there on his journey from the coast, and so had Joséphine on her way from Milan, but there was a royalist element in the city where an uprising in favour of the exiled Bourbons was always a possibility.

Colonel Charles Latour and his friend Tavernier received a pass enabling them to dine in Lyon by the simple expedient of requesting it from General Bonaparte. They drank 'Confusion to the Austrian!' and feasted royally *Chez La Mère Ambrosine* and returned to sleep the sleep of weary men in the barracks beds reserved for them at the respectable hour of eleven o'clock.

At eight next morning General Bonaparte summoned all officers of field rank to meet him in the same barracks, where he proposed to give them some details of his plan of campaign.

He still hoped, he said, to take the enemy by surprise; but since it was impossible to conceal the movements of so large an army from unfriendly eyes, it was reasonable to assume that their whereabouts were now known at Austrian head-quarters. Meanwhile the French *estafettes* had reported some useful information.

First, there had been a change in the Austrian command. The Austrian Emperor's brother, the Archduke Charles, whom they had expected to encounter, had fallen ill and relinquished his command. At this the French officers exchanged looks: the archduke was rumoured to suffer from epilepsy. 'The arch-duke has been replaced by General Alvintzi, whom we defeated at Arcole,' Napoleon said.

At this mention of one of his most spectacular victories there was applause, and Napoleon did not think it necessary to remind his audience that after Arcole Alvintzi had defeated the French at Caldiera.

'So you see the need for haste is great,' Napoleon said. 'Alvintzi will require a few days to get a grasp of his new command and to move across Lombardy from Alexandria. What I propose to do is to move across the Alps and take him on the flank. Don't look so astounded, gentlemen! It's not original – Hannibal did it before me, encumbered by elephants! And there is a way prepared for us ... over the pass of the Great St Bernard. The Chief of Staff is conversant with all the details. Kindly address your questions to General Berthier.'

Several of the field officers followed Napoleon from the room, all of whom had had a share in organizing the reinforce-ments, regiments held in reserve at Lyon, as others had already been taken in at Châlons-sur-Marne. Those who remained asked no questions. The daring concept of crossing the Alps (and who was Hannibal? thought the uneducated among them) had taken their breath away. Hypnotized, as always, by Napoleon, they were not elated. The unspoken feeling was that they would be lucky if any of them were left alive to fight the Austrians.

After Lyon the advance continued at an accelerated pace and followed the pattern of the first days out of Paris. In the morning the field kitchens came up and dispensed coffee; at noon there was broth, apples, bread and cheese, and wine; at night cold beef, more bread and last season's fruit, sometimes a bunch of grapes offered by a pretty country girl in the red skirt and white bodice of Provence. There was no objection to flirtation as long as it was confined to compliments, but sympathy was not permitted, as being destructive of morale. Any girl who felt sorry for the young soldiers weighed down by weapons and equipment, and expressed it by exclaiming, '*Ah, les pauvres gars! Les braves gens!*' was apt to find herself shouldered off the roadside by one of the sergeants who, during every halt, were responsible for order in the ranks.

Napoleon kept a sharp eye on these exchanges. He went tirelessly up and down the columns, sometimes on foot, more often on horseback, applying his remarkable memory to recollecting the names and even the records of his men. Now and then he took one of the staff, or an ADC, to ride by his side. When the army, now 30,000 strong, left Lyon, it was Colonel Charles Latour whom Napoleon called to ride by his side, and flattered by asking his opinion on how best to transport heavy pieces of artillery over the mountains under snow. Latour had been worrying about this since he first heard about the plan to cross the Great St Bernard, and in the hope of pleasing the general he was sympathetic to a hint that Napoleon would like to cross the pass himself, not on a war horse, but on a mule.

When they left Lyon they took the road to the north-east which led to Switzerland, and there their reception was decidedly cool. As a peace-loving nation the Swiss felt that the French, when they appeared, brought trouble with them. General Masséna had driven the Russians out of Zurich, but he had pursued them across the country into the Grisons, which was then given up to bloodshed and strife. Nothing better was expected from General Bonaparte, who was said to be planning a confederation of Swiss cantons on the same lines as the Confederation of the Rhine, in which a number of minor German states had been turned into French departments. Fiercely independent since the days of William Tell, the Swiss were determined that this must not happen to them.

Whatever they expected, no political demonstrations attended the arrival of General Bonaparte's army. It circled the Lake of Geneva and headed south into the Valais, whence the men had their first sight of the white peaks of the great frozen barrier called the Alps. The peaks were called by unfamiliar names on the flimsy maps some of them had bought in Lyon. 'Piz' was one, 'monte' was another, and the most evocative of all was 'Corona'. But whatever the prefix, the figures of the height above sea level were always the same, between 2000 and 3000 feet. And this was what Frenchmen with no experience of mountaineering were expected to climb!

It was from the town of Martigny that all the religious pilgrimages and holiday excursions set out for the Monastery of the Great St Bernard. The town's resources were strained to the utmost by the French 'pilgrims', all in need of shelter from the bitter cold of the mountain night, and some in need of medical help after fractures sustained in falls on the frozen roads. They were pronounced to be 'good fellows', for they were generous with gifts of spirits and tobacco, and even produced some sweetmeats for the children.

The staff were not idle. By the light of torches they explored the countryside and recruited a number of stalwart countrymen to help the aspiring climbers, and felled and prepared the hollow trees which Latour had recommended for the transport of artillery. The weaving of stout cords to haul the logs occupied the evening. Finally, when General Berthier himself produced a stalwart young farmer, with all the reliability of Switzerland in his honest face, to lead the mule, guaranteed sure-footed, across the Alpine pass to the monastery with Napoleon Bonaparte on its back, it was agreed that the ultimate in security preparation was complete.

Such was not the opinion of Jacques Louis David, whose work had so far commended him to Napoleon that he was now the unofficial court painter, and had been commissioned to paint a picture of this historic crossing of the Alps.

'You can't let yourself be painted on mule-back, General!' Latour, who was in the vicinity, heard David say. 'What would the public think?'

'They'd think I'm a careful fellow!' said Napoleon. 'Those sketches of yours make me look like a circus rider.' The sketch he held up showed him in a scarlet coat, on a white horse, with a poised sword in his outstretched hand. The horse had its hind hoofs teetering on the verge of an abyss.

'Perhaps you would care to suggest another pose, sir,' said David. 'But please remember – David does not paint mules!'

When the artist had left, Napoleon looked round, saw Latour, and waved him to his side.

'You heard all that, I suppose?' he said. 'Well? D'you think I was right?'

'Absolutely, sir.' It was his honest opinion, and he knew how to back it up. 'David is a good painter,' said Charles, who knew nothing about painting, 'but Marie hated the thing he did of Marat stabbed in his bath tub, and she much prefers his sketches of you to Antoine Gros's picture of you as the Victor of Arcole.'

'Ah,' said Napoleon. 'So do I. One can always rely on Marie's judgement.' Charles scowled. 'My dear fellow, will you do me a favour? Will you lead the way up to the monastery? And when you get there will you find the Father-Cellarer and ask him to help Berthier get the men in line as they pass the gates, fill their mugs with wine and give them each a hunk of bread? There's enough money in this bag to pay for it,' he added, producing a leather bag from the skirt pocket of his grey coat.

'À vos ordres, mon général. The men will be grateful,' said Charles, and saluting, he left in search of General Berthier, to inform him of the part he had to play in the distribution of Bonaparte's bounty. Then he embarked on the upward climb, slipping and slithering on the frozen track until he found assistance in a stick he had been given with a pointed iron ferrule. Presently he felt confident enough to turn and look back when he saw Napoleon riding the mule led by a rope held by the Swiss guide. He was chatting with the man and appeared to be in high spirits. All very well on the way up, thought Charles, but what about the way down? If his weight makes the mule slip . . .

There were half a dozen young priests waiting outside the monastery, and the Father-Cellarer was quickly identified. He was proud of his charge, and when Charles said he hoped they had enough wine for 30,000 men the Father led him into a building just beyond the gates where there was a satisfactory array of barrels, from one of which he drew a glass of strong, coarse red wine for Charles. 'Would you prefer brandy?' he said, for five of the famous St Bernard dogs were lying on a pile of sacks, each one wearing round his neck the little wooden barrel carrying brandy to revive the travellers he was trained to rescue from the snow.

'Thank you, I like the wine,' said Charles. '*Allez!* I see you've got an assistant.' A man in a black cassock, who had been looking out of a window, now dragged a wine barrel through the door.

'Very welcome, but a new brother,' said the Father. 'I never saw him before.'

The man's face was held in the sunlight of outdoors, revealing a birthmark at the corner of his upper lip, and Charles knew where *he* had seen him before.

'Call that man back!' he said urgently, and next moment a shot was heard. The dogs began barking and scratching at the door. Charles dashed out. One of the young priests was lying on the ground, and a man in a cassock, pistol in hand, was running down the track which led to Lombardy. Charles dragged his own pistol from his belt and fired a shot, which went wide.

General Berthier was by his side.

'There's been an assassination attempt,' he panted. 'The general –'

'Yes, for God's sake – the general?'

'A priest was wounded. The general is unhurt.'

'Thank God,' said Charles. 'I know the assassin. He was the *commissaire de la République* at Reims. His name's Anatole Laguerre.'

9

While Napoleon's expeditionary force was making its way towards Fort Vincennes, Marie and her friend Madame Beauchet were walking westward in the opposite direction, up the rue St-Honoré.

Marie knew every cobblestone in that street. She had walked it as a child, going to catechism class at her parish church, St Roch; as a girl she had seen Queen Marie Antoinette going to the guillotine in the great square beyond the rue Royale – and how many more victims in how many other tumbrils? And as a young woman she had begun her first studies in pharmacy in Professor Guiart's *officine* at the corner of the rue du Louvre. But for her the heart of the ancient street was still the shop with a residence above it where she had lived and worked with her Uncle Prosper until he went to the guillotine and she was sent to prison, and when she was near enough to the shuttered shop to see the name of her grandfather, who founded it – *Michel Fontaine, pharmacien* – on a plaque above the upper windows, she felt a sincerer sense of home-coming than she had ever felt at Vesle, or even at the Quai Voltaire.

A gentleman was standing outside the door of the shop whom Marie greeted as Maître Favart, and to whom she introduced Madame Beauchet. Etienne Favart had been her uncle's attorney, and was now her own; when he greeted her with a low bow she curtsied and said she was glad her message had reached him in time.

'At eight o'clock last night,' said Favart. 'Madame Favart was quite alarmed when the maid admitted such a very grand flunky from the Tuileries who presented your letter. I was very glad to hear that you intended to come back and live in your own house. Colonel Latour is not with you?'

'Colonel Latour has gone to war,' said Marie. 'He was one of the contingent which left from the Tuileries yesterday.'

'I was busy in the office all of yesterday,' said the lawyer, in a tone dismissing Colonel Latour to all the danger of the battlefield. Marie smiled. She remembered the time when Maître Favart himself had been her suitor and intensely jealous of his successful rival. A few months before, Favart had been married to the daughter of a country squire who had held on to his estate through the Revolution and had given his only child as good a dowry as any girl could expect in the France of 1799.

'Have you brought my keys?' she asked.

'Madame Rocroi delivered them this morning. Shall we go in? I don't expect we'll find anything amiss, but we must check.'

The heavy key creaked in the lock, the door swung open and Marie was surrounded by the odours of her childhood: the medicines, the chemicals, the lotions and potions which were the stock in trade of the Pharmacie Fontaine. The stone floor had been washed, so had the drugget which covered it; the bottles and jars on the shelves had been dusted – a tribute to Madame Rocroi's housekeeping. The living room was tidy too, but the small laboratory, down a short flight of steps and entered by a separate key, bore witness to all the unsuccessful experiments Louis Rocroi had conducted in his search for a soporific. Marie said nothing. There was hot water available and the place could be cleaned up.

Up a wooden stair there was a big bedroom facing the street, with clean bedding in a cupboard, and two smaller bedrooms, one used for storage, facing the back yard. Marie saw that Madame Beauchet was trying to see over the wall which divided the yard from the neighbouring garden, where they had both played games with the Noailles children before the rue St-Honoré got the name of 'the Street of the Tumbrils'.

When he took his leave the attorney expressed the hope

that 'Madame la Marquise de Vesle will soon do Madame Favart the honour of calling on her.' He also presented her with a certificate of residence for the Second Section of the City of Paris, declaring that the premises known as the Pharmacie Fontaine were now occupied by Citizeness Latour, niece and sole legatee of Prosper Fontaine, deceased.

Marie and Madame Beauchet then discovered that, not surprisingly, there was not a crumb of food left in the house.

'Madame Rocroi must have been afraid of mice,' said Marie, looking ruefully at the empty larder. 'Never mind! There are lots of shops selling cooked food on this street. Here's some money and a jug. Would you mind running out to the next crossing and buying some *café au lait* and some bread and butter at the Coupe d'Or, and get whatever you would like for supper? I'll light the fire and we'll have a cosy afternoon.'

But Marie first intended to indulge herself. She opened the back door to air the living room, and then ran upstairs to the bedroom she had occupied almost since the time after her parents' death when her uncle had brought her home. She had left a dress in the cupboard: an old dress, not in good repair. It would be interesting to see if Madame Rocroi, in her compulsive tidiness, had thrown it out.

She had done better. She had placed Marie's dress on one of her own hangers, and there it hung limply, a reject of Marie's mother refurbished by herself for the most important gaiety of her life before her marriage.

'*La Patrie est en danger!*' The call had gone forth, and Prosper's only son, Michel, had given up his job at the Botanical Gardens to be conscripted into the army. He fell at Valmy in his first engagement, which was the first victory won by the young French Republic against the enemies pressing upon it from all sides of Europe, and since then Valmy had been a sacred name to Marie.

Not long after that a young officer had appeared at the Pharmacie Fontaine. He was a Lieutenant Buonaparte, known also as 'Tom Thumb', or 'Puss-in-Boots'. He was suffering from a stomach complaint, which Fontaine's medicine cured. He struck up a friendship with the older man, who said that the young man (he was not much more than twenty) was very well read for his age. Marie thought he talked very well for any age and was fascinated by his stories of his Corsican birthplace.

She had never had a sweetheart, nor did her uncle encourage her to join the girls and boys who met to dance in the ruins of the hated Bastille, and so the youth with the brilliant eyes and the black hair falling in 'dog's ears' to his shoulders was so rare a spirit that he hypnotized her as he hypnotized her uncle and later, his armies and his law-givers.

Fontaine declared that 'the boy' gave him a better game of chess than any man in the Second Section. They played in the Café de la Régence, at the other end of the rue St-Honoré. There Buonaparte gave a supper party and invited Marie, as well as her uncle, to celebrate his promotion to captain. That was the occasion when she wore the blue muslin dress with a yellowing lace fichu and a white rose in her hair. There had never been a second occasion, for Buonaparte had gone off to Italy and married Marie's friend from prison days, Joséphine de Beauharnais.

On this May morning Marie wanted to renew other memories of Napoleon than those contained in the folds of an old dress. Deep in her heart she kept the sound of his voice, telling her in his Corsican garden that she was the girl he should have married years ago, when they were both young. She laid the dress down on the bed and went to the open window. There it lay beneath her, that ideal setting of their youth, the yard where they had talked so often, as he liked to say, 'among the lettuces and the pot-herbs.'

Would they ever sit in that garden again? Or would a shot end the story on some Lombard battlefield?

Marie went downstairs to tend the fire.

A few weeks later a headline in the *Moniteur* announced, with telegraphic terseness 'Great French Victory at Marengo.' The details, which were lacking, arrived by courier a few days later, and included the regrettable news that General Desaix had been killed in an action which, while it completely defeated Alvintzi and his troops, had cost 'thousands of French casualties'. It was now Madame Beauchet's turn to soothe Marie with platitudes like 'no news is good news'. The casualty lists began to be printed, and Colonel Latour's name did not appear.

The battle had been fought on 14 June and ten days later Marie decided that if no more information were forthcoming by that afternoon she would go to the Tuileries and find out what Joséphine had heard. She withdrew to the labo in the basement and started to scour the sink, the basins, the walls and the floor. She had opened the shutters of the shop, and the bell on the door never ceased to ring, so that *Citoyenne Marie*, as they called her now, had to come upstairs again and again to attend to customers, some of whom had brought children in need of first aid, all of whom wanted to know what Marie, a well-informed woman and a neighbour of long-standing, thought of the news from Marengo.

Then at one o'clock there was a special edition of the *Moniteur*. The editor had compassion on his readers and printed a despatch just received from the Chief of Staff. General Berthier explained that the Austrian army was totally annihilated, but there had been heavy casualties on both sides and casualty lists would follow. General Bonaparte, who had come through the action unharmed, had feared that he might be out-numbered, and had ordered General Desaix, arrived that day from Egypt, to withdraw ten miles and prepare to attack the enemy on the flank. Then Alvintzi and his men appeared in strength. Colonel Latour was ordered to ride after Desaix and bring him back. Unfortunately, just as the gallant Desaix appeared he was shot dead by an Austrian sharp-shooter.

The concluding stages of the battle were fought with the 'French fury' of old days, the *furie française*, to avenge Desaix.

Marie saw that several copies of the *Moniteur* were circulating among the people on the street, and that all looked as bewildered as she felt. It was an unusual battle of order and counterorder, not conducted with Napoleon's usual conviction. A general sent off to – what did it say? – to execute a flanking movement; and then that general brought back almost at once to ride into an ambush of sharp-shooters! And the man who brought him back was her own husband! Had he been in danger too? But Napoleon was 'unharmed' – there was comfort in that!

There was a lot of noise in the rue St-Honoré now: raised voices, shouts of exultation and cheering, laughter and singing. There was the sound of wheels as a cab drew up at the pharmacie, and a young man in uniform got out.

'Captain Le Marois!'

'Madame Latour! I've just left Charles at the Hospital of Val-de-Grâce! I was coming to find you – '

'He's wounded?'

'Not seriously,' said the youngest but one of General Bonaparte's ADCs. 'He got a bullet in the wrist, the left wrist. He spent last night at Fort Vincennes not very comfortable – '

'And I didn't know! Why – '

'And Dr Larrey wants him in hospital for observation. You'll see him tomorrow, madame, don't worry . . .'

'How can I help worrying? Ah, here's my friend. Captain Le Marois, this is Madame Beauchet.'

'*Enchanté, madame.*'

Marie-Josèphe was holding a tray with a black bottle and a glass.

'Marie-Josèphe, Charles is wounded,' said his wife.

'Ah, I'm sorry. But this gentleman doesn't look well. Would he accept a glass of brandy? I brought it in from the *Coupe d'Or*.'

'Very welcome,' said the ADC. He was very pale, and his hands were trembling, but he still tried to reassure Marie.

'I promise you, madame, Charles is all right, and longing to see you. He's none the worse for his adventure.'

'Adventure?'

Better to say nothing about Laguerre.

'He was worried about getting the general down the mountain. But Bonaparte knew the way to go. He sat down in the snow . . . and then he slid the whole way down to the valley . . . on his *derrière*!'

10

News from Captain Le Marois was not the only information Marie received of her husband. At eleven o'clock the next morning a footman from the Tuileries, in a shoulderknot of gold lace, delivered the kind of letter which Joséphine sent to her women friends: pink writing paper cut in the shape of a heart and sealed with a posy of artificial roses. It read:

> *I have just returned from Val-de-Grâce hospital, where I saw your dear Charles. He is fairly well and longing for you. The First Consul is grateful for his attempt, however abortive, to save him from that murderous attack, and will accord him two months' leave with pay. I hope you will spend at least one month of the two at our country home, La Malmaison, which is well suited for convalescence.*
>
> *I am ever, dear Marie, your loving Joséphine de la Tascher Pagerie Bonaparte.*

Somehow the signature, more than the text of the letter, succeeded in irritating Marie. The formal recital of all her surnames seemed to make Joséphine more condescending than she had been when Marie knew her in prison, when she signed herself boldly 'Marie-Rose, Marquise de Beauharnais'. Then there was the sting in the beginning. She had been to the hospital, where she had seen Charles Latour as if forlorn and neglected by his friends.

Running headlong downstairs and calling out her destination to Madame Beauchet, Marie hastened to the Val-de-Grâce.

She was lucky enough to find one of the porters on the

125

gate who knew her, and who while he was glad to have met
'Madame Bonaparte – the first lady in France, madame!' –
was willing to take Marie to Dr Larrey, an old friend whose
'wheeled ambulances' she had helped to introduce for the use
of the wounded in Egypt.

Dr Larrey rose to greet her with a solemn face, but he was
presently full of good cheer. Only a few bones in Colonel
Latour's wrist had been broken by an unlucky bullet. It was
now in plaster, and he knew madame was capable of band-
aging it until the healing process was complete. A month for
convalescence at La Malmaison would be ideal.

Yes, Dr Larrey believed that the colonel had been aware of
an attempted attack on the general, but he was unhurt and
the miscreant escaped. Would Marie go and see her husband
now?

She followed the doctor down the passage, with the distinct
impression that the least said the better as far as the attack
on Napoleon was concerned. Well, she must wait for Charles,
even if his attempts at reprisals had been in Joséphine's sting-
ing word 'abortive'.

Charles was lying propped up on pillows with a hospital
nightcap on his head. It did not occur to her that he looked
slightly ridiculous – she was too sorry for him for that – and
with a cry of 'Oh, my poor darling!' she took him in her
arms.

'How did you find me?' he whispered with his lips on the
pulse in her throat.

'Captain Le Marois told me and most of the rue St-Honoré
too. And Joséphine told me in a letter today.'

'I thought she might. She was here this morning – very
gracious and very possessive, you know her style. She wants
us to go to Malmaison. Would you like that?'

'Yes, but not yet. I want to nurse you at the Pharmacie first.'

'Yes, Doctor,' said Charles Latour. Everything Marie said
seemed a proof of the real concern for him which he sometimes thought had vanished from their lives. She does love
me, he told himself. I haven't deserved it, but I will.

'Joséphine told me someone had tried to kill Napoleon,' Marie said. 'Is that true?'

There it was – the implicit confession, the truth she could never hide. Napoleon was the man she really cared for, Charles thought.

'What do you know about it?' he asked. 'What did Joséphine say? Did she accuse anybody?'

'Not by name,' she said.

'A man in a cassock followed Napoleon up the mountain and fired at him in a crowd of others and killed one of them. Then I fired at the man and missed, but I was the only person who could name him, and you may well wish I'd shot him, because you know him too.'

'Who was it, Charles?'

'Anatole Laguerre, commissioner of the Republic at Reims.'

'*That* man? He spoke about Napoleon that night as if he hated him.'

'Probably jealous.'

'So he ran off after you missed him?'

'Don't rub it in, Marie. Yes, he did. They sent dogs, as well as the Swiss guides, out after him. He went down into Lombardy and disappeared.'

'Wasn't Berthier afraid he might be lying in wait for Napoleon at the bottom of the mountain?'

'I don't know about Berthier. *I* was! Darling, you'll never know what I felt when I saw the general disappear over the edge. Thank God our advance guard was waiting at the mountain foot, and when I got down they had Napoleon's bottom in dry breeches and were turned about to face the Austrians on the field of Marengo.'

Marie choked on a laugh.

'Then the worst thing of the day happened,' said Charles, his eyes set and staring. 'General Bonaparte sent me to fetch back Desaix, who hadn't gone very far. I put my second-in-command in charge of the guns and rode off. Desaix had heard firing and was ready to return. But an Austrian sharpshooter got him just as we came up with the French. The fellow didn't fire again thank heaven, for Napoleon was rushing back to pick up the body of Desaix, and then, Marie, we saw something we never saw in Egypt, he cradled the poor devil's head in his arms and wept.'

There were tears in Marie's own eyes at the thought of Napoleon's grief at the death of his friend. She remembered Desaix at the French Institute in Cairo: always lively and optimistic, even when times were bad. It was well for Marie's self-control that a knock fell on the door at that moment and Marie's '*Entrez*' admitted two Sisters of Charity.

'The condition of *monsieur le marquis* is favourable today,' said the older Sister, who carried a woollen robe over one arm. 'Dr Larrey is prepared to discharge him into your care after a supplementary examination, and then he will have a talk with you.'

'This is great news, *ma soeur*,' said Marie.

'A tribute to the colonel's constitution. Now Colonel Latour, do you feel able to get out of bed? We only have to go next door.'

There was no doubt about the strength in Charles's muscles or in his thighs as he took the Sister's hand, pushing his way out of the narrow bed to stand on the mat, to assume the robe and a pair of slippers, biting his lip while they adjusted his wrist in a sling hung round his neck. Then he called out, 'Wish me luck!' to Marie, and let the nurses lead him from the room.

Dr Larrey did not keep Marie in suspense. In a quarter of an hour he was with her, repeating the compliments on her husband's constitution and laying down some rules for his convalescence, both in Paris and at La Malmaison. He had been running a fever since he was wounded, and with a view to reducing it he was to follow a strict diet, and drink not more than one pint of wine a day. He was not to play the game of 'prisoner's base', very popular at Malmaison, for more than half an hour each day, and he was not to be tempted into any excesses. He, Larrey, was expected now to attend on Mademoiselle de Beauharnais, who was suffering from a migraine.

Madame la marquise was pleased to wait in the porter's room for her husband, and for the ambulance which would take both of them to her home.

Charles arrived at the *loge* on her heels, very smart in a blue uniform which had been brushed and sponged, and very eager to say how well he felt. He greeted Madame Beauchet like an old friend, was interested in her news of a letter from Madame de La Fayette, and agreed that bed was the best place for him. He was to have the big room once occupied by Prosper Fontaine.

'Are you going to Malmaison?' was Madame Beauchet's first question when Charles had gone upstairs.

'Yes, but I don't know for how long. Don't worry, it won't make any difference. I'll want you to stay on here as my housekeeper. I don't want you going back to the rue de Courty all alone. And I'll tell Maître Favart to keep you in funds.'

'You're very generous, Marie. Would your husband like a cup of tea or chocolate now?'

'Chocolate, I think; he's got a sweet tooth.'

Marie put on a white apron to carry up the tray and kissed her husband when she set it down. She was feeling guilty about Charles, much as she had felt when he lost an eye at Jaffa after she told him to go away and never come back.

She asked Charles what he thought of the migraine Hortense de Beauharnais was said to be suffering from. Could it be put down to this wretched engagement to Louis Bonaparte her mother was urging upon her? She was surprised when Charles shook his head.

'I don't think you're quite fair to Joséphine,' he said. 'You were so much in her confidence that I should think you'd guess the reason why she wants to see her daughter married. You know how anxious she is to have a child by Napoleon –'

'You mean going every year to drink the waters and take the cure at Plombières?'

'Exactly. And her excitement when Joseph Bonaparte's wife had a little girl after six barren years? Score one for Plombières!'

'Do you know that Joséphine lied to Napoleon about being pregnant when they were first married and she didn't want to go to join him in Italy?'

'No, I didn't know that. How did she expect to get away with it when he found out?'

'She meant to tell him she miscarried.'

'*Garce!*'

Marie thought the oath was not undeserved. But Charles had not finished. 'That doesn't affect my point,' he said. 'If Joséphine can't have a child, but if her daughter marries a Bonaparte and had a child by him, that makes them both part of the family and the child could succeed his uncle in the hereditary consulship. *Now* do you see?'

'What I *don't* see,' said Marie, 'is how healthy any child of Louis Bonaparte's is likely to be.'

Charles came downstairs for supper, and Marie smiled to see him prowling round the shop, remembering the first day he came there in pursuit of a 'spy' he wanted to arrest. It was the same day as looking down from the steps of St Roch's church she had seen Queen Marie Antoinette in a tumbril on her way to the guillotine, and it was an odd coincidence that Latour's 'spy' was pledged to save the queen if he could. He was an Englishman posing as an American, by his right name Boone or Bohun. Latour was then a sergeant in the National Guard, and went by the name of Vautour, the Vulture. Like a bird of prey he had pecked at Boone, and even at Prosper Fontaine, whose shop the 'spy' had entered to get help for a shoulder dislocated when he was savaged by the National Guard. Marie had spoken to Vautour sarcastically, but in spite of her rebuffs he had pursued her ... Marie shrugged her shoulders. What was the sense of raking all that up now?

Marie and Charles were on the steps of the pharmacie by ten o'clock next morning, the hour appointed for the start of the expedition to Malmaison, and ready when one of the carriages from the Tuileries, drawn by two white horses, and with a wreath of bees, Napoleon's personal symbol, depicted in gilt on the panels of each door, duly drew up. A man in uniform was seated beside Joséphine, too tall to be her husband but at once identifiable as her son, Eugène de Beauharnais.

Hortense sat next to her brother. He was nineteen but looked older because, like many of Napoleon's junior officers, he wore a sweeping cavalry moustache. With a dolman slung over one shoulder and the sash of an ADC, he looked like a romantic horseman from the great Hungarian plain. He was the favourite of his stepfather as well as of his mother; Marie had been wondering if there were any marriage plans in the making for Eugène.

As they drove out of Paris through the Porte de l'Etoile, Eugène asked Charles a hundred technical questions about the battle of Marengo, which he was very sorry to have missed. He would fain have extended his enquiries to Napoleon's unorthodox descent from the height of the Great St Bernard, but perceiving from his mother's face that she disliked the topic he changed it to the shot fired by the man Laguerre, on which Joséphine had plenty to say. How was it, she complained, that an army of 30,000 men in full battle array could fail to apprehend a villain who had tried to murder their commander-in-chief? Could he have taken refuge among the Austrians? (This was a very popular theory.) Eugène asked if the gunners had performed well under Charles's second-in-command and the talk became so abstruse that the ladies lost interest and began to discuss the purchase of new furniture for Malmaison.

Marie was well aware of the problems caused by the acquisition of the new property. Some of them had appeared while the Bonapartes were still living in the rue de la Victoire and Napoleon had told her in Egypt of the other in which Joséphine had involved him. He believed she had pledged his credit for the full purchase price of 271,000 francs. This was reduced in 1799, and Joséphine herself paid the new price by the unusual means of borrowing from the man charged with selling the dilapidated estate.

Hortense, who was looking so well that Marie wondered if the migraine was a fiction meant to put off her engagement, had of course been to Malmaison before. But Marie had been to Croissy, where Joséphine rented a country house during the Revolution, and was already familiar with the charming scenery of the road which ran by the side of the rippling Seine.

It led them to the gates of Malmaison, beside which newly built guard houses sheltered members of a company of lancers, the bodyguard of Madame Bonaparte, who turned out to salute her. From there a long avenue of gravel led up between beds of roses of many colours to a structure which still looked more like a farmhouse than a palace, although new buildings had already been begun. Under its red-tiled roof the walls of the long, low building were white and inset with tall casement windows overhung with flowering creeper. The effect of light and gaiety was enhanced by the presence of half a dozen ladies in pretty summer dresses whom Joséphine introduced to the newcomers as her ladies of the palace. Marie curtsied to Madame de Montesson, who interested her not so much as the mistress of the first post-Revolutionary salon as 'the wife of the regicide' – the Duke of Orléans who had voted for the King, his cousin's, death when it came up in the Convention. How did she feel about waiting on the wife of the man whom some people felt had usurped the King's position?

Then there was Madame Récamier, dressed as usual in white and holding a bunch of lily of the valley – purity personified! Marie had disliked her since the day in the previous December when Napoleon Bonaparte was officially welcomed back to Paris after his victories in Italy. Madame Récamier, like Marie, was present at the ceremony in the courtyard of the Luxembourg. Napoleon was never happy with a civilian audience, and his lame speech was disrupted when the beautiful Récamier started up from her place in the audience. She *said* it was to see him better: Marie thought it was in order that he might see herself.

So here she was at Malmaison, and Marie was glad when Hortense took her by the arm and motioned her through the open front door into a white marble entrance hall with no other furniture than an oak refectory table on which a crystal bowl of roses had been placed.

'How beautiful!' said Marie. 'It's so cool and spacious. Hortense, you must be very happy here.'

'Of course I am, and so's my mother,' said Hortense. 'But isn't Juliette Récamier outrageous? Did you see her flirting with your husband and my brother, both at the same time?'

'No, I didn't notice,' said Marie. 'Eugène is looking well.'

'So is Charles. I was so sorry to hear about his wound. He ought to rest this afternoon.'

Chatting pleasantly, the two girls went up a steep narrow staircase, quite unlike the splendid stairs of the Tuileries, and found themselves in two salons, of which the first held a full-length painting of the First Consul in his rosy consular uniform, and the second, one of his mother in a black robe, looking young and free.

'Madame Letizia,' said Hortense. 'Have you ever met her?'

'Just once, at the rue de la Victoire, before I went to Egypt. I liked her very much,' said Marie.

'Oh so do I! She's been so nice to my mother and me. I wish her daughters were more like her. But they act as if Maman were a criminal to marry their precious Napoleon.'

'What will they say if you marry Monsieur Louis?' Marie ventured.

'It's none of their business.'

'Oh, Hortense! You're really going to go through with it?'

'Why not? Louis is sometimes misunderstood. He's moody, and he cares more for poetry than for sport, because he hurt himself quite badly playing prisoner's base here at Malmaison. But the general thinks the world of him and perhaps he'll make him his heir to the consulship . . . so don't look so disapproving, Marie . . . yes, I'm going to marry him.'

11

Marie woke up next morning in a pretty bedroom decorated in the 'young lady' colours of pale pink and palest green, reflected in the big bowl of roses on a table painted in white enamel. There was a tapping at the bedroom door to which she said, 'Come in!' and Hortense entered with the abrupt statement that she had heard Marie's husband calling out.

'Oh, poor man, his wrist must be hurting. I'll go at once!' said Marie, and Hortense, saying a footman called Victor had been told to look after the marquis, tugged at the embroidered bell-pull hanging on the wall. Marie got out of bed and slipped into the white velvet dressing gown she found folded over a chair.

Charles was lying in an iron bed with a huge eagle on the top (surely a more appropriate symbol than a bee?) and holding up his face for Marie's kiss, like a child. He said his wrist hurt, and as the footman came in at that moment Marie sent him off for hot water and other necessities. Marie was relieved to see that Charles had had a good night. He complained of the chiming of the stable clock, which now struck eight, but the bedclothes were not dishevelled and he must have lain at peace for hours.

Victor came back with hot water, a pair of surgical scissors and a length of linen, which Hortense held taut while Marie made it into a bandage. Hortense, too, picked up the pieces of plaster as Marie cut them off. The wounded wrist was very much swollen, but was bound up firmly and strapped across the patient's chest. Victor promised to feed him with the bread and milk which Marie ordered for his breakfast, though Charles wanted an omelette.

'You shall have an omelette for luncheon but this is better for you now,' his wife assured him. 'Try to go to sleep again, and no visitors until this afternoon.'

She was satisfied with his smile and a murmur of thanks, and heard Hortense whisper that their own breakfast had been taken to Marie's room, where coffee and rolls, with butter, jam and honey, had replaced the roses on the table.

The two girls ate and drank in silence until Hortense said: 'Eugène will be sorry to hear about your "No Visitors" rule for Charles.'

'Until this afternoon. Complete rest was what Dr Larrey prescribed and I'm so grateful to your mother for letting him have it in this lovely place.'

'You must explore it by and by.'

'Hortense, tell me about Eugène. What does he think of your engagement to Louis Bonaparte?'

'Oh, Eugène is always on the side of the heavy battalions – Mother and Step-papa. He preached me a most affecting little sermon, saying we must always do what will please General Bonaparte because he has done so much for us.'

'And Eugène is quite sure that this will please him? Are you?'

'I'm not sure. The general has other interests. His mistress has arrived in Paris.'

'His mistress!' Marie's ejaculation was strangled. For a moment she thought Bellilotte, Napoleon's Cairo lover, had arrived from Egypt.

'Yes, didn't you know? Signora Grassini, principal soprano of the Italian Opera. It began in Milan, rumour says, when the lady paid tribute to the victor of Marengo. Mother and I saw her creeping into his rooms on tiptoe in case she roused the house.'

'Here?' said Marie, appalled.

'No, of course not here. At the Tuileries.'

'What did your mother do?'

'She began to cry, and she knows she cries beautifully. She

135

said, "No wonder he likes theatre girls – he's such a good actor himself." Shall we get dressed and go out?'

The same carriage as had brought them all to Malmaison on the day before was standing in front of the château with its shafts resting on the gravel drive. Hortense said briefly, 'Napoleon is here,' and drew Marie's attention to two pairs of beautiful white swans, sailing tranquilly on an artificial body of water to the right of the drive.

'Part of Maman's menagerie,' said Hortense. 'She's got monkeys, parrots, even a flock of sheep.'

A short distance further on, in the shade of a group of trees, they came on Maman herself, stretched on a chaise longue in the same relaxed and indolent attitude as Marie had seen her in her room at the Tuileries. She was not so richly dressed, being attired in plain white muslin, and wore no jewels, nor was she attended by any ladies of the palace. Only the swans, swimming closer seemed to be paying her the respects of her menagerie.

'Isn't she beautiful?' whispered Marie. 'Exactly as she looks in the painting by Prud'hon.'

'Oh, is that the one?' Hortense whispered back. 'I don't always remember their names. She loves having herself painted.'

The sound of a heavy step on the gravel made them both look up at the drive. Napoleon was standing there and signalling to them. He was wearing uniform with breeches made of leather under the tricolore sash and riding boots.

He said in a low voice: 'Young ladies, don't stand there muttering. You'll waken Joséphine. Hortense, the sun is too strong for you. Go indoors for a hat, and prepare to take leave of your charming guest for a short time. I need Marie all to myself for the next half-hour. I have some projects I want to discuss with her.'

Neither girl thought of disobeying, though Marie accepted his proffered arm with reluctance. So, she said to herself, he tells me he loves me, and comes to me straight from the

136

embrace of his Italian paramour! Joséphine was right: he *is* a great actor – a master of dissimulation!

'Well!' said Napoleon. 'What do you think of Malmaison?'

'After all the fuss you made about it at Nasriya, it's better than I expected.'

'Plain speaking, as usual. How's your husband?'

'He had a good night, thank you. How about your projects?'

'Let's sit down.' Bonaparte led Marie to one of the charming summer seats which had been placed all through the gardens of Malmaison, very often with rose beds on each side. Napoleon produced a pocket knife and cut a perfect dark red bud which he handed to Marie. Then, in the tones of a schoolmaster, he announced that his 'projects' were two-fold: first to stabilize the future of France and second to stabilize the future of Europe. The precondition for both of these was a lasting peace.

'Peace?' said Marie incredulously. 'No more battles?'

'Do not despise a good battle,' said the man who lived to fight. 'Marengo had its uses. It took the life of Desaix, and the lives of thousands of others on both sides, but it disgusted the Austrian Emperor, Francis I, so thoroughly with his advisers and his generals that he was willing to conclude the Peace of Lunéville with me, and to use his influence with England, which has been subsidising him, to accept my peace negotiations too.'

'Oh, Napoleon!' cried Marie, giving him his old name. 'What wonderful news! How happy everybody will be, and how they will all admire you! I'm sure the English are longing for peace – all our correspondents among the *émigrés* tell us so – and as for France, it will have time at last to catch its breath and develop. Young men will be set free from the dread of conscription. They will go to college and study for the professions –'

'And among the colleges I intend to found,' said General Bonaparte, 'will be a military college, to advocate a new and enlightened officer class.'

'And if it produces men in your own image there will be

137

blessing upon it,' said Marie fervently, and Napoleon kissed the hand that held the dark red rose.

'The rest of what I plan for France will be an affair for the jurists, or "the nobility of the robe", as they used to be called,' he said. 'The Convention, in its beginning, tried its apprentice hand at drawing up a code of civil law. That came to nothing, but at least some guidelines were laid down, and the Second Consul, Cambacérès, is enthusiastic about following them . . . under my own direction. It will do us all good to have rules for our behaviour and the punishment of crime clearly defined, don't you agree?'

Marie Fontaine, as he thought of her once again, would have agreed to anything he said.

'Now, my dear,' said Napoleon, 'I hope that when peace is established I shall get some practical help from Charles and yourself. Has Charles ever lived in England?'

'You know he was no *émigré*,' said Marie reproachfully.

'No, I mean he never went there on a visit?'

'Never.'

'But you have acquaintances there, as well as his mother?'

'And her attorney. Yes.'

'I would like you to consider paying a visit of sympathy to the Dowager Marchioness.'

'I'd better start learning English,' said Marie.

Napoleon did not discuss his third project for the stabilization of France with Marie. It was too serious to be first unfolded to any woman, for a woman's prime function was to be what he called 'the warrior's rest', and he was secretly afraid that the light of mockery which he sometimes suspected in Marie's dark blue eyes might be turned on his own if she thought him a poseur as regards religion. For the third project had a religious issue; being nothing less than the restoration of France to full communion with the Roman Catholic Church.

The French Revolution – of which Bonaparte was called the Son – had been the enemy of the Church. Priests had to take a civic oath or lose their office; churches, even the most famous, were locked or rededicated to the worship of such fictitious deities as the Goddess of Reason; the Feasts of the Christian Church were abolished, while Church lands and buildings were declared National Property and put up for sale.

Bonaparte, as he went about the country, observed that their spiritual deprivation had affected the lives of the people for the worse. He himself had never been a devout man, but his mother's teaching of prayers and psalms on Sundays had impressed him as a child, and the revolutionaries had replaced Sunday as the Day of Rest by a secular Tenth Day, or *decad*.

As he saw the restoration of Church worship and Church privileges as synonymous with the restoration of the Gallican Church, and therefore a matter of civil law, Napoleon opened talks on the subject with the Minister of Justice and Second Consul, Jean-Jacques Cambacérès.

The first thing he asked this confidential colleague was, what would people think of him, with his past record of bloodshed and violence, for being the one to introduce this Christianizing measure. Would the next plebiscite held for his re-election to the hereditary Consulship for life show the same overwhelming majority as had been the case in the past? He knew that a number of his senior officers, brought up to believe in the strictest tenets of the Revolution, might laugh and jeer if obliged to attend a Mass, and one thing he dreaded was derision. His consular colleague assured him all would be well, but the Minister tangled the Gallican issue with such a cloud of legal niceties that Napoleon thought he needed a simpler mind, and should consult Marie after all.

A few days after their first talk, then, he asked her to take another turn in the gardens with him, adding that he would look in on Charles and see if he was able to accompany them. 'You go ahead and wait for us,' he bade her, and Marie ran downstairs and out into the fine summer morning.

There was a young cedar tree opposite the front windows, planted and named in honour of the victory of Marengo, and near it a lady was sitting bolt upright on a chaise longue, not

139

lounging or reclining, as Joséphine had sat for her portrait; a lady who looked, in her black robe and lace veil, more like a European aristocrat than the Corsican partisan she had been in her youth. Marie recognized the general's mother, Madame Letizia.

She approached with her pretty curtsy and a, 'Bonjour, madame,' which received a similar reply.

'It *is* Madame la Marquise de la Tour, isn't it?' said Madame Letizia.

'I'm still Marie!' the girl said firmly, just as Napoleon came out of the house alone.

'*Maman chérie!*' he exclaimed, and gave her a great hug. 'How did you get here?'

'Joseph drove me over,' she explained, and the man looked round the cedar tree as if his brother might be hiding behind it.

He said: 'Then I suppose Joseph is somewhere about? I'll go to look for him.'

In fact Joseph Bonaparte was part of his Church problem. While Ambassador to the Vatican the general's brother had got on so badly with Pius VI as to put France in great disfavour with the Curia: a disfavour only increased by the removal of many of the Pope's art treasures to what was called 'the greater security of France'.

Madame Letizia said quickly, 'Monsieur Joseph said he was going to inspect the hot-houses and ask your gardeners for a bouquet for Madame Julie and the baby, that's where you'll find him. But what about the marquis? Isn't he coming out?'

'I'm afraid not. That young Dr Larrey sent over from Val-de-Grâce finds him fevered and in pain, and has ordered him to spend a few more days in bed. It's disappointing, but I'm afraid it's the fortune of war.'

'How the fortune of war, eh?' said his mother. 'What's the matter with him?'

'Colonel Latour was wounded at Marengo, Mother. His wrist was badly smashed.'

'Pooh, a broken wrist,' said Madame Letizia irascibly.

'That's nothing to make a fuss about. When your father and I were fighting a guerilla war in Corsica only months before you were born, we saw worse than that any day of the week.'

'You were Spartan warriors, madame,' said Marie with a smile.

Napoleon cut in: 'I want to consult you about my third project, Marie . . .'

'I'm flattered, sir.'

As eloquently as possible, Napoleon repeated the same arguments as he had used to the Minister of Justice: would reconciliation with the Church please the people, or the contrary? Would they deride him? Would it affect the vote, when a vote was called for? His mother was as enthusiastic as he expected of one whose brother was Cardinal Tesch, now, after a spell as an army contractor, the Archbishop of Lyon. Marie was equally so.

'What a wonderful thing you will do for France, General!' she said. 'Why do you think it will affect your popularity, or your vote? The old people and the sick will be given new hope if the Sacrament of Holy Communion is restored to them, and think of the beauty you would bring back to their lives instead of the ugliness of recent years! Why should the French deride you? You've given them back their old ideal of military glory – why not our forefathers' ideal of goodness too? The Church will have great preachers again, like the Abbé Bossuet and great musicians like the organists of Notre-Dame and good men like the priests of St Roch, to teach little children –'

'Did they teach you, my dear?' said Madame Letizia, moved by her emotion. 'Was your uncle a religious man?'

'My Uncle Prosper was an agnostic – a free thinker, madame,' said Marie, 'but he took me to be baptized at St Roch, and attended my First Communion there, and perhaps some day my neighbours and I will hear Mass in our parish church of St Roch again!'

All Napoleon said was, 'Thank you. I'll talk to Cambacérès.'

Madame Letizia waited until he had been gone for ten minutes before she said, 'Come and kiss me, Marie.' When

Marie was in her arms she went on, 'You were a dear good child to say that, and so clearly too, for Bonaparte.' She never called her son 'Napoleon' now, or even by the Corsican name of 'Nabulione'. Perhaps she thought the harsh vocables of 'Bonaparte' more suited to a military genius. 'You understand him so much better than his brothers and sisters. I'm not surprised he loves you.'

One of his aides-de-camp, Auguste-Frédéric Marmont, wrote of Napoleon's 'ever-increasing sense of his own importance'. For this the constitutional structure of the Consulate was largely responsible. He might plan to discuss the Church problem with Cambacérès and Lebrun, and they might express their opinions in writing, but the final decision was the First Consul's alone. So he proceeded with his project of a Gallican Church, in other words a Church which should give precedence to the civil power invested in himself.

He acknowledged his brother's scruples over the Pope's complaints about the art treasures removed from the Vatican by publishing his instructions from the then governing body, the Directory, to levy a tax in art treasures on the Italian Church and State and subsequently to admit its appointed commissioners to do the levying (otherwise known as 'looting'). His own conscience, and by inference Joseph's, was therefore clear, and the many fine pictures which decorated the walls of Malmaison were explicable as the free gifts of various Italian cities to Joséphine.

Regarding Napoleon and Joséphine, this same Marmont, who had been with them in Milan, wrote of the husband that 'a love so true, so pure, so exclusive, had never possessed the heart of a man.'

Very little of this great love remained in the Malmaison days. There had been forgiveness for Joséphine's infidelity and shady money transactions with 'Wideawake Charlie' (Captain Hippolyte Charles) and the Bodin Company, and since then passion had been replaced by an affection as easy as an old shoe. Joséphine's opinion on Church matters was not sought.

A valuable opinion was that of Cardinal Caprara, the Archbishop of Milan, now the Papal Legate to France. He promised to use his influence with the new Pope, Pius VII, and with the Officiality of Paris, as the high clergy of Paris was known. A concordat was signed re-establishing a Gallican Church in France, and some months later Cardinal Caprara commemorated the event by celebrating a pontified Mass in the Cathedral of Notre-Dame.

The restoration of the Catholic Church to an official position in the state was marked by the salute of sixty salvoes of cannon and by the presence of four battalions of infantry. Consuls, ministers and ambassadors attended a carriage procession, led by Napoleon in a carriage drawn by eight horses. Inside the cathedral, as he had foreseen, some of his officers revealed their revolutionary enthusiasm – or their ill breeding – by giggling and ridicule. Joséphine was not present, nor was Marie. The latter had been gratified by being able to attend Mass in St Roch's church, the officiating clergy being her old friends, Father Carrichon, who had given her uncle his blessing on the steps of the guillotine, and Father Vincent for whom she had organized a first-aid post on the bank of the Seine.

Charles attended the service with her.

12

Over the following months, while the ladies of the palace, strolling gracefully in the gardens or gossiping lightly in the salons of Malmaison, did not fail to comment on the friendship which had sprung up between Madame Letizia and Marie, Joséphine kept her own counsel about it. She suffered one or two 'nervous crises' and even one attack of hysterics, so that her husband felt compelled to send for his personal physician, Dr Nicolas Corvisart, asking him on the same occasion, to have a look at Charles Latour.

Dr Corvisart uncompromisingly told Joséphine that her hopes of motherhood were illusory, though she might take the waters at Plombières again; they had been doing good since Roman times. To Bonaparte he said Joséphine needed a change, and some of the gay society she loved; perhaps a few weeks in Paris would do her good. To Charles he was even more forthright, especially after a talk with Marie, sitting dejected in an empty salon.

'Marquis, you're in danger of becoming a real *malade imaginaire*,' he said. 'That charming wife of yours is pining for you, and all you can talk about is the pain in your wrist, though the injury is much healed now.'

'All she can talk about is pharmacy,' said Charles sulkily. 'Did she tell you she's gone back to her uncle's laboratory, though she knows I disapprove?'

'Yes, she did,' said Corvisart. 'But pharmacy isn't her only interest. I found her deep in an English grammar, bought at Galignani, the English bookshop in Paris. She has a very good brain and a variety of interests. I wish I could say as much for some of my other patients at Malmaison. Now get out of bed, Marquis, go down to dinner and treat your wife as if you were courting her, and tomorrow take her on a little excursion – to Rueil, perhaps: there's a fine church there, well worth a visit. And if you love her, no talk of war or wounds.'

So Charles and Marie set off for a picnic on an island in the Seine, and while they were away a carriage procession started for Paris, so that when they returned to the château they found it almost empty. Napoleon had decided he should spend a week at his office in the Tuileries and take Joséphine to the city, with his permission to buy as many hats as she liked. The ladies of the palace would go to the Tuileries too and support her at a splendid evening reception.

In Paris Napoleon summoned a meeting of the Consulate to discuss the preparation of a new Code Civil, a compendium of civil law for the guidance of the justiciary and the legal profession. It had had its origins in the National Convention of Revolution days but was now amplified and elaborated by Cambacérès, but while the Minister of Justice took the credit, the new statute was usually known as the Code Napoléon.

The First Consul's personal interest was education. His aim was to establish the *université de France* to include every place of learning from primary schools through the lycées to the Polytechnique and the Sorbonne, to the ten schools of law and six of medicine which he himself created along the lines of the *École des Arts et Métiers*.

From his own pocket Napoleon paid the indemnity demanded by the monks of the Great St Bernard for the shooting of one of their number by Anatole Laguerre, with a warning to the remaining commissioners of the Republic that he would not be responsible for paying for a similar crime.

He smiled as he sent this notice to be copied in a legible hand. There was no reason to expect the repetition of such a crime, for Laguerre had completely disappeared, though he was reported to have been seen in Vienna. And France was at peace. Banditry had been stamped out, and the one outbreak of civil war, in the west country, had been settled in January 1800 by his own Treaty with the Vendeans.

When he looked at the map of Europe the man who sought to stabilize France had reason for self-satisfaction. He was in the act of creating what he thought of as the 'Grand Empire', a group of client states around the mother country which might by force or diplomacy prove to be the beginning of a European Union. There were the States of the Rhineland, there were the Cisalpine and the Ligurian Republic; further along the Mediterranean shore there was the city of Genoa, which had once 'owned' Corsica. He was now turning the Swiss cantons into a Helvetic Confederation – although he dared not bring too much pressure to bear on the hard-headed Swiss! They were nearly as bad as the English – and France had to face it, England was still the chief obstacle to her dreams of glory.

During 1801 the Latours were constant visitors to Malmaison and in receipt of Napoleon's confidence. The Peace of Amiens, he told the Latours, would be announced in the following spring, and would certainly be followed by a rush to cross the Channel in both directions. 'My dear Marquis,' he went on with studied formality, 'I don't know who has a better reason to visit England than yourself. The only comfort of a widowed mother, please prepare to start for the house in London then. You are acquainted with madame's attorney, I believe?'

'We have exchanged letters, sir. Mr Duthie has a great many clients among the *émigré* population.'

'Ah! He will of course introduce you to his acquaintances. And that is what I need from you – your impartial impressions of the French in London: their loyalty to the man calling himself Louis XVIII and the other Bourbons, their newspapers, so full of libellous attacks on myself, their English paymasters, and – oh! anything that occurs to you . . .'

'I understand,' said Charles. 'You want me to become a kind of super-spy.'

'No, Charles, let me say simply to be my eyes and ears. Do you speak English?'

'Enough. And Marie has been studying that crazy language and really has made progress.'

'Exactly what I should have expected,' said Napoleon with a smile. 'You'll be a great help to your husband, my dear girl.'

'I don't see how, if this work is to be among the French! Isn't there something *practical* I can do?' said Marie.

'Certainly, you can buy me a portrait of Milord Nelson.'

Napoleon's wish to have a portrait of Lord Nelson, which presumably would not be hard to find in London, was not a surprise. Marie was led into his study by his mother while he was in Paris, and saw the bust of Nelson which stood upon his desk – a surprising tribute to the admiral who had inflicted a crushing defeat on the French in Egypt in the naval battle of Aboukir Bay. Marie believed Napoleon had a certain sympathy with Nelson because of his notorious love affair with Lady Hamilton. Looking at the sculptured face of Nelson and assessing the mixture of spirituality and sexuality in the features of England's national hero, Marie wondered if Napoleon saw any similarity between Emma Hamilton and Joséphine.

Marie and Madame Letizia, walking in the gardens and the pastures of Malmaison, knew little more of Switzerland than that it was the home of the merino sheep Joséphine kept for distribution among her favoured farmers in the district. Marie found them more decorative than the sheep Charles had established at Vesle, and when he walked out to view them he agreed with this himself, but more because of the pretty girl shepherdesses and the stalwart young shepherds who attended them than because of the merinos. The shepherds wore the peasant dress of the Canton Grisons, from which Masséna had chased the remaining Russians, and spoke its Romansch dialect, so that communication was impossible except by smiles and imitations of their greeting, which sounded like 'Gruetzi!'

Marie would have liked to ask Napoleon's mother what she had meant by that cryptic remark all those months ago, 'It's no wonder he loves you.' Was it possible that Napoleon had opened his heart to the mother he so closely resembled and told her of his and Marie's confession of love in the garden at Ajaccio? She didn't think it was likely. She thought it far more probable that Madame Letizia's keen dark eyes, so quickly observant, had detected the truth. He loves me still, exulted Marie.

Nor did Marie hear what the older lady thought of her son Louis's betrothal to Hortense de Beauharnais. It was celebrated with great rejoicing in January 1802. Marie attended the religious marriage performed by Cardinal Caprara, and noted that an attack of vertigo caused the bridegroom to stumble as he walked and a throat constriction made his responses almost inaudible. Her prayers for Hortense's health and happiness were heartfelt.

At least their bridal journey was not long – only as far as the rue de la Victoire, where their wedded life was to begin in the former home of Napoleon and Joséphine. The populace turned out to shout *'Vive la mariée!'* but the cheering was as nothing compared to the cheers which rent the skies on the night in March when Napoleon, during a diplomatic reception, announced that he had signed the Peace of Amiens with England.

The French people, having survived the Revolution, had been as greedy for *la gloire* as he was himself, and glory had cost them thousands of dead and wounded men. Now they were equally eager for *la paix*, and peace was as popular across the Channel as it was in France. Napoleon had had for some time a 'representative' (discreetly so-called) in London, and on the night peace was proclaimed a team of exultant Englishmen drove to his residence in Portman Square to take Monsieur Otto and General Lauriston to Downing Street to shake hands with the Prime Minister.

The proclamation was read aloud, and Otto's house was illuminated. Figures representing Amity and Peace were lit up, surmounted by a star, and so was the whole of Portman Square. This blaze of light appeared to give great satisfaction to a new member of Monsieur Otto's staff. He had a post in the military section. He had had an undistinguished army career, but now held the rank of general. His name was Anatole Laguerre.

It was, however, to be another two years before Charles and Marie received their marching orders for England. Their travelling plans were abruptly postponed when Charles's health deteriorated. He really was no *malade imaginaire* after all. The wrist wound, which had never fully healed, became infected, the infection became debilitating, and the Latours left the highly charged atmosphere of the court for the tranquillity of Vesle. For Charles this was a wearisome period of convalescence, for Marie a chance to take up again the country life she had embraced so wholeheartedly. Finally, on a bright day in late February 1804, Charles – fully fit at last – and Marie returned to Paris, from there to journey to England.

A coach was set aside at the Tuileries for their journey to Calais, and a cabin on board one of the boats which now discreetly crossed the Channel between Calais and Dover. Charles also had a reservation made for them by his mother's attorney in London, Mr John Duthie, at the Ship Inn at Dover, which was well spoken of.

There was no time for a reply to arrive from Mr Duthie, nor did any letter come from Charles's mother, so Charles filled in the time before their departure by long talks with his Paris lawyer, Maître Vial. Marie spent hours at the Quai Voltaire, dispensing medicines at sale prices to her neighbours and helping Madame Beauchet to anticipate every possible household crisis. At nine o'clock one morning in early March the postilions cracked their whips in the Carrousel, and the Marquis and Marquise de la Tour were off to the Channel coast.

On the way to the port, where they paused for a late lunch, Marie was amazed to find how often they met with traces of Napoleon's presence in these country districts at times when he was supposed to have been in Paris. She said as much to Charles while they were having coffee. He laughed and said the inspection of an invasion fleet was a good excuse for getting out of Paris.

'Wait till we get to Calais and see what you think then.'

From the hotel there with a view over the *avant-port* and other basins and canals, the scene was one of war. Every waterway was crowded with shipping, more than Marie had seen in Toulon harbour when she sailed for Egypt, and that was supposed to have been the greatest fleet assembled in Toulon since the Crusades. And it was a fleet in which ships' carpenters and artificers were working, and making the devil of a noise about it, as Charles said. This was a fleet preparing to put to sea, and when they were at sea what would they do? Invade England. Then what would the English do?

Invade France.

'It's such a little strip of water, Charles,' said Marie next day when they had embarked upon it, and the sea was rough, and Marie was cold in her warm overcoat and queasy in her stomach. 'But I've often heard Napoleon say the English Channel is England's best defence.'

'I suppose the last time it was defeated was when Norman William crossed it in 1066, as I was taught at school.'

'Suppose some day there's a tunnel built below the Channel and an enemy army can march through beneath the water, with horse-drawn artillery, ambulances and field kitchens and all.'

'Don't be silly, dear, the English aren't such fools as that.'

It was dark before the packet berthed at Dover, and the sight of lamplight and firelight streaming through the casement windows of the Ship Inn was a very welcome sight to the travellers. There was a cheery taproom where a log fire was blazing and Marie ordered a hot meal with a good deal of aplomb. 'I'm in England! They're speaking English to me and I understand it,' she exulted.

Charles had flung himself on a letter bearing the name and address of John Duthie. He read it several times while platters of Dover sole were put before them with the inevitable pot of tea, and then he tossed it into Marie's lap. 'How's that for a warm welcome?' he said, and walked out of the taproom.

My Dear Lord, [Mr Duthie began]

Thank you for your letter of even date to hand. The Dowager Marchioness was pleased to hear of your intended visit, and hopes you and your lady will dine and sleep at her house in Edwardes Square on the 8th inst. As the house is some distance from London I shall be pleased to take you there myself. Madame was surprised to hear of your address in Dover, where the Lord Warden is by far the better known hotel. I suggest you travel to London by the coach which passes the Ship at 8 a.m. and will put you down at Nerot's Hotel, St James's, where I have reserved rooms for you.

I am, my dear Lord, your obedient servant, John Duthie.

Marie thought this letter showed the lawyer's excellent French *and* the Dowager Marchioness's coldness of heart. She might have written to poor Charles herself, she thought. He's wanted it for so long! No wonder he rushed out in a tantrum . . . he's probably walking up and down the beach in distress, and catching cold . . . She was relieved when Charles came back, very calm and hungry, and with no more comment than that the Dover sole looked good. She resolved to be very civil to his mother when they met.

Next day's ride to London up the Dover Road in the mail coach, with the postilions so lively in their red jackets and the post-boys' horns so merry in the spring air, the Kentish fields and thickets so bright on either side, was pleasant to remember in the sombre magnificence of Nerot's Hotel, where their suite was furnished in black oak and black horsehair. Mr Duthie, who appeared before the Latours had time to wash their hands, was a good deal more amiable than the tone of his letter had led them to expect. He was a Scotsman from Aberdeen, which meant that Marie's shaky knowledge of English was defeated by his accent and Charles begged him to speak French.

'Her laddyship, yer gweed-mither, ma'am,' was how he began, 'is fair lukin' forrit tae seein' ye baith. She's invitit anither veesitor to ate his denner the nicht and jalouses ye winna objeck tae meetin' the Pranz de Condy.'

Charles looked his admiration as Marie said that of course they would be charmed to meet the Prince de Condé, and he bowed his assent. He had hardly expected his mother to be in such close touch with the senior among all the Bourbon *émigrés*, but rejoiced in this early opportunity of carrying out Napoleon's instructions.

Mr Duthie had ordered a closed carriage from a livery stable in the Haymarket to take all three of them to Edwardes Square. Explaining that he drove a gig when visiting his clients but was 'feared that to drive in an open thing might ruffle the young laddyship's hair' he ushered them ceremoniously into the carriage, and told the driver to leave London by the Hammersmith Road. Marie was pleased to be in a protected vehicle. She was wearing a new dress of smoke-grey chiffon with a rose-coloured satin sash with a matching pelisse and a fillet in her hair and hoped to arrive unruffled by wind or weather. She had locked away her grandmother's pearl parure, but her white kid gloves were immaculate.

Mr Duthie, with a too-frequent use of Charles's title, was telling him that for the past eighty years the social élite of London had chosen to live in Grosvenor Square. Edwardes Square, their destination, was less distinguished. On two hundred acres of land sold in 1768 by William Fox, first Baron Kensington, to Henry Fox, first Baron Holland, two rows of typical Georgian houses had been built north of the Hammersmith Road. The Georgian 'box' was twenty feet wide by thirty feet deep by four storeys high, and while commodious was not too expensive for an *émigré* family of sufficient means, and Mr Duthie boasted that he had bought, as a real estate agent, a corner house and garden for 'the Dowager Marchioness de la Tour' at a bargain price.

Marie had half expected that Charles's mother would be at the door to embrace her son, but they were admitted by a manservant, who led them up one flight of stairs and announced them by name and rank to a lady reading in a high-backed chair. Without haste, she placed a leather mark between the pages of her book, took off her spectacles, and murmuring, 'So there you are,' held out her hand for her son to kiss.

He paused for a split second, inhibited by the sight of a mother who, in spite of her grey hair and widow's cap, reminded him of the portrait inscribed 'Marie-Sabine de Polignac' which had been vandalized at Vesle by the addition of a black moustache. Then he bent forward and daringly kissed her cheek.

'This is my wife,' he said, and led forward Marie, who without a word spoken, smiled and curtsied low.

'Pretty dress,' said the dowager casually, and asked the manservant, who entered carrying a silver salver with decanters and glasses, what had become of Mr Duthie.

The man replied that monsieur begged to be excused, he had a carriage waiting at the door.

'Mr Duthie has been a great help to me in my bereavement.'

'Oh, my dear mother,' Charles burst out, 'if only Edouard had been spared to you!'

'And had been here to meet you today,' their mother said, with her handkerchief to her eyes.

'Marie knew Edouard, *Maman*. She helped him once in Paris, when he was hurt.'

Madame de la Tour closed her eyes.

'So?' she said. 'You must tell me how it came about, madame, that you – fell in with both my sons.'

13

In the 'typical Georgian box' which was her dwelling, the dowager paused on the narrow landing and looked upstairs and down. Servants were moving in and out of the dining room on the ground floor, and from the basement rose the savoury smell of roasting meat. There was a sound of men's voices from the room they had just left.

'I take it the Prince de Condé has arrived?' said Charles's mother to a hovering footman.

'Yes, madame, accompanied by his grandson.'

'Very good. Make sure the gentlemen have everything they need.' And to Marie: 'We dine early here, but not until more than an hour from now. I suggest we go to my own room for our little chat. There will be a fire there – and I noticed you were looking a little chilly in the salon.'

'Thank you – it's a rather windy afternoon.'

Marie followed her hostess up another narrow stair to a bedroom floor where a door standing ajar admitted them to a room in which a log fire in a burnished grate was reflected in a walnut bed whose pink silk curtains hung from a circular brass rod, and where a grey Persian cat was comfortably asleep on the pillows. The single window looked on the back garden, which was obviously in the process of being replanted with flowerbeds and fruit to suit the new tenant. More than the cat and more than the flowers, what caught and held Marie's attention was the portrait above the fireplace of a beautiful woman, dressed in the height of a fashion of about twenty years back.

'Do you recognize that portrait?' said her hostess.

'Yes, because I've seen it before. Or at least I *think* I've seen it, or one very like . . . It is Queen Marie Antoinette.'

'Madame Vigée-Lebrun, the artist, painted Her late Majesty many times. Where could you have seen another example of her work?'

'When my uncle sent me with a bottle of medicine to the Vicomtesse de Noailles when she was under house arrest in Paris.'

Madame de la Tour winced. 'Did you ever see the Queen in real life?' she asked.

Marie could have said, 'I saw her on her way to the guillotine!' but she replied gently, 'I saw her when my uncle took me to the Federation celebrations in 1785. She was very lovely . . . with her little boy in her hand.'

'That poor child! So then you must have seen all the Royal Family . . . and I needn't explain the Prince de Condé to you. Sit down, Marie.' The 'Marie' was almost whispered, but it was an encouragement.

'I didn't know the Prince was in London. I thought his headquarters were in Ghent . . . with the Army of the Princes.'

'He comes here to meet his grandson, Louis-Antoine, who spends much of his time in Baden. His title is the Duc d'Enghien.'

'Is he married?'

'No, but there's a lady in the case – the attraction in Baden, I'm told.' Here the dowager heaved an affected sigh. 'These miniatures might interest you.'

She unhooked two little portraits, done in weak colours, which hung on either side of the bed, and laid them in Marie's lap. One, the picture of a boy about five, was plainly Charles – the dark eyes and black curls had not changed much with the years, and equally clearly had been inherited from the imperious lady now sitting opposite Marie.

'Charles was very like you, madame, as a little boy.'

'You think so? Edouard was more like his father, a true la Tour.'

The catch in her breath made Marie look up, and when she

saw that the older woman's eyes were full of tears she felt a surge of pity.

'Oh, madame! I'm so sorry –' she began. 'Remember, you have another son left to you – a son who loves you very much . . .'

'You mean to be kind, I'm sure. But tell me,' with a return to her earlier, chilly manner, 'when are you going to give me a grandson?'

'I wish I knew.'

There was something so resigned and so depressed in the simple words that Madame de la Tour, as she rose to light the candles in the girandoles beside the fire, drew a caressing hand over the girl's bright hair and decided to say no more about sons or grandsons. Instead she said she hoped the young people would not object to the presence of strangers at her dinner table.

'For really the poor old prince can be a great bore,' she was surprised to hear herself saying. 'He used to drop in far too often for my husband's taste. But I knew he came because he felt guilty. It was he who encouraged Edouard to join in that fatal adventure – the invasion at Quiberon Bay – and he couldn't stop talking about it, and blaming himself, until I felt like screaming. I tried to give his grandson a hint, but it didn't do much good . . .'

'It'll be interesting to meet him, I'm sure.'

'Anyway I've asked another guest – a woman – who'll shut him up if he starts on Quiberon – especially if she begins on Women's Rights.'

'Not Madame de Staël, by any chance?'

Madame de la Tour laughed the ringing laugh of a girl.

'No, not the doughty baroness. It's Lady Holland, my landlord's wife. A great admirer of your General Bonaparte, I believe. Who is *not* an admirer of Madame de Staël.'

'I don't think the general believes in Women's Rights,' said Marie demurely, and the entry of a manservant bearing a tea tray put an end to a shared peal of laughter.

Tea was drunk, and the tray removed before anything more

was said about the Hollands, in terms no more flattering than those used to describe the Prince de Condé.

'Is your landlord coming to dinner too, madame?' Marie asked.

'Not he. He was asked but politely declined, saying he's caught a chill. My belief is he'll spend a happy evening in his library, while the fair Elizabeth disports herself elsewhere.'

'Isn't their marriage a success?'

'In a way it is, but she's just a little bit too much for him. Like a thunderstorm or a tidal wave or some other natural calamity. She's a clever woman and if women could sit in Parliament she would do very well, but in society she's out of place because she has a bitter tongue and can't always control it. You know she's a niece of Charles James Fox, the Whig leader?'

'No, I didn't know that. I know Mr Fox championed the French Revolution.'

'And the American Revolution, and anything that promises to turn the world topsy-turvy. He's been a bad influence in Lady Holland's life, far more so than her first husband, Sir Geoffrey Webster, though he was no gentleman, divorcing her for "criminal conversation" – that's the fashionable term for adultery – after she swept Lord Holland off his feet in Florence when she met the poor boy when he was doing the Grand Tour. Holland was just a youngster, twenty-four to her twenty-seven, but he stuck to his guns like a man and married her three days after the divorce. Even so, she found time to bear him a son before they were married, and then he brought her home to Holland House and a more luxurious life than she ever imagined when Webster married her as a chit of sixteen.'

'Sixteen, was she?' said Marie faintly. In the rush of gossip, and the older lady's obvious delight in it, she felt as if something like a tidal wave had happened to herself.

Within five minutes she was able to appreciate the dowager's metaphor when a footman announced, 'The Lady

Holland,' and the lady not so much entered as stormed into the room.

She was neither unusually tall nor unusually heavy, but she gave the impression of height and weight not ill-suited to her air of self-assurance. At thirty-four she was still a beautiful woman, vivacious in her greeting to Madame de la Tour, whom she called 'Sabine', rude in her detailed inspection of Marie through a tortoiseshell lorgnette and with a twitch of her aquiline nose. She must have left her cloak with the servants for she wore no wrap over the evening dress of scarlet satin, very effective with the black hair she wore braided and swept into the confines of a narrow band of diamonds.

'Well, my dear Sabine!' said Lady Holland – and her voice was too loud for the little room – 'Is this the daughter-in-law you said you didn't want to meet? Why, she's a beauty, an authentic beauty, and Charles is in luck! Come and kiss me, young lady, and be prepared to like me very much – I'm sure we shall be friends!'

Marie approached her shyly and, all too aware of Madame de la Tour's sniff of irritation, held up her cheek for Lady Holland's chilly kiss.

'You'll sweep the young men off their feet at the ball!' said the latter. 'Are you looking forward to it?'

'I don't – I mean I didn't know,' stammered Marie. 'I mean this is the first I've heard of any ball.'

'You mean you didn't tell her, Sabine? You're very naughty!'

'I thought you should have the pleasure of telling them yourself. Charles is invited too, Marie. He tells me you're accustomed to dance together.'

'Paris went dancing mad after *Thermidor* marked the beginning of the end of the Revolution,' said Marie.

'Had the waltz reached Paris by then?'

'Oh yes. It had even reached the country districts; we danced it at Vesle.'

'Wonderful! Now let me explain about this evening. I've been asked to bring a party to a grand ball at Lansdowne

House. Easier said than done. First, Lord Holland has to decline – he's caught a chill. Then a friend of ours, Sir David Boone, is on duty and will arrive late. Next my good friend Sabine de la Tour keeps the ball a dead secret from Charles and you, on whom I *absolutely* counted . . .'

'Oh please, Lady Holland,' said Marie, 'you mustn't blame Madame de la Tour. She had every reason to suppose we would spend the evening with her . . . since we accepted her kind invitation to dine and sleep tonight.'

'Worse and worse!' cried Lady Holland. 'Put them off with a "dine and sleep", did you? Not very forthcoming! This isn't Windsor Castle, or the Prince's residence at Brighton. You can't think much of English hospitality, can you, my dear?'

'It was what we wanted,' said Marie smoothly. 'We were very happy to be asked at all.'

'Thank you, Marie,' said the dowager, 'but if I had understood all the circumstances, I should have insisted on your going to the ball. Lord Lansdowne is an important English statesman, and it could be very interesting for Charles to have the entrée to Lansdowne House. Oh, and, Elizabeth dear, I can increase your party by one man. The Duc d'Enghien is in the house at this very moment, along with his grandfather, and he's always ready for any gaiety that may come his way.'

Lady Holland's reaction was not what Marie expected.

'D'Enghien and Condé, eh? You're aiming high, Sabine! The two leading Bourbons of the day! Don't tell me you're going to be mixed up in one of their silly royalist plots, my dear.'

Madame de la Tour bit her lip to suppress a sob.

'Considering that one of their wretched plots cost the life of my dear son at Quiberon, you must be out of your mind to call me a plotter,' she said. 'Marie, will you pull the bell cord and ask the footman to come? I want to send for Charles. I want to tell him we're all in a muddle here and need a gentleman to put us straight.'

'Yes of course.' Marie got up and dragged at the length of embroidery which did duty as a bell-pull. 'If you're still in a muddle about the ball let me tell you one more muddling

thing. I have nothing suitable to wear at Lansdowne House.'
She waited until the gasps died down and then she added,
'Except of course my wedding dress, and it's hanging in my
wardrobe at Nerot's Hotel.'

Only Lady Holland was equal to saying, 'You weren't married in church, were you? But you were married in white?'

Marie choked down the angry reply: 'Were *you* married in
white, after you'd been through a divorce and given birth to
your lover's child?' Instead she said, 'The dress was white
peau de soie, with a white tulle veil, and I wore white roses
in my hair.'

'Charles should have had you painted,' said his mother,
and with a brisk exclamation of, 'Who's taking my name in
vain?' Charles himself was in the room, having overtaken the
manservant on the stairs.

'Marie was telling us about her lovely wedding dress, which
she thinks of wearing to the ball tonight,' said his mother,
and Marie never admired her husband so much as when his
natural query of 'What ball?' caused both ladies to overflow
with incoherent explanations, which an ADC of General Bonaparte had no difficulty in 'setting straight'.

The difficulty, he said, was the length of time it would take
to get to London, not to mention back again, but if Maman
would lend them her carriage and horses, and since the Holland carriage and four were already in the la Tour stables, he
thought it might be managed. Would Lady Holland permit
him to convey her kind invitation to the Duc d'Enghien, who
was already in evening dress and wearing his decorations?
Certainly she would. And who was her other guest, and why
was he coming on later? His name was Sir David Boone, an
ensign in the Royal Navy.

'We've heard of him, Charles,' said Marie. 'We met his
brother in Paris, do you remember?'

'Yes, I do.'

'Ah, that was another tragic story of plots and plotters,' said
the dowager, touching her handkerchief to her eyes.

'But which had nothing to do with our proposed evening's

entertainment,' said Charles coolly. 'Maman, permit us to take leave of you – unless you're prepared to pair off with the Prince de Condé and give us all a lesson in dancing at Lansdowne House?'

The dowager's indignation at this suggestion sent them all downstairs in good humour.

The Prince de Condé was at the front door to see them start – such a frail, little old gentleman that Marie was not surprised that he, the leader of the *Armée des Princes*, had never ventured to challenge Napoleon. His grandson, the young duke, was more promising: a handsome, well-made man, who as Lady Holland whispered to Marie, was 'every inch a soldier'. Marie, who thought that description applied even more aptly to her husband, was looking round for Charles. He had left her on the upstairs landing when his mother called him back into her room.

Oh, don't let anything go wrong now, when everything was going so well! she thought, and it was almost a prayer. And then Charles reappeared, smiling like a happy man. 'I mustn't fuss,' she said to herself, 'not in front of all those people.' She had counted fifteen servants in attendance on Charles's mother, with four grooms intent on wheeling out a carriage with the crusader's cockleshells on the door panels ('Better than a swarm of bees!') and a cook in a white tunic and a chef's white toque.

Lady Holland's personal maid was also present, who took her place on one of the rear seats of the carriage after wrapping her mistress in a fur cape and offering another cape to Marie.

'I took the liberty of bringing a wrap for you,' she said, 'since I was planning to kidnap you! Are you comfortable?'

'You were very thoughtful, madame. I'm as comfortable as I can be.'

'Good! Now, gentlemen, get in, and let us be on our way.'

Lady Holland took Marie's hand and drew her close. Charles took his place on his wife's other side, with the young duke beyond him. The postilion cracked his whip, the coachman released the brake and Marie, her head spinning, was off on yet another horse-drawn journey.

Certainly Lord Holland's matched bays tackled the Great West Road with more enthusiasm than the hacks Mr Duthie had hired from a livery stable, and their mistress had hardly time to point out the roofs of Holland House on the other side of the highway before they were leaving Hammersmith behind.

Marie was almost dropping asleep when she heard her husband say, 'Lady Holland, won't you please tell us about Lansdowne House? Remember I'm a foreigner with everything to learn about London. Who is Lord Lansdowne and why should he give a ball?'

Lady Holland laughed. 'Because he likes to entertain,' she said.

'Lansdowne House has gone through several changes in a short time,' she explained. 'It was built by Robert Adam for the Marquess of Bute nearly fifty years ago. He sold it to Lord Shelburne, who was the first tenant. He was the Foreign Secretary under Chatham, and changed the name of his mansion to Lansdowne House when he became Lord Lansdowne. He was Prime Minister, and conceded American Independence in a treaty with Benjamin Franklin, signed in the very house we're going to – now when was that? I've forgotten the date.'

'And you haven't told us where the house is,' said Charles.

'Corner of Berkeley Square,' said the Duc d'Enghien. This simple explanation put a full stop to Lady Holland's excursion into history, and all the passengers were silent as the coach rolled through Kensington, turned into St James's, where the lights in the royal palace shone through the gathering gloom, and pulled up outside Nerot's Hotel.

'Don't take the horses out, we're going on to Lansdowne House,' said Lady Holland to the coachman, and almost in the same breath rejected the duke's suggestion that she might want to come back to Nerot's after the ball.

'It's a long way back to Holland House at dawn,' he said.

'I know it, Louis, but I must go home. My little boy is sick, as well as my husband, and they'll both worry about me if I don't appear. I have my maid to keep me company. And now – let's meet in twenty minutes, shall we?'

Murmuring, '*À vot' service, milady!*' the French maid went off to help in the removal of baggage from the la Tour carriage, which had followed them, and Marie, delighted to find lamps all through the rooms and corridors of Nerot's, rushed upstairs to take her dress out of the wardrobe.

A chambermaid followed, to pour out warm water and help Marie with her stockings and undergarments, so that she was completely ready by the time Charles came in from the dressing room next door, and what he thought of the vision he saw was expressed in the stumbling words, 'My bride! My – beautiful – bride!'

'Do you like me?'

'Like you? I love you!'

He had her in his arms then, and with the fervour of the early days at the Quai Voltaire (and to the great danger of the white peau de soie) called her his lovely girl, kissing her lips and stroking her hair, until he was reminded to say, 'I've got something for you to wear.' He released her, and going to the overcoat he had flung down on a chair he took a leather case from the pocket and snapped it open.

'My mother called me back before we left,' he said. 'She wants you to wear it tonight. She said you wore roses on your wedding day. These are to wear instead. She wore these jewels when she was married to my father. Now they're for you to keep.'

The case contained a diamond tiara, with three flowers in the shape of roses in front and six smaller roses arranged on each side. In the lamplight they were as brilliant as Marie's shining eyes.

'For *me*?' she whispered. 'I don't believe it. Why should she give up this – the most beautiful thing I ever saw?'

'Because family jewels go with the family, and now you belong to us. Mother said, "She's young and beautiful, just right for diamonds! And Marie's very sweet and very sympathetic and very sensitive too. You must take care of her, my son!"'

She laid her head on his breast and said, 'And will you?'

'If you'll let me.'

Lansdowne House was certainly at the corner of Berkeley Square, for the mansions and great trees of that aristocratic neighbourhood were visible beyond the pillared façade of Robert Adam's masterpiece. Lady Holland, however, had omitted to state that the gardens and carriageway of Lansdowne House extended to and occupied a part of Berkeley Street, occasioning a congestion of traffic obviously vexatious to the coachman, who was crimson with suppressed oaths as he edged the bays past the other vehicles on the street. He set down his passengers safely, however, at a door where they were greeted by a butler quite as imposing as the intendant of the Tuileries, who addressed himself to Lady Holland.

'Good evening, milady. Lord Lansdowne begs you to excuse him, he was detained at the Foreign Office and has only just returned. I gave him your ladyship's message and a refection has been prepared for his guests who have not dined. May I show you the way?'

He led them through a hall where marble statues struck attitudes before vast oil paintings of military subjects in which the British redcoats were always victorious, into a room on the left-hand side where a table was elaborately set for dinner and a sideboard held bottles and decanters.

The butler presented a whole grilled salmon, set in a bed of lettuce on a silver dish, and a footman followed him pouring champagne, so that Lady Holland, with a greedy sigh, exclaimed, 'What magnificent hospitality!' as an elderly gentleman appeared at the door.

'What a delightful thing to overhear!'

'It's a delightful thing for you to say, considering what an imposition this is,' said Lady Holland. 'But I literally kidnapped three of her dinner guests from the Dowager Marquise de la Tour, and I felt that without some sustenance they would never stand up to a long evening's dancing. May I present her son, the present marquis, and his charming wife? Louis d'Enghien of course you know.'

'I'm always happy to meet old friends, and make new ones,' said Lord Lansdowne, and bowed. Marie dropped a deep curtsy; she was very much impressed by this amiable, elderly gentleman, so dignified and yet so self-assured! She believed that Napoleon Bonaparte was a genius, but Lord Lansdowne had been Prime Minister of Great Britain, and say what you like, there was a difference!

'Please be seated, everybody,' said Lord Lansdowne. 'Hark! The orchestra is striking up,' for the sound of a lively tune was coming from a distant room. 'People for the ball will soon be arriving. Ah! here comes someone now.'

The butler was ushering in a young man in evening clothes which were obviously made in London, in contrast to Charles's white waistcoat and black tailcoat which were equally obviously made abroad.

'Lord Lansdowne, may I present Sir David Boone?' said Lady Holland, and then they all had to rise again while their host, with the respect for protocol which seemed natural to him, rehearsed the style and title of each one. Marie, her attention sharpened, noticed that he introduced Charles and herself as *'nos amis français'*. With Bonaparte's invasion fleet lying off the Channel coast and his Grande Armée encamped at Boulogne, an Englishman was well advised to explain his French guests, even if they were *émigrés*.

She herself was not concerned with that. She was having to accept the fact that Sir David Boone, apparently in his middle twenties, was a younger version of the self-proclaimed American, the 'English spy' who had taken refuge from the National Guard in her uncle's shop on the October day when Queen Marie Antoinette had gone to the guillotine.

'Now, David, give us an account of yourself,' said Lady Holland, who had rapidly finished the chilling salmon on her plate while the butler filled the newcomers' glasses with champagne. 'You said you had another engagement and might be late, and now you're here almost as soon as we were! Pray what was this mysterious engagement?'

'I think your ladyship will agree that it was something special,' said the young man, flushing. 'I had the honour of being invited to a luncheon given by their lordships of the Admiralty, at which Lord Nelson was their particular guest.'

'Special indeed!' cried Lady Holland. 'Pray was Lady Nelson present?'

'Lady Nelson is in Norfolk, I believe. Lord Nelson was accompanied by his intimate friend, Sir William Hamilton. They are sharing a house at present.'

Marie caught the smile which passed between Lord Lansdowne and the Duc d'Enghien, a tribute to the other piece of property which, in their intimacy, Sir William shared with Lady Hamilton's lover.

'It was a great honour for me to be invited,' said Sir David, 'me, a humble ensign in HMS *Vindictive*. That's what my captain called me when he gave me leave to come up to town from Portsmouth, and he said I would hear interesting things at their lordships' table and must not blab about them . . . and it was *true*!'

'You're very discreet, Sir David, but you've whetted everybody's curiosity,' said Lord Lansdowne. 'Luckily there was no such embargo laid on me at the Foreign Office. They too had an interesting story to tell, which will be in *The Times* tomorrow morning and so public property. The French Republic is to become an Empire and Napoleon Bonaparte is to be the Emperor of the French.'

Over the laughter, the derisive applause, and exclamations of 'Good God' from the younger men, the Duc d'Enghien's voice rose clear and high: 'Old Boney will choke from self-importance. But the name won't make any difference. He's the First Consul now – it's only another name for dictator.'

14

The awkward silence which fell on the little company after the duke's explosion was broken, with characteristic aplomb, by Lord Lansdowne's proposal to Lady Holland that they should open the ball together – although the ball, as the music and the sound of dancing feet grew louder, was obviously open already. The lady had hardly placed her hand on his arm when Charles followed his host's example and was saying to Marie that it would be fun to see if they could remember the steps of a quadrille. He was pleasantly aware that he was cutting out Sir David Boone, who perforce covered his retreat by proposing to d'Enghien that they should 'follow the crowd and find partners for ourselves.'

There was no shortage of pretty girls in the ballroom, sitting beside their mamas on the rout-seats set against the mirrored walls. The ballroom of Lansdowne House, on the opposite side of the foyer to the dining room, was oblong-shaped and high, with a musician's gallery at the left-hand side, and on the right an alcove filled with little tables and easy chairs, the walls being used for the shelved books of a respectable-sized library.

Charles handed Marie to a seat. He knew she was miles away from her surroundings and was not surprised, although her voice was not raised, when she burst out: 'That wretched d'Enghien! Miserable fellow! I could have strangled him when he dared to call Napoleon "Boney"!'

'What do you suppose Lord Lansdowne calls him, or will call him, when they meet?'

'Your Imperial Majesty.'

'Perhaps you're right. But if you're in a strangling mood,

you were a very good girl not to show it. Come on, darling, don't spoil it all! This is a great night for Napoleon and his friends. What do you suppose they're doing at the Tuileries?'

'I bet they're dancing there too. Oh, how I wish we were there with – with all of them! Charles, when can we go home?'

'When I've done my job here. When I've found out who Napoleon's enemies are.'

'I thought they were the whole English nation,' Marie interpolated.

'In particular, when I've paid my score with Anatole Laguerre. But now let's celebrate. If you really feel you're equal to a quadrille, let's dance!'

'Am I equal?'

She danced the old-fashioned square dance as if there were wings on her little satin sandals, up the middle and down again, cross hands and set to partners, as if she were celebrating another victory of the greatest soldier of the age, until a rosy flush which was not a schoolgirl blush came up on the face beneath the la Tour diamond roses. Charles scandalized the dancers beside them by kissing her.

'Would you do that at the Tuileries?'

'Joséphine wouldn't let me.'

'Joséphine will be the Empress. Oh, can you believe it?'

'It's a triumph for a girl from a Martinique plantation.'

'Where one of their slaves predicted she would be a queen.'

Marie shivered, as if she were remembering the cell in the Carmes prison where Joséphine had told the inmates about that prediction, and was silent until the time came to join in the applause at the end of the quadrille. Then she said, 'That was lovely!' and took her husband's arm for the walk back to the alcove. As they sat down Charles saw that they had been followed closely by two men, the first of whom was Sir David Boone.

'Sir,' the young Englishman began, 'forgive me. I feel I must lose no time in soliciting the honour of your amiable lady's hand for the next dance.'

'I understand it's a waltz,' said Charles. 'Marie?'

'I accept with pleasure,' said Marie, with a solemnity which appeared to gratify Sir David, who said, 'Thank you, madame,' before stepping back to make way for a man who could not be regarded as a dancing rival.

It was the ubiquitous butler. He bowed low to Marie before he addressed her husband.

'Forgive the interruption, my lord,' he said. 'Lord Lansdowne instructed me to inform your lordship that he desired to have the favour of a private talk with you. He is waiting in the room where you had your dinner.'

'And he isn't accustomed to be kept waiting, eh?' said Charles, getting up. He bent over his wife and lowered his voice.

'Boone can hardly have expected so much success in what I believe the navy calls "a cutting out operation",' he said. 'Now I see he's waiting to *move in*, so I'd better go and see what the old fellow wants.'

'Yes, you had,' said Marie, trying to smile. 'But don't be long.'

'Ten minutes,' said Charles. '*Mes excuses, madame.*'

He bowed, and left her, the butler at his heels. The band struck up, and in a moment Sir David Boone was by her side again.

'Forgive me, madame,' he began. 'I'm afraid your husband was wrong. That's not a waltz they're playing.'

'No, it's an old English country dance, which we used to dance at Frascati's.'

'You're obviously an expert and I should be a very poor partner for you. Would you think me unpardonable for proposing that we forget the country dance and take a turn through the room instead? There are some interesting things in Lansdowne House which you ought to see – statues by Canova in the foyer, and in the Round Room, next to the place where I found all of you, a striking souvenir of the American Revolution. But if you're too tired . . .'

'Of course I'm not too tired. Quite a few people seem to be

walking around instead of dancing, so let's do the same. I'd like to see the Canova statues.'

She preferred visiting the foyer to visiting the Round Room. It would be dreadful if Charles thought she was following him! Besides which, she had once heard a guest at the Tuileries, described as an art critic, speak of Napoleon's 'Canova profile'. But whatever the man meant by that, Marie could see no trace of Napoleon in the *Loves and Graces* which the sculptor had executed in marble, and which appeared to great advantage in the oblique lighting of well-arranged lamps.

She sighed, and then allowed Sir David to lead her to the Round Room, where she was glad to see the heavy door leading to the dining room was firmly shut. Her companion pointed out a document in faded ink, under glass, framed and hung on the left-hand wall to commemorate the historic visit of the American statesman.

'I thought the treaty recognizing American Independence was signed at Paris,' said Marie.

'Perhaps it was, and this was only a preliminary document signed while Mr Franklin was in London,' said Sir David.

'Benjamin Franklin is dead now, but he's still very popular in France.'

'Did you ever meet him?'

'No, but I met his successors, Gouverneur Morris and Mr Thomas Jefferson, who is the President now,' Marie said.

She saw the man's look of chagrin, and felt she had not been as enthusiastic as he expected about this piece of paper, hung on the wall of the Round Room like an art treasure.

'It's a long time since the American Revolution, Sir David,' she said. 'We've had a revolution of our own since then. And the Americans declared their neutrality in our wars that followed. Perhaps that was to punish us for sending them the Marquis de La Fayette.'

Sir David Boone let the sarcasm pass. He had already decided that the Marquise de la Tour was not the ingenue she appeared to be. He said: 'You had a bad time in the Revolution, didn't you?'

'It was a great shock to most of us.'

'But right at the start, when everything was a shock, you were able to feel compassion for others who were also shocked? Weren't you called Marie Fontaine?'

'And you are Adam Boone's brother? I was sure of it!' said Marie.

'Adam Boone. Was that the name you knew him by?'

'Wasn't it his name?'

'That was his name on the memorial tablet my mother erected in our village church in Kent.'

'And that is the name a good priest put on his grave in Brittany.'

'So . . . he is buried in consecrated ground. You are sure of all the facts, are you not, madame?'

'They are in the archives of Nantes, Sir David, and were told to me by an attorney named Antoine Fouquier-Tinville.'

She saw the name meant nothing to Sir David Boone: he had never heard of the Public Prosecutor of the Revolutionary Tribunal in Paris, whom fate had taken to Nantes on the very day when a Breton fisherman named Pierre Malouet was accused by his neighbours of giving shelter to 'a foreign enemy of the Republic'.

'Adam, an enemy of the Republic? Rubbish!' said his brother.

'Of course, but you know there was civil war in the west in those days, and Adam bore arms in a skirmish with the government troops. He was sent to prison for that, and died in custody. And . . . and I'm really sorry, Sir David, but that's the way it was.'

'So now we know the truth,' he said. 'Thank you for telling me. My mother will be grateful that we heard it from the girl poor Adam wrote about in his last letter from Paris, on the day he met you and your uncle at the Pharmacie Fontaine and thought you were both wonderful.'

'Did he really?'

As Marie spoke the door yielded to a violent push and her husband was in the room.

'What, not dancing?' was his greeting, and to Boone's stammered excuses about the country dance he merely said, 'Well, they're waltzing now. That's "Dreams of Danube" the band's playing, can't you hear? But excuse me now, please, I must go. The duke is waiting for me outside.'

Charles de la Tour knew that he must have appeared to be distraught, and that it would be difficult to explain to Marie why a 'private talk' with Lord Lansdowne should have had this effect on him.

What happened was that when Charles sought him out in the little dining room he found not only Lord Lansdowne but the Duc d'Enghien seated at a table from which the cloth had been drawn. Each had a full glass before him, and a crystal decanter in a silver wide slide stood on the polished surface of the table.

'There you are, my dear fellow!' said Lord Lansdowne. 'Good of you to come along so quickly. Pray be seated. We're drinking brandy, would you like a brandy?'

'Thank you, I would,' said Charles, and watched while his host filled an empty liqueur glass from the array of glasses by his side.

'The fact is, my dear de la Tour,' continued Lansdowne, 'something rather disagreeable has been brought to my attention – something that for the sake of fair play I should like to discuss with you. Lady Holland informs me that according to your mother you are here as an agent of – of the First Consul Napoleon, and that your visit to England was planned and financed by him.'

Charles's mouth was set in an angry line. 'Lady Holland is a busybody,' he said. 'A busybody and a false friend. Whatever my mother told her was intended to be a confidence, which she has betrayed.'

Lansdowne raised his eyebrows. 'Rather than vilify the noble lady,' he said, 'you should confine yourself to disproving her statements – if you can.'

'Upon my honour,' Charles cried, 'the only one who could

do that is Napoleon himself. And if I could bring him to my side in a country where he is vulgarly known as "Boney", he would tell you that he has on several occasions urged me to visit my mother, to persuade her to abandon her *émigrée* status and return to France. I am here not as a secret agent but as a devoted son.'

'Well spoken!' Lansdowne exclaimed. 'Frank and straightforward – that's how a young man ought to be. Don't you agree, my dear Duke?'

The Duc d'Enghien who had been listening attentively while he sipped his brandy, now prepared to enter the discussion. With a deferential bow to Charles he observed that '*Monsieur le Marquis*' was probably wondering what the devil he was doing there at all ... 'especially since I apparently offended you, sir, by calling the First Consul by an unsuitable nickname. For that I ask your pardon. I am afraid I shall offend you again if I suggest a solution which I already mentioned to Lord Lansdowne, which is, to refer this whole matter to General Anatole Laguerre.'

Charles appeared to struggle for breath.

'Gentlemen,' he said, 'I have the honour to be one of the First Consul's ADCs. Before I followed him to war in Italy I worked in Plans. Both are positions in which it is essential to know the name of every rank and every officer holding that rank in the French army. I am able to tell you confidently that there is no such name as General Anatole Laguerre in the Army List. He was the *commissaire de la République* at Reims when I knew him first.'

'In that case,' said the duke, 'he has the right to call himself "general". By a law passed in November 1798, that rank was conferred on all *commissaires*.'

'Extraordinary!' said Charles. 'I didn't know that. In November '98 the Directory was on its last legs; no one paid much attention to its *projets de loi*, and I was fighting in Syria.'

'At Jaffa!' said the duke. 'Wasn't that where you –'

In delicate reference to Charles's blind eye, he touched an index finger to one of his own eyelids.

'Yes it was.'

'Then if Lord Lansdowne will excuse us, I think we ought to talk apart.'

He left Lansdowne House by a side entry, saying now was a good time to see to their horses, and Charles left by the Round Room, where he found Marie.

The Duc d'Enghien was in the gardens, strolling in the carriageway which bisected the flowerbeds. He was smoking, and offered his cigar case to Charles.

'Have one?' he said. 'These are rather special. My grand-father gets them from Havana.'

'Where's that?'

'In Cuba.'

Miserably aware that he had spoken like an ignoramus Charles jerked his chin at the corner of an alley running behind the house where a group of men in livery were talking and laughing. 'Let's keep away from the servants, shall we?' he said.

'Good idea. Some of the grooms are French, who might not approve of your strictures on General Laguerre.'

'And you – do you disapprove?'

'Oh, I'm not one of the fellow's admirers, who are women for the most part, with Lady Holland in the lead.'

'She would be, but I didn't suppose a Bourbon prince would champion a murderer.'

'A murderer? Laguerre? De la Tour, do you know what you're saying?'

'Yes, with half the monks of the Great St Bernard to be my witnesses.'

In quick, nervous sentences Charles sketched the unforget-table scene at the monastery for a horrified listener: Laguerre firing at General Bonaparte, the shot going wide and killing a young monk ('for whom my general paid an indemnity'). Charles himself firing and missing, Laguerre himself dis-appearing until he fetches up in England, posing as a hero.

'My God!' said the duke. 'That's quite a story. I can't wait to tell my grandfather.'

'With all respect to the Prince de Condé,' said Charles, 'Laguerre should receive his just deserts at the hands of a younger man.'

'Meaning yourself?'

'Perhaps.'

'How would you set about it?'

'Is he married?'

'No. De la Tour, you think of my grandfather as an old man, and of course he is, but he's very wise, and he detests Laguerre. Months ago, after he superseded Monsieur Otto at the embassy, Laguerre published a statement beginning, "Frenchmen, I am taking you under my protection!" My grandfather was outraged. He thought the only man entitled to say such a thing was the late King's brother, the Comte de Lille, the claimant to the throne.'

'I thought the Comte d'Artois was the more aggressive of the two.'

'Not as Laguerre is aggressive. But yourself? You haven't told me what you plan to do.'

'What I'd *like* to do,' said Charles emphatically. 'If the man were married I'd try to reach him through his wife. But that's out, so I must write and issue a challenge in form – according to the code duello.'

'No,' said the duke. 'No letter-writing. The written word can be dangerous in an affair of honour. Tell me, which do you favour as a weapon, the rapier or the sabre?'

'Neither,' said Charles. 'My bullet missed the target in the mountain, I hope to have better luck in London.'

'Ah, the time-honoured scenario. Dawn breaking over Lincoln's Inn Fields, and the gallant marquis, there with his seconds and a doctor and an implicit belief in the tried and true maxim of "pistols for two and coffee for one"! My dear boy, don't ever change! You're quite perfect for your part in the scenario you've chosen. You're like a character from an historical romance – one of the Three Musketeers.'

'I've never heard of them. Are you laughing at me?'

'I wouldn't dare. No, I don't think you're laughable; I do

think you're being rather silly. Doesn't it occur to you that if you do call your man out, and drop him, you would be treated as a murderer? There's no guillotine in England, but there's a public hangman, who's very good at his job, I'm told.'

'Shut up!' said Charles. 'I see you've something to propose. Let's hear it!'

'I propose that we go together to Portman Square early tomorrow morning and you tackle Laguerre directly with the murder at the monastery. You threaten to give the story to the newspapers if he doesn't leave the country and join the Armée des Princes at Ghent. That should appeal to him, for he has organized a little private army of his own. He's won great favour with Mr Pitt by offering to incorporate it into the English army which is standing ready to repel an invasion by Napoleon.'

'A private army? What does he call it?'

'*Les Français de Grande Bretagne.*'

'Sounds like the Trojan Horse to me,' said Charles.

'That isn't funny. Mr Pitt wouldn't think so, which is another good reason for your leaving the country too.'

'Run away, you mean?' said Charles. 'Go to Ghent?'

'Good heavens, no!' said the duke. 'I want you to save yourself, *and* your wife, *and* your mother, from any possible unpleasantness when the story gets out. You're a dangerous firebrand, and I want you out of the way. Go back to Paris!'

15

When a carriage stopped at the door of Nerot's Hotel that evening, one of the porters opened the door for Charles to get out.

'Good evening, sir,' he said cheerfully. 'Madame came back about ten minutes ago. I believe she went straight upstairs.'

'Thank you,' said Charles. His voice did not sound normal, even to himself, but the man was a stranger and might not notice anything was wrong. He looked at his mother's coachman, sitting foursquare and reliable on the box, and said, 'You heard what that fellow had to say?'

'Yes, sir, and very glad I was. Another case of "All's well that ends well", seems to me.'

'Quite so. Well, better put up your horses, Jennings.'

Jennings descended to the pavement, looped the reins over his arm and came to stand next to Charles.

'Begging your lordship's pardon, am I to put 'em into the stables here or at Lansdowne House?'

Charles looked up and down King Street. There were few people to be seen and nobody was listening. So why are we muttering like a couple of conspirators? he asked himself.

'I've given you your orders for tomorrow,' he said, 'and you appeared to understand them. Repeat them now!'

'I'm to pick you and His Grace up here tomorrow at eight in the morning along with two of his servants, and drive you to Portman Square. After I bring you back here I take you and her young ladyship out to Hammersmith.'

'Well done! And no mention of Lansdowne House in that programme?'

177

'No, sir. You told me you weren't going back to Lansdowne House.'

'So use the stables here. I did tell you I'd booked a room for you in the annex.'

'Very good of you, I'm sure. But if you don't mind, when I've seen to the horses I'd like to go back on foot to Berkeley Street. With your permission I'd like to go out with Lady Holland's man. He's a mate of mine, and we usually spend our free evenings at a show. Tonight we thought we'd go to Astley's.'

'Astley's. Is that a theatre?'

'It's a kind of cross between a circus and a music hall. Last time we was there, before they had the fire, they had a representation of the Battle of the Pyramids. Very life-like with Old Boney scarifying the Mamelukes a fair treat . . .'

'I wish I'd seen that,' said Charles. 'I was in that battle, and I was pretty scared myself.'

'Not you, my lord. I can't believe that you were acting scared.'

Charles knew the man had seen him 'acting scared' that evening and was trying to reassure him. A decent fellow, Englishman or not!

He asked, 'Do they serve food and drink at Astley's?'

And when the coachman said they did he took a golden sovereign from his pocket and put it into the man's hand. He said, 'Jennings, you don't need my permission to enjoy a free evening with your friend, you've earned it. Get yourself a good supper, that's all – and don't be late tomorrow morning.'

Charles went into Nerot's Hotel, not walking fast. His talk with Jennings had occupied a few minutes, and there was no putting it off any longer. The confrontation with Marie! As he entered the hall he saw a man he recognized behind the reception desk, and thought of another way to occupy a few more minutes before he need challenge Marie to give him an explanation of her extraordinary conduct. He marched straight up to the desk; the man bowed.

178

'Good evening, sir,' he said. 'Have you come to reclaim the little case you deposited here earlier?'

The case of the diamond tiara – of course! He had almost forgotten the circumstances.

'No,' he said, gathering his wits together, 'I'd rather leave it in your care for the present. My lady has returned to the hotel, I understand?'

The man looked at the grandfather's clock in a corner of the hall. 'She came back about a quarter of an hour ago,' he said.

Charles took the stairs three at a time. He was all ready now to talk to Marie, to discuss returning to France with her, to tell her about Laguerre . . . He came to their bedroom door, turned the handle without knocking, and went in.

She came out of the dressing room and stared at him. Then she came towards him at a fast run, with her head lowered like a battering ram, how efficiently he didn't know until it struck him in the ribs with a confusion of fair curls and pink satin ribbon which made him catch at the back of an easy chair to keep his balance.

'*Zut alors!*' gasped Charles Latour. 'Marie! What the devil do you think you're doing?'

'Did I hurt you?' she said. 'I'm sorry. I didn't mean to. But when I came back – and you weren't here – I got so frightened –'

It sounded lame, but it was better than confessing that she had only meant to throw herself into his arms. After all the tender things he'd said earlier that evening, Marie had been almost shocked senseless by her brief glimpse of Charles's face as he came in, set in such harsh lines of ill-temper as made her feel guilty of some unexplained crime, which destroyed the confidence she was beginning to feel in the success of their visit to England. Her first impulse was to coax him, to caress him, to kiss him if he would welcome kisses . . . and now here he was *glaring* at her!

'No, you didn't hurt me, don't be silly,' said Charles, who believed he was absorbed in pulling down his waistcoat and adjusting his cravat. 'Frightened because I wasn't here, were you? Nothing to the fright you gave me when I had to ask a lot of horseboys, grinning in the gutter with quart pots of beer in their hands, if any of them had seen my wife, and was told, yes they'd all seen my lady picking up a hackney coach coming out of Berkeley Square and driving off to God knows where, all alone in London!'

'Then your friends the horseboys probably heard me tell the man to take me back to Nerot's –'

'Why didn't you ask my mother's coachman to drive you? Jennings? He was there.'

'Jennings was not there.'

'Yes he was. I saw him with that crowd just before I went in. After I said goodnight to d'Enghien.'

'Was that before or after you were drinking in the bar?'

'That was after I'd been upstairs to look for you. Misinformed by that dead bore Sir David Boone.'

'He's not a bore! I suppose you're angry because he asked to dance with me!'

'Don't be a fool!' This is ridiculous, thought Charles. We're squabbling like two children, sniping and scoring off each other . . . well, at least she isn't whimpering the way she sometimes did at Vesle. And being in a temper suits Marie. She looks magnificent.

She was still wearing the wedding dress, rumpled by the adventures of the evening, and her hair was dishevelled (and no wonder) but her colour was high and her eyes were bright.

Charles was willing enough (or soft enough, as he thought of it) to suggest to Marie that they should kiss and be friends, when a genuine grievance occurred to him, and he said angrily, 'Marie, you came back here less than half an hour ago. Two people said so. But Jennings said you were in Berkeley Street one hour ago. Where did you go, what did you do in the interval? Tell me, Marie, I demand to know.'

'You demand to know! Watch your language, Charles, or else go back to your horseboys and your Jennings and act like a real secret agent – spying on your own wife.'

'You're talking like a crazy woman!'

'Very well then, I'll tell you where I went. Not because you demand to know, but because I want to tell you. Because I think you're in danger of forgetting that Napoleon sent us here to do certain things for him. I didn't forget that he asked me to do something that sounded very simple – to bring him back a portrait of Lord Nelson. So I asked Sir David Boone –'

'Aha!' said Charles. 'I thought Sir David would come into your story sooner or later.'

'Don't speak to me like that!'

Charles had the grace to look slightly ashamed of his spiteful remarks.

'I'm sorry, Marie,' he said, 'go on with what the fellow told you. Was it something about Lord Nelson?'

'I know you think Sir David is a bore, but I think he's a brave man. He was in the naval action off Copenhagen with the admiral.'

'Well?'

'So I asked him where I could buy a portrait of his chief.'

'Did you say who wanted it?'

'Of course not.'

'Good girl. And did he?'

'He told me the King's printseller, Edward Orme, had a good selection of aquatints at his shop in Bond Street, at the corner of Brook Street. So when I hired a cab, that's where I told the driver to go first. Luckily they stay open late.'

He didn't think she was fibbing – her gaze was too straight for that – but some demon of perversity made Charles Latour say he would like to see the picture. He regretted it when he saw how carefully the print shop had made up the parcel for Marie, producing it from the wardrobe, unpacked it in five minutes, and they gazed in silence at the great man's portrait.

'By gad!' said Charles, 'he really looks like a national hero, doesn't he?'

Marie nodded. It was not the stars and medals on the blue uniform coat which proved the heroism so much as the empty sleeve pinned across it; not so much the patch on Nelson's

181

sightless eye (not shown in a portrait taken in profile) which told of another sacrifice for king and country, as the hint of a smile round the thin lips which was evidence of a happy nature disciplined by a great service and the burden of a guilty love.

'An expensive hero for France,' Marie said.

'He knocked hell out of our ships at the Battle of the Nile,' said Charles, and seeing her enquiring look, corrected himself. 'At Aboukir. The Battle of the Nile is what they call it here. Nothing went right for us in Egypt after that. Desaix told me General Kléber thought we'd have to surrender to the English.'

'Kléber!' said Marie. 'Poor man, he's dead now, murdered on the same day as Desaix died at Marengo, but he was never fit to succeed General Bonaparte in Cairo.'

They had proceeded from squabbling into talking like two friends who had been through the whole Egyptian campaign together, and now Marie had to spoil it all by uttering one of the silly praises of Napoleon which proved where her heart lay! Charles choked down his irritation by asking Marie if she was going to pack up the Nelson print.

'I'll do it if you like,' he said, 'but in that case I'd better get on with it. I don't want to have a rush of packing tomorrow morning. I have to go out early.'

'No, no, I'll do it,' said Marie, and began smoothing out the sheets of wrapping paper. 'Where are you going to so early?'

'To Portman Square. D'Enghien and I thought we might pay a morning call on General Laguerre.'

There was no denying Marie's distress now. She sank limply into the nearest chair, as if she could no longer stand upright, and with her hands clasped over her heart she gasped, 'Oh Charles! Is that wise?'

'It's absolutely necessary. D'Enghien thinks so too. He's coming along tomorrow because the Prince de Condé wants to offer Laguerre a commission in the *Armée des Princes*!'

'I don't believe it.'

Marie had dropped her melodramatic attitude, the hands folded on the heart, but her face had taken on the mulish look he hated, a blend of obstinacy and conscious superiority which always irritated him.

He fired at her: 'Why the devil do you always pretend to know more about politics and war than every man older and wiser than yourself . . . unless he happened to be your hero Bonaparte?'

'Whom Anatole Laguerre tried to kill, as he may try to kill you tomorrow if you're silly enough to put yourself in his power. Why should the Prince de Condé reward a man with his record by giving him a commission?'

'Because the prince, like his grandson, is a Bourbon of the Bourbons, you little fool. Because he knows Laguerre's pretensions and even his presence in London are offensive to his own royal cousin, the Comte d'Artois. We'll get him away to the Low Countries and see if he's the fire-eater he claims to be. And don't worry about us tomorrow; we're going armed.'

The tide of Charles's impassioned speech beat on Marie's head like hammer blows. Neither the husband nor the wife was aware of a gentle knocking on the door. When Charles ended on the ominous word 'armed' a louder knock sent him to the door with an abrupt 'Yes, what is it?' to the footman mutely proffering a letter on a silver salver.

'Charles, what is it?' echoed Marie, as he tore the letter open.

'It's from Mr Duthie, Mother's attorney, he's in the lobby. Wants to know if we'll have dinner with him here – tonight.'

'Oh Charles, that boring little Scotsman! I can't understand a word he says!'

A dinner party thus inauspiciously begun continued more successfully half an hour later. A curt 'Behave yourself!' from Charles ended Marie's strictures on Mr Duthie's Scottish speech, and his own proposal to send a message to his mother by her attorney met with Marie's objections that to do so would be disrespectful. Then both gentlemen met (in the lobby, where Mr Duthie was drinking sherry and reading *The Times*) in a torrent of apologies, Mr Duthie for giving them such short notice of his invitation. Those exchanges revealed to Marie that her husband meant to return to France without delay, and in her happiness at the prospect of going home, she was ready to forgive him anything.

They went into the dining room, where more than half the tables were filled, and an unctuous head waiter proposed some resolutely English food: roast beef and Yorkshire pudding and gravy, boiled potatoes and boiled cabbage; apple tart with cream. But the wine list was French, and Mr Duthie ordered a good bottle of burgundy. 'Empty your glass,' he urged Marie. 'You're looking a wee bittie tired tonight. Too much dancing at the Lansdowne Ball, maybe?'

'Not really,' she replied. 'I enjoyed dancing the quadrille. I felt wonderful, too. My mother-in-law gave me the most lovely jewel to wear –'

'Her diamond tiara, maybe?'

'How do you know? Did she tell you?'

'I once saw her wearing it, when she and the late marquis got me an invitation to a reception at the Palace of Versailles. She looked magnificent.'

'I'm sure she did,' said Marie, before Charles cut in with, 'I didn't know you'd ever been to France.'

'I've been back and forth a good deal in the last few years.'

'May I ask what took you there?'

'Business for the late marquis at the *Émigré Office*.'

'I see.'

But Charles's speculative look was far from comprehending. He asked for advice on the best cross-channel route to try, and was told it was certainly Dover–Calais, as they had arrived.

'Don't take a boat from Newhaven,' said Mr Duthie authoritatively. 'The crossing is longer, and the coach connections with Paris are not good. I presume it's Paris you'll be bound for?'

'Yes, and that's another worry. Since the Revolution you can't find a livery stable in every country town, so I can't be sure of having a carriage, or even of letting our friends in Paris know what time we'll arrive.'

'You mean . . . the people at the Quai Voltaire?'

'Of course.'

'Another advantage of going into Calais. They have a Chappe telegraph station there.'

'You mean that semaphore thing?'

'Yes, have you never used it?'

'I've had it explained to me by General Bonaparte himself, but Monsieur Chappe's invention was not used on campaign, either in Italy or in Egypt. So what can I do, without credentials – just walk up to the Calais station and ask to use the semaphore?'

'Oh fie, lad,' said Mr Duthie tolerantly, 'you've got your credentials here in England, and you are wearing them tonight! You're an ADC to the First Consul, aren't you, and you've a bonny blue, white and red sash to prove it. Get madame to tie it round your arm before you go up to the Chappe station (poor lassie, she's right near asleep) and you can send any message you like – I guarantee it!'

'Mr Duthie,' said the Marquis de la Tour, 'I wish I knew you better.'

Marie, who had, she said, 'only closed my eyes for a moment', became aware that Charles was pleased about something and that he was apologizing for her. The men were still discussing details of tomorrow's journey. Mr Duthie was to join them at Nerot's and accompany them to Hammersmith ... and then Marie was lost in remarks about livery stables, sparing Jennings and his horses, an endless stream of platitudes turning like wheels in her head until she was aware that Charles had picked her out of her chair (at which she struggled and insisted that he put her down) and was holding her arm while she found words to thank Mr Duthie and apologize for being so tired.

'My Lady Dowager will be angry with me when she sees how I've wearied you,' said the host. 'She was planning on taking you on a shopping expedition. You'll be sorry to miss that.'

'I saw some beautiful shops in Bond Street,' said Marie, 'but what I'm really sorry to miss is Dr Edward Jenner's lecture on vaccination. He's going to give it in the Royal Institution in Albemarle Street.'

She wasn't thinking straight: she knew this was just the sort of remark to enrage Charles, who would call it 'showing off'; but as he said nothing and only kissed her cheek, she clung to him and begged him to be careful tomorrow. Yes, she told them both, she would go to bed, and yes, she could get upstairs by herself.

They watched her go, and then Charles said he would accompany Mr Duthie as far as Piccadilly, for the acceptable English purpose of getting some fresh air. They talked about nothing at all until they parted at the top of King Street, when Mr Duthie said, 'Whatever you're going to do tomorrow that needs care, for God's sake *take care*! Don't run any risks!'

Charles walked back slowly, brought up against what he had been trying to forget: the problem of Anatole Laguerre.

Marie was in bed and sound asleep. He could see by the shaded light of a lamp that she was lying in a straight line on her own side of the bed, with her fair head burrowed into the pillow. He undressed quietly, blew out the lamp, and slipped into bed on his own side and whispered, 'Marie!' There was no gesture, no word of welcome. She never moved.

At once his mind was filled with horrifying images. Mountain peaks and a bank of snow, a man in a cassock fleeing from a pistol shot that missed. D'Enghien's face . . . and where was he now? He had started something he didn't want to finish . . . or did he? His handsome face contorted in pain, dissolving and remoulding into the hated features of Laguerre.

Laguerre's face burnished by a gentle, sleeping breath. Marie had turned towards him and her hand had slipped into one of his. On purpose? A mute invitation? What?

Such a little hand. He dared not take advantage of it, although he was aware, by the merest pressure of his fingers, that it was her left hand he held. He could feel the outline of her wedding ring. He remembered buying it at a famous jewellers in the Place Vendôme, and the salesman's joke about the smallness of the worsted ring he had taken along for

186

sizing. 'Your girl must have small hands, citizen!' Yes, they were small hands but competent and capable of healing. And that was the quality he had denigrated, made fun of, belittled, ever since she had first responded to his kisses in a doorway of the rue du Bac. Her wedding ring! He remembered putting it on her finger in the shabby official room of their marriage in revolutionary Paris, and in the silence, in the freedom of London, he swore another vow.

Marie, if I survive tomorrow, I'll be a different man.

16

When the chambermaid's tap fell on the door at six next morning Charles Latour was already awake. He lay still for a minute, so close to Marie that he could feel her sleeping breath on his cheek and then slid out of the bed and made for the dressing room. When he went down to breakfast he found that it was served in a separate room, filled with businessmen and presided over by last night's head waiter, who graciously took Charles's order for coffee and scrambled eggs on toast.

When he was halfway through the meal a door on the lobby opened and the Duc d'Enghien appeared. He was wearing a white riding coat with a tiered shoulder cape, a style as popular in London as it was in Paris, and a pair of black riding boots polished to a mirror's gloss. He was completely relaxed yet obviously tingling with vitality, ready for anything the day might bring. Charles admired him very much. He had no idea how often, in the years to come, he was to remember that handsome, vigorous and entirely masculine young figure, whose very presence seemed to bring light into the room. He did think, as he heard the murmur of recognition which d'Enghien acknowledged with a smile, that the royalists were fools to attach so much importance to the Comte de Lille and the Comte d'Artois as heirs to their brother's throne, when in Louis-Antoine de Bourbon-Condé, Duc d'Enghien, they had a successor who could win the minds of men.

Then the duke recognized him in the crowd, and Charles was standing up to shake hands, exchange greetings and propose coffee, which three waiters hurried up to offer in vain. 'Thanks, I had breakfast with my grandfather. I'm staying with him in Grosvenor Square,' said the duke.

'Did you have a talk with him?'

'I did this morning, and he thoroughly approves of our plan. But tell me, how *is* Madame de la Tour?'

Under cover of the polite enquiries they got out of the room, and Charles was glad. They had been talking rapid French and there was no danger that they had been understood, but he was strung up now, and longed to be getting on with the job. Two men came up at once.

'Grandfather insisted on reinforcements,' said the duke. 'These are two sergeants from the regiment we're recruiting for today.'

They were two big fellows in civilian clothes, with the thews and muscles of prizefighters. Jennings, approaching and saluting the gentlemen, accepted them as 'His Grace's men' and said they could sit where the footmen sat, at the rear of the carriage. It was closed, for a thin rain was beginning to fall.

'I'm going to Antwerp on the boat, and on to Ghent,' said the duke casually, and as Charles said nothing he went on, 'It's as good a place as any for transport to Baden, where I want to go to next.'

Charles nodded. Baden was on the German side of the Rhine, and there, in the castle of Ettenheim, lived the lady whom d'Enghien loved, the beautiful Charlotte de Rohan. It was said she was his wife, but it was unlikely that the bearers of the two greatest names in France would have been married in secrecy; what many Bonapartists believed was that the proximity of Baden made it the probable headquarters for a royalist invasion of France.

'I'll talk to him about the invitation to join the army,' said the duke, and Charles knew that by 'him' he meant Laguerre. 'Then you come in with the monastery story.'

'Very good. Do you think he'll have many people in the house?'

'Perhaps some of the men he calls "companions". Pompous fool, pretending to be William the Conqueror!'

'What happened to Monsieur Otto, after Laguerre got him out of Portman Square?'

'He was offered a job editing one of Laguerre's newspapers, and of course declined it. He's living in the country now.'

'Which newspaper?'

'*L'ambigu.*'

Laguerre was thorough, you had to give him credit for that! Using the press as a weapon had been done in France *before* the Revolution; in the days of the Terror it had been found more expeditious to send newspaper owners to the guillotine. Bonaparte, who believed in the freedom of the press, had no such redress, but Charles Latour knew that nothing made the general so angry as tolerance of such squibs at himself as the cartoons of Gillray and the falsehoods about himself which appeared in the pages of *L'ambigu*. Another thing Laguerre must pay for, he told himself.

The carriage rolled out of Bond Street, down Oxford Street and after some turns into Portman Square. Everything was silent, except for where some front doorsteps were being washed.

Charles's attention was caught and held by two men strolling up and down in front of what was now Laguerre's office, the windows of every floor closed by shutters. He wondered if the men belonged to the fighting force Laguerre claimed to have raised, for they wore paramilitary uniforms: black hats and trousers with red jackets, and as they walked in cadence they swung aggressive-looking nightsticks attached to their wrists by leather straps.

Charles touched the duke's arm and mouthed the question 'Troops?'

The duke waited to reply until the two men had walked the whole breadth of the garden front and then replied, 'No, bodyguards. The kind you get by the Prime Minister's favour. Members of London's embryonic police force, the Bow Street Runners. The residents call them Robin Redbreasts, because of the jackets.' Then while Charles was still sighing over the frivolity of the English, he added, 'They may come in handy. Now, I think, might be a good time to ring for admission.'

The doorbell was answered by a footman, who responded

to Charles's request to see Monsieur Laguerre with his 'regret that the general will not be available until three o'clock'.

Whereupon the duke came forward and said with authority: 'I regret if we cause inconvenience, but our business is urgent. I am the Duc d'Enghien, and I am the bearer of an urgent message from the Prince de Condé.'

Whether the footman was impressed by the two great names, or by the sight of the two sergeants who had now entered the entrance hall was open to doubt, but he said: 'Does this gentleman accompany Your Grace?'

'This is the Marquis de la Tour.'

'Will you both be good enough to wait in the outer office?'

'Certainly.' A door on the hall was opened, and at a gesture from the duke his men took their places on either side of it. Charles followed him into a small room furnished only with a table, chairs and six filing cabinets.

'Stuffy in here,' said Charles. 'Shall I push the shutters back and open the window?'

'Go ahead.' The duke was examining the filing cabinets. 'Just keep your eyes on the Redbreasts, will you?'

Charles had thought the wooden shutters were on the outside of the building, but in this room they were on the inside, and bolted. When the bolts were drawn and the window opened Charles saw the two members of London's embryonic police force chatting to each other at the far side of Portman Square.

The sound of metal jarring on metal made him turn sharply. The Duc d'Enghien had succeeded in opening the top drawer of one of the filing cabinets and was leafing through a paper file. Charles saw that it was lettered with the name CONDÉ.

'What are you doing?' he said, in instinctive disapproval of the break-in in what looked like private property, but the duke replied, 'He's got most of the Frenchmen in England on file here. I wanted to see what he thinks of my grandfather. Not much, I'm afraid . . . Hush! Here he comes now,' for the flagstones of the corridor were resounding to the martial tread of a man whose name in English meant 'War'.

191

Anatole Laguerre's opponents lamented that by the accident of his family name he was credited, especially in the popular press, with the attributes of Mars. The man who now marched into the office was not like the god of war, except perhaps in size, supposing Mars to have been tall, for he was several inches taller than a six-footer like Charles Latour. But his great height was not complemented by a taut body, for his belly sagged until he was unable to fasten the belt of his uniform, and the loose leather ends prevented him from wearing a pistol or a sword. His figure was disproportionate from the small head to the big, womanish hips, and the big nose stuck out aggressively from cheeks the colour of day.

'Good morning, Monsieur Laguerre. I am happy to meet you at last,' said the duke.

'And good morning to you, Monsieur le Duc d'Enghien,' said Laguerre. 'You are the bearer of a message from the Prince de Condé, I understand. I'm flattered. It is the first time His Highness has condescended to acknowledge my existence.'

'His Highness has been unwell,' said the duke. 'That is why he and I had to refuse your invitation to a reception for your group, *Les Français de Grande Bretagne*.'

'So the poor old gentleman has been unwell, has he?' said Laguerre. 'He has probably over-exerted himself in leading the *Armée des Princes*.'

The duke ignored the sarcasm. He said, 'Ah well, he has thought of that. His message to you is, please to accept my escort on the morning boat to Antwerp, thence to Ghent, and there to join him at the head of his army.'

The day-coloured face was suffused with blood. Laguerre stammered out his reply, an unequivocal refusal.

'I think you had better accept,' said Charles. He took his pistol from his pocket and laid it on the table.

'Who are you?' said Laguerre.

'I am the Marquis de la Tour,' said Charles. 'We met in Reims over four years ago.'

'What, the *aristo* from Vesle?' said Laguerre. 'You've risen

192

in the world since we first met.' He looked significantly at the duke, who took his own pistol from his pocket and laid it in front of himself. Laguerre looked at the weapons and shouted, 'Gustave! Jacques! *À moi, à moi!*'

'Save your breath,' advised the duke. 'They won't be let in.'

'So!' said Laguerre. 'You wish to imprison me in my own office, after making free with it.' He glanced at the open filing cabinet. '*Monsieur le Duc*, this is not the conduct one expects from you. You are known to be a fair-minded man. Do you really expect me to submit to a kidnapping at gunpoint, to abandon my responsibilities as the Leader of All Free Frenchmen and the ally of the English Government, to go with you on some wild-goose chase to the continent? Do you? Answer me!'

'I think the marquis has something to say to you first.'

'I want to remind Laguerre of our second meeting, at the Monastery of the Great St Bernard,' said Charles, 'when he fired at General Bonaparte – and killed a monk.'

'It's a lie!'

'We can leave that up to the law,' said Charles. 'Look out of the window and you will see two Bow Street Runners patrolling up the square. If we hand you over to them and charge you with murder, you may have to spend some months in Newgate while witnesses are brought from Switzerland, but then you'll go before an English judge and jury and be given a fair trial.'

I shouldn't have said that, he thought. I shouldn't have mentioned the likelihood of a delay. He'll find some way to profit by it, that's what he's thinking now.

Laguerre was smiling as he turned to the duke. 'I'll take my chance with an English jury,' he said. 'Twelve good men and true, and all of them envying me the chance to take a shot at Boney – as I'm sure you do yourself, do you not?'

The duke flushed angrily. 'I'll gladly meet Napoleon on the battlefield,' he said. 'I will never be a party to murder.'

'Unless you leave this house *now*,' said Charles, 'and go

quietly and comfortably in the duke's carriage to the Antwerp package, we shall have to resort to violence.'

Laguerre looked at the two pistols on the table. He weighed the threat of immediate violence against what he might gain by delay: the influence of his supporters on the government and the influence of Mr Pitt on the opinions of judge and jury; the dubious evidence from Switzerland and the possibility of an escape from Ghent, all were rapidly appreciated by the adventurer. Eventually he said to the duke, 'Very well. Under duress, I accept your invitation.'

17

The events of the morning had passed so quickly that it was still only eleven o'clock when Jennings drove Charles back to Nerot's Hotel. There he encountered a chambermaid who told him she had just taken a pot of coffee and a jug of hot milk to 'milady', did he want to order anything more? No thanks, said Charles, who wanted nothing but to hold Marie in his arms while she listened to his story, though he hoped her embrace would be less violent than on the day before.

It was. She came into his arms as gently as a breath of summer wind, whispering, 'Oh, my darling, are you all right? I've been so worried,' while tears filled her eyes and trickled down her cheeks, proving that it was true.

She worries about me! She really does love me! he thought happily, and remembering the tenderness of the night he kissed the little hand that wore his wedding ring, and saw that above it she had slipped the diamond circlet he bought her in Cairo, which she very seldom wore. So that was a good omen for a happy future! Charles kissed Marie, and accepted the cup of coffee she poured for him. Until he began to drink it he had no idea how thirsty he was.

They had settled side by side on the sofa before Charles brought the story of Anatole Laguerre's defeat to a close. 'It all ended very quietly,' he said. 'I told Jennings to follow the duke's carriage to the docks and he saw all four of them – the duke, his two men and Laguerre – go aboard the Antwerp paddle-boat and find seats in one of the public rooms. I've a feeling Jennings would have liked to go too.'

'I wish he had.'

'Why?'

'The more people to keep Laguerre in custody the better. He's a dangerous man!'

'I told you he came along like a lamb.'

'After he'd been made to look like a fool. After he'd yielded to two men with guns . . .'

'Don't be silly, Marie. You sound as if you admire Laguerre.'

'I don't, I don't, I hate him! But that's why I worried so – I was afraid the meeting would turn into a gun battle . . . I'm so thankful it didn't but I'm still afraid of what Laguerre may be planning to get even with you and the Duc d'Enghien. The duke will be safe in Baden, but you – oh Charles darling, I wish we were going to France this very minute!'

He thought her reasoning was a prime example of feminine folly, but in his heart he knew he wouldn't have been sorry to be setting out for Dover instead of posting off to Hammersmith as an act of filial piety which would probably not be appreciated! But Marie certainly had good reason to keep on the right side of the old lady.

Charles went downstairs to reclaim the diamond tiara from the hotel strongroom. Having told Marie what he meant to do, for safety's sake he went inside the strongroom, away from prying eyes, and fastened his jacket securely over the leather case deep in his breast pocket.

When the la Tours came out at midday, ready for the drive to Hammersmith, Jennings and the carriage were waiting in front of Nerot's, which Charles had expected, and Mr Duthie was making his way briskly down King Street, which he had not.

'Oh my God!' he exclaimed, stopping short. 'Here comes the Scotsman! I'm sorry, Marie. Yesterday I couldn't think of anything but Laguerre. I quite forgot to tell you my mother had asked Mr Duthie to come back with us today.'

'Don't worry, Charles,' she said, 'I'll be as sweet to Mr Duthie as I know how to be.'

'Which is *very* sweet indeed,' said her husband, and was rewarded with a smile and a blush. 'Just don't mention the

Laguerre episode to my mother, or her attorney, do you understand?'

'Perfectly,' she said, and then, as Mr Duthie bowed before her: *'Bonjour, monsieur. Comment allez-vous?'* speaking for the first time in her own language – a compliment he repaid by replying in the credible French he had learned at the University of Aberdeen, where he had taken his law degree.

They were all talking French by the time the drive to Hammersmith began, for Marie, as if to prove she could be tactful as well as sweet, drew Mr Duthie out on the subject of his visit to the Palace of Versailles with Charles's parents on what had obviously been a red-letter day in the Scotsman's life. They heard him praise the 'condescension' of King Louis XVI and the beauty of Queen Marie Antoinette. They also heard him praise the young man then known as Count Edouard de la Tour.

'I never knew you'd met my brother, Edouard,' said Charles.

'The Flanders Regiment was on guard duty at the palace that night,' said Mr Duthie, 'and my young lord was in attendance on the King. He spoke to me in a verra friendly way, and he looked magnificent. Poor young fellow! It was a weary day when he set out for Quiberon Bay.'

'His death broke my mother's heart,' said Charles.

'Oh, I wouldna jist say that,' said Mr Duthie. 'She's verra proud o' you. When your Paris man of business – Maître Vial, is that his name? – wrote to tell her you had been decorated with the Cross of the Legion of Honour, she was uplifted to the skies.'

'She never told me so,' said Charles, but Marie saw that he was pleased. She resolved to make another attempt to persuade his mother to visit them in Paris.

When they drove up to Edwardes Square any conciliatory action seemed foredoomed to failure, for the residence of the dowager marchioness was in the throes of a domestic upheaval. A delivery of coal to a cellar in the area, a sunken locality clearly defined by iron railings and a cement bridgeway leading from street level to front door, had shed a miasma of coal dust over ironwork and stonework indiscriminately and reduced the cook's cat to a frenzy. This animal, a big ginger tom with one chewed ear which showed how well he fought a legitimate feline attack, was in the habit of taking his siesta on a cushion placed on the inside of the kitchen window sill, but Cook had closed the window against the coal dust, and Tom was on the wrong side of the glass. His yellow fur was soon a filthy black, and the coal man reacted to the animal's squalling and spitting by bombarding it with small lumps of coal, soon replaced by one large enough to drive the wind from the cat's body in a gasp of pain.

'*Oh, pauvre minou!*' cried Marie. 'Charles, stop this horrible man! Don't let him hurt the poor cat again!' For the coal man, pleased with his aim, was selecting another missile.

Charles found his English quite unequal to the occasion. He had spoken up to a 'horrible man' in Portman Square that morning, and routed him completely. What was it about this Englishman, a poor labouring wretch – some quality of character, some tenacity of purpose – which warned the Marquis de la Tour not to start a fight, even a fight of words with the coal man?

Mr Duthie touched his arm, and muttered, 'The fellow's drunk!' Certainly the man was swaying, and had grasped the iron paling of the bridgeway, while a smell of spirits filled the air, but in spite of this Charles cried out, loudly enough to surprise himself, 'Drop that coal, *canaille*! Leave the poor beast alone!'

His adversary yelled back: 'Shut your bloody jaw, Frenchy! I wouldn't take no orders from you – no, not if you was Old Boney hisself!'

Mr Duthie, who had memorized the name written upon the tilt of the coal cart, now entered the fray.

'Don't be insolent, my man,' he said, 'I shall inform your employer of the way you speak to his customers . . .'

'And do a poor cove out of a job, would you?' said the coal man. He seemed prepared to enlarge upon the theme, but was startled by the dragging open of the heavy front door and the appearance of Madame de la Tour on the threshold.

'Who's making all that noise down here?' she said.

The coal man jerked a grimy thumb at Charles and said laconically, ''Im.'

'It was all my fault that Charles was shouting. I asked him to,' said Marie. 'The man was throwing coal at a cat, and I begged Charles to stop him.'

'A cat?' said the dowager. 'A ginger cat?'

Marie said it was – 'And there he is now,' she added, as a stout woman in a dusty apron, carrying a cat in her arms, came lumbering up the basement stairs.

'Good afternoon, Mrs Gibbons,' said the dowager. 'I thought I should find Tommy at the bottom of the disturbance. Is he all right?'

'Yes, madame, thanks to my young lord and lady,' said Mrs Gibbons. 'I'm very grateful to them both.'

'Cook them a good lunch, then. How are you getting on with it?'

'I'd just begun to prepare the vegetables, madame.'

'Then before you go any further, put on a clean apron! And take your – pet – back to the kitchen and *keep him there*!'

'Thank you, madame.'

'She's an excellent cook,' said her mistress, 'and a faithful servant; but Gibbons is a perfect fool about that cat. Come, dear, shall we go upstairs?'

'Please, there's something I should like to say first . . .' said Marie. '*Chère madame*, I'm very sorry you were disturbed, perhaps you were lying down, but please don't be angry with Charles. It really was my fault. That man was throwing great lumps of coal at the cat, and hitting him too, and Charles tried to stop him when I – when I began to cry, and oh – I am a fool!'

'No, you're a tender-hearted child, Marie,' said her mother-in-law. 'I'm glad Charles obeyed you. It's more than my husband would have done for me. But you look tired, my dear; was the Lansdowne House ball too much for you? Lady

199

Holland looked in this morning, and she said you looked sensational.'

'Thanks to your magnificent gift,' said Marie. 'Lady Holland wore nothing half as fine. I enjoyed the ball, we both did, but London was tiring in many ways.'

'And I was sorry when Jennings told me you mean to go to France immediately.'

'Oh dear! Charles won't be pleased with Jennings. He planned to tell you himself.'

'Did he indeed,' said his mother with a sniff. 'I was hoping he'd want to pay me a longer visit, and get on really friendly terms with our royalist society in London – so much more influential than the Corsican . . .'

'Who will soon be the Emperor of the French,' snapped Marie. 'But as far as the royalists go, Charles is already on very friendly terms with the Duc d'Enghien. He came to our hotel quite early today, and he and Charles spent the whole morning together.'

'I'm very glad to hear it. Now, Marie, be a dear and ask those men to come indoors. It's time they had something to drink.'

Marie obeyed, but as she went towards the door she thought: she tries to be very grand with her precious royalist society, but when she came out in that shabby dress and those awful boots she looked like one of those poor women from the streets behind the church of St Roch who used to beg ergot and pennyroyal from my uncle – not like an aristocrat at all!

She waved to Charles and Mr Duthie, who were walking up and down in Edwardes Square. The coal cart had disappeared and all was quiet.

Madame de la Tour ushered them into the dining room and asked Charles to pour some wine. Mr Duthie, ensconced in an easy chair, said the rain had stopped and he had enjoyed getting a breath of fresh air. 'Though I've been wasting my own breath,' he said, 'trying to persuade your son here to prolong his stay in England.'

'I expect he's rushing back to France to celebrate with the

200

future Emperor,' said the dowager. 'Pray, Charles, where does the Corsican intend to be crowned? In Reims Cathedral?'

'Reims is Bourbon territory for crowning,' said Charles lazily. 'I imagine General Bonaparte will choose somewhere more spacious, like Notre-Dame de Paris.'

Having reduced his mother to a fermenting silence, Charles advised Mr Duthie to 'drink up' and reminded him that they had planned to go to a livery stable and hire a carriage for the return to London. He had no intention of hanging around to be heckled about 'the Corsican', and asked Marie if she would like to accompany them.

'No, no, Marie must stay with me,' said his mother, 'she's too tired to go traipsing after you. Perhaps we'll get some fresh air in the garden. I was working there a little while ago' (that explained the boots), 'and everything smelled so sweet after the rain.'

The scent from plants and bushes was still sweet twenty minutes later, when after a reminder that luncheon had been ordered for one thirty Madame de la Tour and Marie said goodbye to the gentlemen and went out through a tidy scullery into a large garden divided by paths edged by boxwood hedges in the French style into plots where the spiked green leaves and buds of daffodil had appeared.

'It's lovely, *chère madame*,' cried Marie. 'Charles and I have made a pretty water garden at Vesle, but we hadn't any bulbs. I suppose we could get some from Reims?'

'You like it at Vesle, don't you?'

'Very much.'

'I never was there in my life.'

'Then why don't you come to us?' Marie was inspired to say. 'Come in June – you'd love it then, and we'd love to have you.'

Madame de la Tour laid a finger on her lips. 'Hush, my dear,' she said. 'I shall never leave England again. Only one thing would bring me back to France – if you invite me to a christening, and let me take my grandson in my arms. Is there no hope of that?'

With stiff lips Marie said, 'None.'

'Now tell me, and tell me truly: you have never done anything so foolish – and wicked – and dangerous – as a denial of life?'

'*Madame la Marquise*,' said Marie, 'I have cared for sick and wounded men but I never took the Hippocratic Oath. My uncle read it to me. It says to a doctor all human life is sacred. I swear to you that if new life is ever confided to me I will defend it with my own and at the cost of my own if need be.'

18

When Marie was a little girl, and her cousin Michel was a big boy, his father, her Uncle Prosper, took them both to see a primitive magic-lantern exhibition arranged by his friend Professor Guiart. It made her nervous. The grown-ups and the Guiart youngsters laughed at her, but Michel was kind as always, and explained that there were no strangers at the back of the room to cast their shadows as she feared; the shadows on the white screen were cast by little figures painted on slides and reflected in the light of the lantern.

Presently there was a magic lantern in the Place de la Revolution, and the living figures stumbled up the steps to the scaffold and died in the light of the guillotine. When that Terror ended Marie forgot the magic lantern for half a dozen years. But on the day they left England and returned to France she felt so faint and her imagination was so vivid that she felt as if the sequence of events was moving as swiftly as the slides in Professor Guiart's parlour, in the days long before he taught her pharmacy.

His eldest son was his assistant, and when the professor signalled with a Rap! on the little wooden clapper he held young Hubert slid a new slide into the slot and added a new detail to whichever story of La Fontaine the magic lantern was telling. There was no clapper on the way to France, but in her dreamy condition Marie thought the Rap! preceded every change of scene. Rap! – they were leaving the house where Charles's mother was clinging to him and crying and all the servants were waving goodbye – Jennings with his hat in his hand and Mrs Gibbons with her cat in her arms. Rap! – and they were being driven down the familiar miles to

London, when without the benefit of any clapper-sound the highway turned into the Dover Road, and before them lay the blue line of the English Channel.

Then rap! – they were in a ship at sea and Marie was nauseated. It was a period of humiliation, of Charles holding her head and calling her *ma pauvre chérie*, of Charles making her drink brandy from his flask, of Charles saying, 'Where the devil is the steward?' and pulling on the bell. The man came promptly, and Marie shrieked when she saw him. He was very trim in a cotton shirt and trousers, like the summer uniform worn by the French army in Egypt, but he was no ship's steward: he was General Berthier, Napoleon's Chief of Staff.

Berthier's welcome was diminished by the spectacle of Marie's confusion, but after Charles explained how bad the crossing had been he seemed prepared to make the best of it, and told Marie she must try to sleep in the carriage he had brought to take them to Paris. As soon as she saw the carriage, by the lights of Calais Maritime Station, the vehicle's shining panels sprinkled with golden bees, she knew who was the owner and also the commander of the cavalry bodyguard which formed up around them after a wait at Calais, she knew not how long. Marie was warm and comfortable between the two men. Her head was much clearer, and she could follow what they were saying about the founding of the Empire. It had been done by a *senatus consultum*, and then the senate and the remaining consuls had waited on Napoleon at the Palace of St Cloud, where he had staged his famous *coup d'état*.

'Of course the army was represented,' said Berthier, 'and we all stood round him in a semi-circle and heard him acclaimed as Emperor of the French. By God, Latour, I remembered some of the early nights of the campaign in Italy, when we saw him wrap himself in that old grey overcoat and lie down to sleep beneath a cannon, and I thought how far he's come since those days . . .'

'I wish I'd been there,' said Charles Latour.

'There'll be plenty of great occasions in the future,' said Berthier. 'He revels in planning them. The coronation – that's a headache already. He wants to get the Pope to crown him in the Cathedral of Notre-Dame!'

'Didn't I tell you so, Marie?'

'Tell me what, dear?'

'That the coronation would be in Notre-Dame?'

'Look here,' said Berthier, 'hadn't we better stop talking and let your poor wife get some sleep?'

'But it's so interesting, I'm not sleepy!' said Marie, and Berthier laughed and told her to close her eyes and she would drowse off in five minutes, and presently he was proved right.

She was in a deep, refreshing sleep when the carriage stopped to the sound of orders and counterorders and she heard the captain of the bodyguard barking out that these were persons of importance on their way to Paris, who must proceed without let or hindrance, *'by order of the Emperor!'*

They were in a clearing in the forest where two roads met. One was the highway to Paris, and the other a side road leading down to a dry moat in front of a pile of heavy old buildings which appeared to be fortified.

'Who are these men, and what is this weird place?' asked Marie.

'The men are part of the garrison, and as nervous as cats,' said Charles. 'That's Fort Vincennes, where I did my training under Murat, before we left for Italy. *Mon Dieu*, that's a long time ago.'

'Nine years ago,' said Marie. 'Is Fort Vincennes a prison now?'

It was General Berthier who answered. 'Only for political prisoners on remand,' he said. 'It's mainly used for courts martial nowadays.'

'I pity the soldiers sent for trial in such a noisy place.'

'Noisy, madame?'

'Yes, that dog barking would drown the most convincing speech for the defence.'

'I don't hear barking, madame,' said Berthier, and Charles backed him up with a terse, 'You're dreaming, Marie.'

The barking dog in distress was so clear that Marie thought

of asking the captain of the bodyguard, standing alertly beside the carriage door, if he were deaf to it too, and then she felt by the movement of Berthier's arm that he was tapping his forehead in the world-wide sign which meant 'Delusions!' and realized that he thought she was in the same state of confusion as had distressed her on shipboard. She heard Charles ask the driver for another rug; felt him wrap it around her, take off her bonnet and draw her head to his shoulder. 'Go back to sleep and dream again,' he said.

It was late when they reached Paris, for the bell on the clock of Notre-Dame was tolling, but whether it struck ten, eleven or twelve strokes Marie could not have told. Her head was perfectly clear, and she knew it *was* a clock and not a dog barking, but she had to give her whole attention to what Charles was asking her to do.

'Awake? That's right,' he was saying. 'Put your hair straight, dear, we'll be at the Tuileries in ten minutes.'

She found a comb in her pocket and dragged it through her golden hair. 'Am I respectable?' she said, and Charles replied, 'You're lovely.'

Then they reached the Tuileries, a great pile which made her think of Fort Vincennes with the moat, except that the palace was brilliantly lit with lamps in every window. The bodyguard swung off the fresh mounts obtained at a post-house on the way, there was a great creaking of leather and stirrup irons, and their captain was helping Marie out of the coach. Four sentries held up flaming torches as the doors were pulled open and in the lighted hall two figures were revealed like leading actors on a stage: a man in the rose carnation of his consular uniform who was Napoleon, and a woman in an imperial robe of white satin who was his wife, Joséphine.

Charles led Marie forward, and as they crossed the threshold of the Tuileries she took her hand from his and bent her knee to the ground in a grand obeisance, breathing rather than speaking the words, 'Your Majesties!'

Then Napoleon took her hand, and pressed upon her cheeks the three kisses of ceremony while Joséphine, abandoning her pose of a beautiful effigy, flung her arms about the girl and cried, 'Welcome home, darling! You've been very much missed – both of you!'

Charles was encouraged by this to tell her about 'the wretched crossing – Marie so exhausted she ought to go straight to bed', much of which was lost on Marie, who was listening to Hortense de Beauharnais.

Madame Louis Bonaparte had been standing behind her mother, also dressed in white satin and looking pregnant. She now came forward to embrace Marie and tell her she was 'wonderful!' 'That curtsy, darling, was a lesson to all of us! We're a little bit shaky on the nice points of protocol!'

After Hortense's exuberant greeting many more people came up to welcome Marie and Charles, people astute enough to see that the la Tours were in high favour with the Bonapartes. Marie was kissed by the ladies of the palace (she shrank back from Madame Récamier, having never liked that young lady's pose of perpetual virginity) and had her hand kissed by Talma, Napoleon's favourite actor and by Eugène de Beauharnais, Hortense's brother, whom she was very glad to see. When Joséphine came up and told Hortense to 'take Marie up to her room, she was ill on the crossing, and I want Dr Corvisart to see her,' she made no protest, though she suspected this was due to Charles's interference – the sense of being taken care of was delightful!

Hortense led her up a wide staircase to the first floor, where bedrooms opened off the Galerie de Diane and a servant acquired in Egypt stood guard at the door of Napoleon's study. The room reserved for the la Tours was large and airy, with an applewood fire burning in the grate, and the pink brocade curtains drawn across the window matched the pink curtains drawn round the four-poster bed.

A pretty maid was waiting to point out the marble bathroom, and the warming-pan she had put inside the bed. Might she unpack for the lady and the gentleman?

'Where is the gentleman?' asked Marie, and Hortense said, 'Can't you hear him? He's walking up and down the Galerie de Diane with Bonaparte, giving him a report on English politics.' Bonaparte – it was what her mother called the man, and Hortense had always stumbled at the name of 'stepfather'. Well, he was her brother-in-law now, and Marie, thinking of the Bonaparte who was even closer to Hortense, asked sharply, 'How is Monsieur Louis?'

'He hasn't been well lately, but he's much better now. I had a letter this morning.'

'A letter? Isn't he in Paris?'

'Dr Cuisart ordered him to the south for his health. He won't be back until the baby comes in October.'

'Oh, is October the date?' said Marie lamely.

Hortense did not seem anxious to continue the subject. Except that she asked if Marie had seen a French paper called *L'ambigu* in London.

'I heard about it, but I didn't see it.'

'The editor, a man called Peltier, wrote a vile thing in it about me. He said it was well known in Paris that Napoleon was the father of my child. It was copied by the English papers, too.'

'Oh Hortense! Oh, how disgraceful! Don't cry. Monsieur Peltier won't be able to do much more harm. He was only "the front man", I think they call it, for a real villain called Anatole Laguerre, who is at the bottom of all the libels about Napoleon, and my husband and the Duc d'Enghien ran Laguerre out of England on Saturday.'

19

At the castle of Ettenheim, in the margravate of Baden, all was very quiet on a certain night in March 1804. The margrave of Baden was not well-known in his principality, which for most of his life had been a unit of the Rhineland Confederation organized by Napoleon Bonaparte as part of a future European Union. Many Badeners, especially the country folk, believed the Rohan family were still the lords of the land, in spite of the involvement of a Cardinal de Rohan in a great court scandal which helped to bring on the French Revolution. That a young lady of the Rohan family had a lover, and lived openly as his wife at Ettenheim, seemed as little blame-worthy to the country folk as the controversial scandal of the Queen's necklace.

The spectators of the love affair felt that a Bourbon of the Bourbons, who in an ideal world might some day be the King of France, was the right mate for a Princesse de Rohan, and quite apart from his ancestry he was such a likeable fellow! Handsome and witty, the Duc d'Enghien was an excellent shot and proficient in all the manly sports. His horsemanship was outstanding, and those who saw him returning from a long ride with Princess Charlotte that afternoon and holding hands while they rode, expressed their approval of the liaison by a grunted, 'They look great together!'

By early evening they felt great together, like a comfortable married couple who, after bathing, had changed into lounging garments and dined before the fire in Princess Charlotte's boudoir. The dinner-table had been removed, and the lady, in a primrose-coloured négligé, was working on a petitpoint embroidery of tropical flowers and foliage, while the duke, who had helped himself to more coffee, was dividing his attention between the cup and the fawning of his pet spaniel, whose long silky ears he was fondling.

'He hasn't forgiven you for leaving him behind this afternoon,' said the princess.

'Poor old fellow, we went too far for him!' said the duke with a laugh. 'Never mind,' he said to the dog, 'you *shall* come with me next time I go riding, and that's a promise.'

'You'll take him to Ghent?'

'*Juste ciel!* I'd forgotten all about Ghent!'

'Don't go, then.'

'I must go, dear. I can't leave Grandfather alone much longer with that man Laguerre.'

'I thought you told me there were plenty of people there to keep Laguerre in order.'

'So there are.'

But the girl kept her head bent above her embroidery, and was silent so that d'Enghien left his easy chair and went over to her sofa, where he took the petitpoint from her hands and folded them in his own.

'Charlotte, why don't you come to Ghent with us tomorrow? With me and my dog?' – who was listening as if he understood, and beat his tail in approval. 'Then you can see that Laguerre is perfectly harmless now – and after that we can be married.'

'Married in Ghent? Oh, Louis!'

'Why not in Ghent? There's a Catholic church, and – and my grandfather would be there –'

'Would you be doing this to please your grandfather?'

'No, but because I adore you, Charlotte!' cried the duke. 'I've loved you since the day I saw you first. I've told you so a thousand times, and you keep putting me off and off. Come now, give in! Let me take you to Ghent tomorrow, prepared for a future worthy of us both.'

She stretched up her arms, the golden sleeves fell back, and as he buried his face in her golden flesh he hardly heard her whispered, 'Yes!' But his whole body thrilled to it, and they were deaf to any sound but that, when a troop of cavalry came riding into the quadrangle of the castle of Ettenheim.

The duke and his sweetheart scrambled up and hurried to a window.

'Soldiers!' said Charlotte. 'What are they doing here? Oh, I can guess. They're from the *Armée des Princes*, come to escort you back to Ghent.'

But the duke saw that the guidons the soldiers carried were not showing the Bourbon fleur-de-lis.

'Look at the little flags they carry,' he said. 'They're showing the Tricolore. Those are Bonaparte's men.'

'I don't suppose he has a monopoly of the Tricolore. What's that uniform they're wearing?'

'It's too dark to tell. Dark green tunics – they could be the *Chasseurs* of the Guard. Hark! Here's someone coming.'

It was the butler, self-important and anxious, who entered with a bow.

'I apologize for disturbing Your Highnesses,' he said. 'A French officer is here in command of the troops who have just arrived, who begs to speak to you, monseigneur, if you please.'

'I don't know that I do please,' said the duke. 'In command of a section of *Chasseurs*, is he?'

The butler said he believed so. 'His name is Ordener, *monseigneur*, and he and his men have come from Strasbourg.'

'That's quite near,' said Charlotte in an undertone.

'Too near, unless . . . I don't know him,' said the duke, 'but I think I'd better look into this. Show this person up in fifteen minutes,' he said to the butler, 'and in the meantime call my valet and tell him I want to change into uniform – quickly. And send for madame's maid, please.' He took Charlotte's hand. 'Darling, I want you to change into evening dress. The green will do beautifully – no jewels.'

'I don't see why I should bother to change, just to receive a Bonaparte officer.'

He knew how to humour her. He said, 'It's not for that. It's because I should be madly jealous of any man permitted to see you *en négligé*. That's my privilege and mine alone!' She

211

gave a little affected gasp, and then, seeing that they were alone, she kissed the tips of her fingers and laid them across his lips. Then she hurried from the room, while her lover went back to the window and looked down at the troops below.

The next person to appear was his valet, who announced that everything was ready in the bedroom. 'Your Highness didn't say if you wished to wear an Order,' he said. 'I've laid out the St John.'

'That will do very well.' They walked from the room together, leaving it empty except for the spaniel, which was running restlessly up and down and whining.

Ten minutes later they were back again, Princess Charlotte gowned in green and wearing a gold link necklace; her dark hair was brushed into ringlets. The duke was a gallant figure in uniform, wearing the sash of the Order of St John of Jerusalem and at his neck a cravat bearing a golden Maltese cross. The servants took up their positions against the wall, and the butler motioned to a page to open the door on the corridor. A man in a French uniform spattered with mud made an awkward entrance.

'Your Highnesses have permitted me to introduce Captain Ordener,' said the butler.

The man bowed. 'Sir, do you affirm that you are Louis-Antoine de Bourbon-Condé, known as the Duc d'Enghien?' he said.

'I'll affirm nothing until I see your passport,' was the reply.

'Passport? It was not considered necessary for a visit to Baden.'

'Not considered necessary in Strasbourg, you mean?'

'Exactly.'

'But in Strasbourg there are educated men who must know that Baden is an independent sovereign state which unaccredited persons are not free to enter.'

'Baden,' said Ordener, 'is a unit of the Rhineland Confederation, owning the suzerainty of the First Consul of the French, whom I am sworn to serve.'

'Ah, Napoleon!' said the duke pleasantly. 'We have reached

an impasse. Let me resolve it by affirming that I am indeed d'Enghien. What do you want of me?'

'To come back to France with us and remain there for a few days. People are interested in you, duke, they want to get to know you better –'

'Don't listen to him, Louis! Don't do what he suggests!' Charlotte was almost hysterical, and d'Enghien stroked her hand.

'I don't think you understand,' he said to Ordener. 'I am at Ettenheim as the guest of Madame la Princesse, and tomorrow I am expected at Ghent, where my grandfather is quartered. I cannot go off on a jaunt with you to meet some hypothetical friends ... It's all right, Charlotte, please don't cry!'

For Charlotte's tears exasperated Ordener to say: 'Don't encourage him to resist me, madame, or I shall be compelled to use force.'

Not the threat of force employed on himself but of a demonstration which would terrify Charlotte caused d'Enghien to submit. He said, 'Your proceedings are highly irregular, captain, but Strasbourg is so near that I cannot refuse to spend the evening there with you. A longer stay I will not promise.'

Ordener, expressionless, motioned him towards the door. D'Enghien spoke only once again, bidding the servants look after their lady; he saw that the maid already had the weeping princess in her arms.

Ordener's troopers, who had dismounted, scrambled back on their horses when the two men appeared. They were impressed in spite of themselves, not by their captain's skill in arresting the man they had come to seek, but by the splendid bearing and personal attraction of the man himself. They were all promoted *sans-culottes* of the Revolution, for whom a Bourbon, or any *aristo*, was an enemy, and this young man was a Prince of the Blood! If only they were all like him, they thought, as in a respectful silence they presented arms.

He insisted on having his favourite horse brought from the stables, unaware that his favourite dog was looking on from the shrubs planted against the walls of Ettenheim, although he fancied he heard whining when he handed over his pistol to Captain Ordener. Then they were all in the saddle and moving off, and before very long they came to that great barrier between two countries and two cultures – the River Rhine.

Strasbourg, on the French side of the river, was a city in high favour with Napoleon Bonaparte. It had accepted his civic and financial reforms without question, it had accepted the Concordat, and in Strasbourg, a city of such advanced thinkers, Napoleon thought he might find one of the key points of his projected European Union. Certainly Louis d'Enghien, as he rode into the market place, thought his luck might change in Strasbourg, and was disappointed when the troops, instead of halting, rode faster than ever until the city was left behind.

'Where are you taking me?' he muttered to Ordener.

'My orders are – to Fort Vincennes.'

'To prison?'

'Not to prison. To be tried by court martial.'

'Prejudged to the guillotine, like my royal cousins before me?'

'You will have a fair trial. A trial by jury.'

'But on what charge?'

'Sedition and treason.'

'What a farce!'

As he saw the duke's head fall forward on his breast, Ordener thought 'What a shame!' would be a more apt comment, and regretted his own share in the business. You may cheat the guillotine, my friend, he thought, but they have thought of a way. For the soldiers had turned off the highway on to a side road, Fort Vincennes loomed ahead, and in the sand of the dry moat could be seen, with evidence that it had just been dug, an open grave.

Somewhere in the darkness a dog was barking, a blood-curdling sound.

Ordener's nerves snapped. 'Shoot that cur!' he cried out.

'Leave my dog alone!' cried d'Enghien. 'He followed us

from Ettenheim, he shall die with me. If you do him harm I'll strangle you and throw your body into the grave prepared for me.'

'Save your speeches for the court martial,' said Ordener. 'Look! It's assembling now.' A procession of robed and hooded men was moving past them into the main building. D'Enghien was ordered to dismount and two sergeants tied his hands. Inside Fort Vincennes it was very quiet and the sinister procession seemed to have vanished. Louis d'Enghien was escorted to a cell in a high gallery looking over the moat, and there, under the eyes of a man in general's uniform, he was handed over to an elderly warder, whose first question was, did he want anything to eat or drink?

'No, thank you. I only want to be left alone.'

'Very good, sir. Shall I bring you a coat? You seem to be chilly.'

He was aware that he was trembling violently. 'No coat, please.' Louis sank down on the pallet bed but as soon as he heard the cell door close he got up again and went to the window. The glass had been removed, the bars left in, and though he was aware that he would be watched he fastened his hands round the bars and prayed for his love.

'Almighty God,' he said, 'take care of Charlotte, and may she suffer no evil because of this day's work. May she not grieve for me, but live her life in happiness and beauty, keeping me ever in her heart.'

Then he prayed for his grandfather, that he might be told that he, Louis, had died bravely as one worthy of the name of Condé, and then he stood with his head in his hands, looking down at the open grave and the dog lying on its side on the edge of it, thinking of his friends and his happy boyhood.

He heard a bell in the clock tower chiming and checked by his watch. Eight o'clock. The hours were passing very quickly. He heard a voice call, 'Condé!' and the door of the cell was opened. Four men armed with halberds were waiting outside. He placed himself, at a gesture, in the middle of them, and with a firm tread walked down the stairs and into the great hall of Fort Vincennes.

It was lit by torches stuck in iron holders; the flickering light made the shadows seem more ominous and the faces of the judges more cruel. They were all strangers to him and in the brief silence caused by his appearance he used his voice at its most powerful to protest the legality of their court and of his seizure. The Prosecutor, whose face was the same hue as his red robe, called out 'Silence, Condé!' and the halberdiers ranged themselves at his sides. He was not in a dock and there was no sign anywhere of a counsel for the defence.

The judges wasted time by arguing about his identity, and since he had seen that his loud voice irritated them he cut them short by bawling, 'Of course I am the Duc d'Enghien!' and a clerk read aloud the charge of sedition and treason. Sedition, it appeared, was raising a private army, the *Armée des Princes*, to fight the French Empire, which he countered by saying, 'No, it was to act as an auxiliary to the army of Austria'; at which the jury shook their heads. They had simple country faces, and he supposed they had been coerced into taking part in this farce.

Treason, said the Prosecutor, meant enmity to their sovereign lord Napoleon, Emperor of the French. The prisoner was reported to have said in royalist circles in England that next time he entered France he would go fully armed. Was that true?

In a flash of pride and temper he said yes. 'No Condé would enter the France of Napoleon without being armed,' he said, and heard the Prosecutor's exultant, 'The prisoner is condemned out of his own mouth!'

The trial went very quickly after that. D'Enghien was pronounced guilty and condemned to death by firing squad; he asked for a priest and heard his request refused. When the halberdiers approached he refused to let his hands be tied, just as, outside, he motioned away the officer who wanted to fasten a handkerchief across his eyes.

On the verge of the grave Louis-Antoine, Duc d'Enghien,

looked death and man straight in the face, and the last living creature to feel his caress was the spaniel which dragged itself feebly to his side. The last man in the file now forming was a mere boy with a kind face, to whom he said, 'Don't let him suffer!' and was comforted when the lad nodded.

The officer in command of the squad, seeing his lips move, asked him if he wished to say anything. Louis had been trying to remember what a priest might have said of hope and trust, but no words came. But when he stood to attention under the levelled rifles a voice in the crowd called out, 'God bless Your Highness!' and he spoke his faith aloud.

'God save the King!'

The rifles blazed forth, and a Bourbon died.

20

At the palace of the Tuileries, where he had never been, the news of d'Enghien's death caused a deep gloom to fall on the morning it was known in Paris. The bearers of the tale were Napoleon's three sisters, who had reduced Joséphine to hysterics on the day before by saying that she was unfit to be anointed and crowned as Empress, and who had returned to repeat the punishment by asking her why a wife with so much influence over her husband couldn't have used it 'to save the life of that poor young man'.

The ladies of the palace, catching the infection, were all sobbing and crying, and Hortense, declaring that they would wake Marie, made sure that she was well and truly awakened by running upstairs and into her bedroom, followed by the pretty maid. Amélie brought the inevitable coffee, and also the information that *monsieur le marquis* had gone for a ride with General Junot and would be back for luncheon.

When Marie heard Hortense's story of the tragedy at Vincennes she was glad to think her husband was with Junot, just the cheerful company he required. For there were questions Charles Latour must know he had to answer: had he told Napoleon anything about Louis d'Enghien which might have made him send Ordener to Baden? Ordener, according to Hortense, was the villain of the piece. Talleyrand, as Foreign Minister, had said if Ordener had had the sense to carry a passport Napoleon would not be accused of conducting an illegal abduction . . . !

'Is that what they're saying?' said Marie.

'Ordener's great mistake was talking too much in front of the servants. I would really like to know about that poor

Rohan girl, and how she's bearing up . . . What are you doing, Marie?' exclaimed Hortense, as her friend got out of bed.

'Darling, don't be cross with me or think me ungrateful for all your own and your mother's kindness, but I want to go to my own home. Oh, not for long! I'll be back in the afternoon. But I must breathe, and I can't breathe in the Tuileries – the luxury is stifling me!'

'I'm sorry,' said Hortense, and said no more, while Marie made a hasty toilette and put a few items, including a battered leather jewel case, into a little bag. Then Hortense said, with a wry smile, 'It's true what people say, you're very like Napoleon. You make those quick decisions and you act upon them as if a great wind were blowing you along, and what it boils down to is you mean to have your own way and to the deuce with all the rest of us.'

Marie, as they started down the stairs, replied, 'That isn't so, my dear. Tell Charles I'll be back quite soon.'

'But where are you going? To the old Fontaine house? That's your home, or it used to be.'

'No, I'm going to my real home on the Quai Voltaire.'

'May I tell my mother? She'll want to know.'

Marie smiled. 'It isn't a secret,' she said. 'Tell whom you please.'

Only one doubt assailed Marie as she turned across the Pont Royal. Knowing their taste for gossip she dreaded having to hear a repetition of the Vincennes tragedy from the lips of Monsieur and Madame Bélard. But when they both opened the door to her nothing suggested that they had ever heard of the Duc d'Enghien. In their hearty welcome they enquired after *monsieur le marquis* ('He might be along presently? Good!'), after which they belaboured her with questions about London – had she really liked the English – all savages, weren't they? That got them up to the apartment, which looked shabby and neglected; Madame Bélard produced a duster from her apron and flapped it about, while her husband lit a fire of logs laid on the bricks Marie herself had installed in the grate. She assured them that she wanted neither coffee nor wine; she had come merely to look around and see what had to be bought to improve the living conditions at the flat, and for that she would prefer it if they would kindly leave her alone.

She bade them draw back the curtains and open the window and then they went unwillingly downstairs. The old house seemed to close in upon Marie as she sank down upon the end of the day bed, under the faded tapestry, which brought her nearer to the fire, and stretched out her hands to the blaze. She was not aware that a ray of spring sunshine, coming through the open window, had turned her bare head to living gold. She was aware of nothing but the pain the day had brought.

Nearly half an hour had passed, and she was about to fling a handful of pine cones on the fire, when Marie heard the sound of voices and movement in the courtyard far below. Could it be Charles come to look for her? Somebody was coming, certainly. A woman? Hortense? It was Madame Bélard who opened the front door and appeared pale-faced before her.

'Madame,' the woman said, 'a gentleman is here, asking to see you.'

'A gentleman?'

'Madame, it is the Emperor.'

Marie's heart beat fast. She said, in unconscious imitation of the Tuileries formality, 'I will receive His Majesty.'

She stood up. The concierge's wife went out, and there was a heavy rapid tread on the stairs, and Napoleon came in so quickly that Marie recognized the accuracy of Hortense's description, 'as if a great wind were blowing him along'. She curtsied, and attempted a greeting, quite drowned by his own sharp words.

'Marie! What are you doing here?'

'I wanted to be at home.'

'I might have known it. I've only been here once in my life, but I've always understood that this place has a hold on you ... I would have known, even if Hortense hadn't told me, that this was where you'd go to ground. Oh, I'm not angry because you ran away from the Tuileries. The place was like a madhouse today. There were my sisters, screeching like wildcats, and there were Fouché and Talleyrand, nearly as bad. Fouché told me to my face that in condemning d'Enghien I had committed worse than a crime, a mistake! He was jealous because none of his policemen were called on to make the arrest. Talleyrand at least admitted that I acted legally, according to the laws of war, in the invasion of Baden.'

'Oh stop, stop, sire!' cried Marie. 'I'm grieved you've been upset, but do tell me just one thing: your attitude to the duke was not influenced by anything detrimental my husband may have told you about him?'

'Charles said he admired him very much, and God knows why,' said Napoleon. 'Louis d'Enghien must be a man who's made as much of a career by dying as most men make out of leading useful lives.'

'Don't make fun of him, sire,' said Marie. 'He was a very fine young man.'

'Ah yes, you met him, Charles said. Is that why you've joined the legion of his admirers? Was Louis d'Enghien fine enough to touch your cold heart?'

'I don't know you when you talk like that.' Marie had been standing since Napoleon entered the room. Now she sat down again on the day bed and said, 'You sound just as Charles did when he was in the National Guard. He always said no woman could praise any man without being in love with him ...'

'Meaning you by "no woman"?'

'Possibly.'

'Who was the man?'

'You should know.'

'You mean – I *was*?'

'I was in love with you then. I told you so in Corsica.'

In a few hasty steps Napoleon walked round the day bed and stood in front of her. He looked, for once, unsure of

himself, and his first words were unsure. 'I remember everything you told me at the Casa Bonaparte. That was when I
made my second mistake.'

'What do you mean?'

'My first mistake was when I failed to admit to myself how
much I loved you when you were a girl. In Corsica I should
have refused to listen to you. I should have swept you off
your feet and away to a farm I own in the forest . . . and made
you mine for ever. But I didn't have the courage to insist –
and so I lost you.'

'Because you wanted to return to France and play at politics
until you became the First Consul Napoleon. I *wanted* Hortense to tell you where I'd gone – so that we might be alone
together, in my home, while we said our last goodbye.'

'Now,' he said, 'you are going to come away with me. I
have a carriage at the door. I'll take you, not to some forest
hideaway, but to a palace – Fontainebleau or St Cloud – and
you'll be all mine.'

She saw tears in his eyes, she felt the force of his pleading,
but she shook her head.

'Nothing has changed, Napoleon. You are still married to
the lady of your choice, and if the French people found out
that you had run away with another man's wife, I fear that
you would never wear the crown.'

He looked down at her, seeming taller than he was.

'Do you know what d'Enghien said before he died? He
cried, "God save the King!" People think he meant his cousin,
who calls himself King Louis XVIII now. A pretty king! He's
welcome to the crown of France if he can win it, because it's
mine by the right of conquest. The Bourbons left the crown
in the gutter and I picked it up on the point of my sword.
Marie, I love you! Take me as I am, for I am yours!'

She saw the unbelievable happening as he sagged to the
floor and was forced to believe. The Emperor of the French,
the invincible soldier, the master of half Europe, was on his
knees at her feet.

21

When Marie returned to the Tuileries an hour later the palace appeared to be uninhabited. Only the presence of the sentries, pacing in front of the great door, suggested the presence of those within who required protection. Marie asked the nearest man to ring the great doorbell for her: she doubted if she was strong enough to pull the rope. When a footman held the door open for her to enter she was pleased to see the intendant close behind him. The man was meddlesome and pompous, but he liked to be consulted and to share his knowledge. Marie asked if he knew whether the Marquis de la Tour had returned.

'Yes, madame, about an hour ago. He came back with His Majesty, who ordered a light luncheon for both of them to be served in his study.'

Marie was glad to think that the lacerating scene at the Quai Voltaire had not destroyed Napoleon's appetite. For herself, she said, she wanted nothing, only to know if *monsieur le marquis* was still in the study.

Probably not, because the Emperor had come downstairs to talk with Her Majesty, who was indisposed, and then he had gone out alone. Had madame wished to see the Emperor? Or Madame Louis Bonaparte? Marie was glad to settle for Madame Louis, and was ushered into the yellow salon to await her.

Hortense did not keep her waiting long. She came running in, not from her mother's room next door but from the hall, beautifully dressed as usual, lightly rouged, but with reddened eyes which told a story of distress and her first words to Marie were, 'Have you seen Charles? He must have missed you at the Quai Voltaire!'

Marie said, 'Yes, he must have done.' She wished to keep the Quai Voltaire out of any conversation at the Tuileries. She risked saying, 'Charles went out with Junot and came back with the Emperor. Did you see him?'

'Yes, we had a little chat, while the Emperor went to Maman. Oh, Marie, they had such a quarrel!'

'What about?'

'The Emperor means to leave Paris and go to the Channel coast. He's not pleased with Admiral Villeneuve, and he wants to inspect the invasion fleet himself. And he wants to take Maman with him to Aix-la-Chapelle as soon as he has finished his inspection, and she doesn't want to go. She thinks it's too dangerous – too near Austrian territory, especially now when people all seem to be so angry about what they're calling the Duc d'Enghien's abduction from Baden . . . !'

'Don't cry, Hortense,' said Marie. 'It's a big sensation just now, but it'll be forgotten by midsummer – you'll see.'

'I see you, Marie; you pretend to be so very calm and equal to anything, but perhaps you'll cry too when I tell you Napoleon means to take your Charles with him as his ADC –'

'What, to Aix-la-Chapelle?'

'No, to the English Channel.'

'He won't come to any harm there. If there were a declaration of invasion involved I would be seriously alarmed.'

'I don't think Bonaparte means to invade.'

'But he does mean to go to Aix. Why?'

'Oh!' Hortense began in the mocking tone becoming more and more natural to her. 'It's part of the bee in his bonnet about Charlemagne.'

'Charlemagne? You mean that prehistoric old Emperor?' The significance of the title struck her and she corrected it to 'Emperor of the West'.

Hortense said triumphantly, 'Exactly. Emperor of the West. The last ruler of France to be crowned emperor. And Napoleon identifies with him – isn't that the word? I've heard Monsieur Talleyrand use it, haven't you? Yes, *identifies*, that's what he does. He even refers to Charlemagne as "*notre illustre prédé-*

cesseur''. The Bonaparte girls are furious. They say it makes him look like a fool.'

'I didn't know you paid any attention to the Bonaparte girls, Hortense. You still haven't explained about Aix.'

'Why, Charlemagne was crowned at Aix and had his court there, only they called it Aachen then, and that's why *they're* going to Aix, to see the historical places, and perhaps buy some of the relics to use at *our* coronation. I heard Maman say, laughing of course, ''Do you think the Austrian Emperor will sell you any of those baubles after you've been fighting him for years?'' Oh, Marie, don't look so – so silly? You must know Charlemagne had two sons, and left the western part of his empire – that was France – to one, and the eastern part – Austria and Germany – to the other. Poor Bonaparte. He'd be thankful to have just one son to be an heir to *his* empire!'

A wave of pity consumed Marie. Poor Bonaparte indeed! The object of his wife's derision, of his stepdaughter's mockery . . . and rejected, even while he was on his knees to her, by the woman who had loved him! She rose from her chair and went towards the door.

'Where are you going?' cried Hortense.

'I – I thought I heard somebody – coming.'

'Probably Charles come back.'

It was Charles, who said, 'Here at last!' and taking her in his arms kissed her with a vigour which Hortense declared quite shocked her, so that she absolutely insisted on 'leaving the field clear for you two love-birds'.

Charles said, 'Tell me about you. I hear you had a distinguished visitor this morning. What time did you get back to the palace?'

'I left the Quai Voltaire a few minutes after the Emperor did and when I got back *you* were gone. Where were you?'

'Not much further than the stables. I had to fix up transport to Boulogne tomorrow.'

'Did *you* have to do that?'

'It's an ADC's job.' And with obvious pleasure Charles stroked the silk sash knotted round his right arm, the insignia of an aide-de-camp conferred upon him by Bonaparte after the Battle of Arcole. His schoolboy delight in this mark of honour had always seemed to his wife one of the most endearing things about Charles de la Tour and she instinctively crept back to his embrace. He called her 'darling Marie' and kissed her.

'You've heard then that I'm off to Boulogne?' he said.

'Boulogne, is it? I heard Villeneuve is out of favour.'

'He's never been *in* favour since he lost most of the French fleet to Lord Nelson in Aboukir Bay. By the way, Bonaparte says he keeps forgetting to thank you for the Nelson portrait you brought him from London. What did he talk about at the Quai Voltaire?'

'Oh, mostly about d'Enghien's death. He's very distressed about it.'

'So I gather.'

'Charles, do you remember – we passed Fort Vincennes on the way back to Paris?'

'Of course I do. What of it?'

'I heard d'Enghien's dog barking while we were outside Vincennes.'

Charles stared at her, his jaw dropping.

'My dear girl, think what you're saying. The duke's dog was nowhere near Vincennes that night we came up the road. So far as I know he was in Baden.'

'And on the morning after the duke was killed, the dog was found shot dead, lying on the grave of the master he adored –!'

'So what do you suppose the barking was about?' said Charles. 'Some awful warning from the spirit world of what was going to happen?'

'Something like that.'

'Marie, I can't believe this is you, with all your scientific knowledge, talking like a – a gypsy fortune-teller! I tell you there was no barking from Vincennes. I was right there in the carriage with you. Don't you think I would have heard it? Poor Louis d'Enghien was a level-headed fellow: he wouldn't have believed in a rigmarole like this. Now I want you to come right back to our room and let me order you something light for supper. You don't want to dine with the court, do you? Or with the Bonaparte girls and their brother?'

'With the Bonaparte girls and Napoleon – never!' With a desperate attempt at coquetry, Marie said, 'Not too light a supper, darling – I had no luncheon.'

'There you are! Missing a meal next! You're overtired, that's what it is. You were exhausted when we left London and you haven't stopped going since. What am I to do if you won't take care of yourself?'

'But you take such wonderful care of me, darling!'

It was tenderly said, and Charles drew her to the door. But Marie stopped him as he opened it, when they could hear the courtiers gathering for one of the Sunday dinners which were a feature of life at the Tuileries.

She said, 'Charles, please wait. I want to tell you what I'd like to do when you've gone to the Fleet. I'd like to go back and live at the pharmacy with Madame Beauchet. You love to tease me about my scientific knowledge, so I'm sure you'll give me your permission and approval when I tell you I want to study more. I went to see Professor Guiart, who can show me how to help the people in our *quartier* along the way to better health.' While Marie was talking, in a voice which certainly did not sound exhausted, she had kept her eyes on Charles's face across which every expression from assent to disapproval she had seen pass. Then she spoke up with her clinching argument.

'Then, when I've learned part of how to do that, my dear, we can try to help our friends at Vesle.'

22

When she woke up next morning after a good night's sleep, Marie's first thought was for the weather. Charles had left the bedroom. Was he, too, concerned about the weather on the journey to the coast, and had he gone to consult a barometer? Or to consult the Emperor?

By looking out of the window she could see the first rays of sunshine falling across the flowerbeds in the gardens of the Tuileries, and dew lying on the grass plots beneath the chestnut alleys. A perfect morning, and one on which she would not be called upon to face Napoleon! Marie still blushed when she remembered how he had kneeled to her, had buried his face in her lap – and she had not given him one caress, one tender word. Well! They would soon be parted for long enough.

Marie was pulling on her robe of white broderie anglaise, crumpled by packing and repacking, when she heard her husband's voice outside the door and called, 'Come in!' He entered, not dressed for riding, and when she said, 'I thought you'd gone already,' he replied in the sullen tones she knew too well, that he wasn't going. The plans were changed.

'Charles! What on earth has happened?'

'Last night, after you'd gone to bed, a courier came in from the Chappe telegraph station with a message for the Emperor. They'd had his telegram about coming to see Villeneuve, and of course they had to tell him that, a day before, Admiral Villeneuve's squadron had sailed for Brest.'

'What did the Emperor say?'

'Cursed and swore, of course. Vowed to punish Villeneuve for acting without orders – then gave orders summoning him back to Boulogne, but putting off the inspection until later this month . . .'

'Very upsetting for him, Charles, and for you too.'

'Oh I don't matter. Eugène de Beauharnais is with him now. Let's hope he can calm him down.'

'And what about me, don't I matter?' said Marie, stung. 'I told you what I planned to do, and got your approval, and I wrote to Professor Guiart last night.'

Charles whistled. 'Then you'd better let me walk you along to the pharmacy pretty soon,' he said. 'You'll have things to do but I think you'd better have a word with Joséphine first and tell her your plans – will you, dear?'

Hoping she would not have to encounter Joséphine's husband, Marie said she would. Soon after that, coffee, with brioches and honey, was brought in, and after breakfast the de la Tours went downstairs. Marie, as she passed beneath the gilded ceilings of the Tuileries, thought that the palace was a world within a world, in which so many people were living at cross purposes, in the grip of their different hopes and ambitions, and that the man round whom they all revolved – Bonaparte – was no more fortunate than the least of them.

She suggested to Charles that she should ask the intendant to find out if the Empress was willing to receive them both, and was not too surprised when the man came back with a message that Her Majesty would receive Madame de la Tour alone. He added in hushed tones, 'The hairdressers are with Her Majesty.' Then with a quick change of manner, he turned to Charles and said, 'The Emperor requests the presence of *Monsieur le Marquis* in his study.'

'I hope that doesn't mean another change of plan,' said Charles, an indiscretion which Marie covered by asking him to let her know when he was free. Then she followed the intendant into Joséphine's bedroom.

The scene before her eyes was very familiar to her. In the apartment they had shared in the rue de l'Université she had seen the rites of Joséphine's toilette which usually lasted for two hours, and of which the central figure was Joséphine herself, worshipping her own beauty, while the acolytes waving her hair and polishing her nails were her own maids. The same scene had been repeated in their cell at the Carmes prison, where the hairdressing was done by a kindly fellow prisoner, Madame de Beaupré, and the manicure by a young woman 'of easy virtue', as they phrased it then, who thought it was an honour to wait upon the Vicomtesse de Beauharnais.

The actors in the great drama of the toilette had increased and the setting had become unbelievably luxurious. Joséphine was not sitting on a prison pallet, but reclining half-erect on a chaise longue, facing a table with a marble top on which were spread brushes, combs and cosmetics. She wore a white satin robe with a hem of white ermine and with her beautiful chestnut hair streaming over her shoulders she looked every inch an empress.

Bending over her were two of the most expert hairdressers in Paris, Claude and Alexandre, with a youth in attendance to carry their equipment. Also present was a lady of the palace, as required by protocol whenever the Empress was waited on by a man or men, and her faithful servant, Agathe Riblé, was in the background. Agathe and Marie were old friends, and it was she who announced Marie's entrance to the Empress.

'Dear Marie, come and kiss me,' said the soft Creole drawl, and Marie surrendered herself to the embrace that was like no other, so soft, so yielding, so perfumed, and heard herself told that she had come at exactly the right moment, they were going to do her hair in a new style and she wanted to be told the truth about it. Marie promised the truth and sat down on a stool at the side of the chaise longue with her hand in Joséphine's.

Those artistes of the toilette, Claude and Alexandre, each took up a strand of chestnut hair and while Claude took the front piece and puffed it over Joséphine's brow Alexandre swept the back piece smoothly over her head to meet the fullness, and fastened the end (which was braided) with a plain tortoiseshell clasp.

'Of course I shall wear diamonds!' said Joséphine, 'but this will do for tonight. What do you think of it, Marie?'

'It's very becoming. It suits you, really it does.'

'It's exquisite,' cried the lady of the palace, taking up her cue. 'It makes Her Majesty look about twenty – not a day more!' Joséphine, who was then over forty, fairly purred with satisfaction.

She thanked the hairdressers for their handiwork and dismissed them. When Claude asked if he might brush out her hair again, she said, 'Agathe can do that while she's dressing me.'

Marie said, 'It's so pretty, Joséphine! Aren't you going to wear it at dinner?'

'No – or well, just for five minutes for Bonaparte to admire . . . but this is a style for a future eventuality.' Joséphine smiled and Marie understood. It was easy to see how a crown would rest on those silky waves of hair. Joséphine had been rehearsing for the coronation.

And she was sure of Napoleon's admiration. She always had been, since the early days when he came courting Joséphine de Beauharnais instead of Marie Fontaine! In spite of their quarrels about her extravagance, and his brother's revelation of her infidelity, Marie believed that Joséphine still came first with the man who meant to raise her to a throne.

Would Joséphine be so self-assured, so completely basking in her own triumph, if she had seen that poignant tableau in the house on the Quai Voltaire, had heard Napoleon's confession that he loved Marie Fontaine?

Through the blood throbbing in her ears she was aware that Joséphine had asked her a question, and was repeating it.

'I said, why are you wearing your overcoat. Are you going out?'

Marie took the plunge. 'Yes,' she said, 'that's what I came to tell you. Charles is going to escort me to the Pharmacie Fontaine. I thought I might spend a few days with Madame Beauchet. I haven't been to see her since we came back.'

'You'd have plenty of time to pay her a visit and be back

in time for dinner. You're up to something, Marie! I insist on knowing what it is.'

'Well – if you must know – I've asked my old friend and teacher, Professor Guiart, to come and see me there.'

'Ah, the good Guiart! For what purpose, pray?'

'I want him to find me some medical work, within my power to do.'

'Like you worked in that – what was it? – that underground cellar beside the Seine?'

'Exactly like that.'

Joséphine flung up her hands, and cried, 'You never, ever, think of me!'

'Darling, I do, I do! Charles and I are so grateful – to you and the Emperor – for your hospitality and all your kindness – but truly we can't impose on you any longer. We must stand on our own feet now –'

'But I thought you would stay with me and amuse me, at least until I go to Plombières in July.'

'I thought you were going to Aix-la-Chapelle.'

'Who told you that?'

'Hortense. I told her my own plans. I didn't expect this would be such a shock, because I thought she would tell you.'

'Hortense is in bed, Marie, and Dr Cuisart says she must stay there. She's having such a difficult pregnancy, he's afraid of complication. My poor Hortense! My poor little girl!' Joséphine, distracted, burst into tears.

Marie called for the maid, who had gone into the next room.

As soon as the maid saw the state Joséphine was in she turned in her tracks and ran back to the bedroom she had just left. Marie heard her rummaging about in the bathroom and knew she was looking for the medicine prescribed for Joséphine's fits of hysteria. When she came back she was carrying a little silver tray which held a green glass bottle, a glass of fresh water and a silver spoon. Her eyes opened wide when she met Marie's, and she breathed rather than spoke the words, 'Well! Here we go again!'

It was not very respectful, but then the two young women

232

had been through similar scenes fifty times. In the rue de l'Université days it had been toothache which laid Joséphine low – and her teeth were certainly in a wretched state – once or twice it had been a heavy chest cold. But never before had hysteria followed a successful session with the hairdressers, and Marie was not surprised when Agathe, busily chafing her mistress's hands asked in a stage whisper, 'What is it this time?'

'Worried about Hortense.'

'I don't wonder. But Hortense is in bed and sound asleep, I've just looked in to see.'

'She means to write to the husband tonight. You must allow time for that before she goes to bed herself.'

'I will, and if you're all right alone I'd like to go and get the bed ready. I shan't be long.'

'Just look out and if you see my husband, tell him I shan't be long either.'

When they were alone she tried to compose Joséphine's limbs into a more restful attitude on the sofa on which they had laid her. Spoiled, selfish and shallow – she was all of those things to a fault. But good heavens, she was beautiful! That pure profile, those tender lips! And she loved her children; what woman would not weep to see her tears for poor Hortense, captive in a worse than loveless marriage – especially if the woman knew that the marriage was of her own making. Impulsively Marie leaned forward and took Joséphine's cold hands in her warm ones, and as soon as the clear hazel eyes opened on her own she began to speak.

'Joséphine,' she said, 'I'm sorry to be going away when you want me to stay, but I'm not going far, and I'll come back whenever you send for me. And if there's anything I can do for you, great or small, you only have to tell me, and I'll do it. You have my word on that, my absolute sworn solemn promise, to do whatever will make you well and happy.'

23

'Is something the matter with Joséphine?' Charles asked, when he and Marie had entered the Tuileries gardens and started up the broad central path. Agathe had admitted him to the salon after she took the Empress away.

'Why do you ask that?' said Marie.

'Because of Agathe's face when she looked round the door at me. It seemed as if she'd seen a ghost.'

'Yes, well, she was rather upset. Joséphine was saying how worried she was about Hortense and the coming child. The father is to be sent for, won't that be nice?'

'Perfect!' said Charles. 'That's all we need at the Tuileries – Louis Bonaparte stumbling around, insulting everyone to prove his own importance!'

'Perhaps Eugène de Beauharnais will keep his brother-in-law in order.'

'Ah, Eugène may well exert himself, he's in great spirits today.'

'Why? Has he received some new mark of the imperial favour?'

It could only be a guess, of course, but it was a characteristically shrewd guess, and the whole story would be in the *Moniteur* tomorrow, so Charles told Marie that the Italians, who wanted Napoleon to be King of Italy as well as Emperor of the French, would be asked to accept his wife's son, Eugène de Beauharnais, as his Viceroy with command of the army and a palace at Milan.

'The Bonaparte girls will be furious,' said Marie.

'Especially when they hear that Eugène is to be known as

"le Fils de France",' said Charles with a laugh which Marie echoed.

'The Son of France? How thrilled Joséphine will be! Eugène is her favourite, you know, and this will take her mind off Hortense's woes. The next excitement will be planning a wedding for His Highness the Viceroy of Italy!' Marie's peal of laughter was a girl's laugh of delight at the anticipated prospect of rejoicing: of dancing, music, orange-flowers and feasting. 'But what are you stopping for?' she exclaimed, for Charles had halted before they reached the rue St-Honoré, in the middle of the narrow street which joined it to the Gardens. 'This is our own garden gate, but we can't get in this way, it's always kept locked. We have to go round the corner and go in through the shop.'

'Yes. I know,' said Charles. 'But I think I'll be getting back to the Tuileries. When do we see you there again?'

'Not tomorrow. Professor Guiart is coming at ten in the morning –'

'Marie!' Charles's hands were on her shoulders, and in the darkening street his face was close to her own. 'This thing – that you want to work at with Guiart – it won't be too much for you? It won't undermine your own health or tire you out?'

'It's my kind of work, dear. I'll be all right.'

'I admire your strength of purpose.' It was said sincerely, and Charles drew Marie into his arms and kissed her. It was their first spontaneous embrace for a long time.

Charles did not prolong the leave-taking. Murmuring something about seeing her soon, he left her on the corner of the rue St-Honoré, where on two windows, lighted from within, raised letters of white enamel spelled out the name of the Pharmacie Fontaine. The words altered her original plan of hurrying into the arms of Madame Beauchet. Marie crossed the narrow street which she remembered as the Street of the Tumbrils, turned on the opposite pavement and looked around at the shop front. There, still visible in the sunset glow, she read her grandfather's name: *Michel Fontaine – pharmacien.*

After Michel, Prosper had come, and after Prosper, Marie.

She could not have defined the warm but wordless feeling which flooded her brain as prayer, for in the formal religious instruction of her Catechism class at St Roch she had been taught to think of prayer as inseparably allied with the repetition of the Rosary, and where her beads had been laid after her uncle's death by the guillotine she could not tell. Yet prayer it certainly was, this tumbling, incoherent entreaty that she might be found worthy to serve her fellow beings in her chosen field. Then, with a stifled word of blessing on her husband, Marie rang the bell of the Pharmacie Fontaine.

The door was flung open in an instant, and Marie was seized in the embrace of Madame Beauchet, so rapidly as to make her think that her old friend had been hiding behind it – which happened to be the case. Both women were entangled in an outburst of feminine incoherence, such as the repetition of the word 'wonderful' and the exclamation of 'How well you look!' until pause and definition was given by Madame Beauchet, who said with a gasp that she had been on tenterhooks for an hour, ever since Professor Guiart had stopped by to say that Madame de la Tour would be coming round to the pharmacy from the Tuileries.

'Professor Guiart? What did he want?' Marie asked sharply.

'Oh, he looks in regularly, in case I can't cope with any problem in the pharmacy. But this time he wanted to leave a message for you. He said you'd asked him to see you here tomorrow, but he wanted to put it off until tomorrow afternoon at three, because he has been called into Consultation with Dr Berthollet at the house of Monsieur Boissy d'Anglas, who has been stricken with a tertian fever – '

'Poor old gentleman. No, that's all right, my dear, I'm glad he's going to see Dr Berthollet.' It was the truth, she had worked with the doctor before, and he had sponsored her employment in Egypt; she knew he would oppose any objections Guiart might make to the inclusion of a young woman in what she now thought of as her health project. She shivered in happy anticipation, and Marie-Josèphe blamed herself for keeping her standing in the cold lobby when there was a good fire in the kitchen. Marie must come in and be made welcome to her own house!

She opened the door leading into the shop, and Marie thought of her husband's story of 'one candle burning', for the place was lit by just one candle set on the counter behind which she herself had sold cosmetics. The candle was surrounded by a neat array of the familiar little majolica pots.

'Everything's in apple-pie order, I see,' she said, looking down affectionately at her friend's head. Marie-Josèphe was a small woman, and her head, on which the black curls were brushed neatly under a white goffered muslin cap, reached not quite to Marie's shoulder.

'I hope you'll think the books are too. Maître Favart's been so good, coming in every Saturday to check them out with me. He's been trying to teach me double entry, but it's too difficult for me. Business has been very good, Marie. I have quite a respectable profit to show you!'

'I'm sure you have, but let's leave the books until tomorrow, shall we? I hear the sound of a kettle boiling . . .'

'Boiling over, more likely. Would you rather have tea or coffee?'

'Coffee, please. Charles wanted us to stop for coffee on the rue de Rivoli, but I was anxious to get home.' And how good it was, she thought, as she followed her friend into the kitchen where a bright fire was burning, to find Marie-Josèphe so much at home in the old pharmacy, as she drew up two easy chairs to the fireplace and began to prepare the coffee, though she was rather chilled by her friend's next remark.

'I'm glad the marquis is learning to look after you.'

Marie said irritably, 'He looked after me beautifully in England!'

'You were very brave to go there, with him, to an enemy country. How did you get on with his mother?'

'Very well. She's rather stiff, you know, and very *ancien régime*, but she was very kind – I liked her.'

'Did you meet any French people?'

'Quite a few.'

'Did you come across that poor young man who was murdered at Vincennes last week?'

'The Duc d'Enghien? Yes, I did.' Marie hesitated. 'That seems to be a leading topic here. What are people saying about it in our *quartier*?'

'That he was the victim of Napoleon's jealousy.'

'Oh, that's ridiculous!'

She spoke more sharply than she meant. It was second nature for Marie to rush to Napoleon's defence and particularly when the imputation of jealousy was made in this place. True, they had never sat together by the fireside: her memories – and his too – were of summer evenings when they had talked in the garden 'among the lettuce and the pot-herbs', as he liked to say, and it was not too dark to see that garden now. It was too early for spring vegetables yet, but some green shoots were visible, some new life was thrusting its way into the old yard.

'Have you been planting bulbs, Marie-Josèphe?' Marie said. 'May I look?'

'Certainly. There's only a few hyacinths, but they will smell so sweet.'

Marie got up, and took the few steps which carried her across the flowerbed. She kneeled down and ran her fingers across the bulbs. What she whispered to herself was, 'Oh, my darling!' and she was not thinking of the scent of hyacinths.

Marie-Josèphe was not a highly educated woman but her sense of perception had been developed through years of association with the Marquise de La Fayette and observation of how that unfortunate lady's moods altered in response to the demands made upon her by an overbearing husband. Gilbert de La Fayette had fought in two wars, far more successfully on behalf of the Americans in their struggle for independence than when he fought for the French in their stand against a foreign invader. That had earned him months of imprisonment in an Austrian dungeon which his wife insisted on sharing as, when Marie came back to Paris, Adrienne still insisted on sharing her husband's exile in Holland.

The worst of this ingrained habit of mind for Madame Beauchet was that it made her think a husband's temper as the reason for every depression on the part of his wife. She could see that Marie was depressed when they came in from the garden and blamed herself for the little jibe about Charles's learning to take care of his wife. She busied herself in buttering some slices of *pain d'épices* and offering them with the coffee, and was rewarded when Marie stopped staring into the fire and turned with a cheerful smile to ask if she had good news of Madame de La Fayette.

Delighted by this fortunate change of subject to her favourite topic, Madame Beauchet embarked on a long, verbatim account of the 'lovely letter' she had received last week from 'my poor dear lady'. She was well and *he* was well, the girls were none the worse for their prison experience. The only bad news was that *he* (La Fayette) was planning to return to his little estate not far from Paris and take my lady with him, in which case my lady would probably find herself doing a servant's work and waiting on his every whim. It was so unfair!

'She'd rather come to Paris?'

'Of course she would!'

'Where she has that big house standing empty next door?'

'Labelled National Property by the revolutionaries.'

'I know, but that order can be set aside. How do you suppose we got to live back at Vesle? Would you like me to speak to – the Emperor about it?'

'Oh, Marie, you're very kind, but no, don't. My lady thought of that herself, when she saw all the returning *émigrés* getting their houses back again, and she asked her cousin to speak to General Bonaparte about it. And when her husband found out he was furious and said it must stop because he refused to accept any favours from the Corsican upstart – I don't know why.'

'What a fool!' said Marie. 'They quarrelled when the General was trying to get him released from prison, as one of the conditions of peace with Austria. All La Fayette got from that was an extension of his imprisonment at Olmütz, and that's how this "no favours" cry began. But don't you worry about Madame Adrienne. She's perfectly safe in Holland. And they have plenty of servants there, I've heard.'

'What else have you heard?'

Marie, who knew that this was her cue to retail any gossip she might have heard about the Marquis de La Fayette, reflected for a few minutes before giving her own opinion.

'La Fayette is a fool and I pity his wife. But the ones I blame are the Americans. They buttered him up and made him think himself a great man when he was only a boy, calling him "the Hero of Two Worlds", though the real French hero on the American side was Rochambeau.'

'I know you always said so, dear.'

This placating reply from her friend soothed Marie's own irritation at the criticism of Napoleon, and she permitted herself to close her eyes while Marie-Josèphe's voice babbled on in recollections of the 'good old days' when she and Madame de La Fayette had played with the children in the stately garden of the great house next door – the house where, before it was sealed up as National Property a band of *sans-culottes* and their women had danced the carmagnole, had drunk and rampaged in some of the worst excesses of the Terror. The subject was alarming but the voice was soothing, and Marie yielded to its charm. She dozed off, conscious only of being protected, thinking that it was her Uncle Prosper who sat in the opposite easy chair, waiting for young Captain Bonaparte to come in and join him in a game of chess.

Or thinking that it was Charles who had entered, dressed in the uniform of the National Guard and was stroking her shoulders, until she opened her eyes and saw that the caressing hands belonged to Madame Beauchet, who was telling her she ought to be in bed.

Marie twisted her head round to look at the clock which Prosper Fontaine had brought to Paris from the family home in Brittany.

'I can't go to bed yet, it's not quite eight o'clock.'

'You've been asleep for nearly two hours. You were very tired, Marie, and you'll be much more comfortable in bed. I've had a warming-pan tucked inside it since Professor Guiart told me to expect you. He and Dr Berthollet are coming tomorrow. You ought to have a good night's sleep.'

After this Marie made no more demur, but waited until her friend spent a few minutes in the kitchen, from which she emerged carrying a china jug with a lid which Marie recognized. Her uncle had made hot bedtime drinks for her in that jug, and once, when they were first involved in politics, he had added a soporific.

'What's in there?' she asked rather sharply.

'Only hot milk,' replied Marie-Josèphe. 'With a sprinkle of sugar and nutmeg, that's all. It was hot already. I only had to heat it up on the little paraffin stove.'

'You shouldn't have bothered,' said Marie, but she acquiesced mildly when she was told that if she talked too much she would wake herself up. She accepted the rebuke, the change of candle in its tin holder, and Marie-Josèphe's arm, before they started up to the bedroom of her early years. Decidedly she was over-tired, for she stumbled twice on the narrow wooden stair, but her white room looked like a haven of rest when the door was opened and Marie-Josèphe spread back bed-clothes as white as washing and drying in the fresh air could make them, and watched Marie sit, propped up on pillows, and drink her hot milk. Before she took away the jug she kissed Marie and said, 'Bless you, my dear. Sleep well,' more tenderly than anyone at the Tuileries had ever spoken to her.

Marie had turned on her right side and was drifting off to sleep when her eyes were caught by the wooden door of the wall cupboard which served her as a wardrobe. Instantly she sat up, her heartbeats shaking her breast. In that cupboard, she knew, there was the blue dress which had been made from a gala dress of her mother's before the Revolution, and adapted by herself in 1793 to wear at a supper party in the

Café de la Régence where she and her uncle had been guests of Captain Buonaparte. She remembered, too, that Charles Latour had been in the café that night and according to himself suffering from jealousy.

Most of all she remembered that the last time she had been in that room she had taken out the dress, pored over it and stroked it – 'As I stroked the hyacinth bulbs today,' she said to herself. 'I'm a sentimental fool! I'll never look at the dress again. It isn't fair to Napoleon. It's like the flirting with him and teasing him which led to that horrible scene at the Quai Voltaire. It's got to stop, and when I see him again I'll tell him so. And it's not fair to Charles . . . He's trying so hard to be nice' – without defining what she meant by a schoolgirl word like 'nice'.

Next morning, refreshed, Marie got out of bed, and with a sigh for the marble bath-tub of the Tuileries, she filled the china basin on the washstand with cold water from the ewer and plunged her face into it. When she raised it, groping for a towel, she heard a step on the stair. Could it be Marie-Josèphe, who had promised to call her at half-past seven? But it was only seven o'clock on the Breguet watch, and surely that was a man's tread on the stair. Could it be Professor Guiart?

I must get dressed! she thought, and snatched up her long white silk petticoat from the foot of the bed. A knock fell on the door and she called out to know who was there.

It was not her old friend and teacher: it was her husband. He was smiling. He leaned forward and kissed her cheek.

'Good morning, darling!' he said. 'How fresh you look, and how rested! Dr Berthollet is here with me. Hadn't you better get dressed?'

24

'He's very early,' said Marie, as calmly as she was able. She saw that Charles was excited, and hoped she would not be blamed for it.

'Is Monsieur Boissy d'Anglas all right?' she asked.

'Ah, you're taking a leaf out of Napoleon's book – pretending to be concerned about the health of a revolutionary – a man who voted in Convention for the King's death. Napoleon would vote for the Devil if he thought it would give him a commanding vote in his infernal plebiscite. Come on now, Marie, hurry up and get a dress on! Where do you keep your clothes – in here?'

He was inside the bedroom, he had pulled open the cupboard door and Marie caught a glimpse of blue muslin, the relic of that summer night of which she had been thinking so fondly, now hanging next to the white overall she proposed to wear that day. She lunged forward and grabbed at the overall just as Charles was about to shut the cupboard door.

'Going to be all dressed up for the day's work?' he said, cocking an eyebrow at the overall.

'I always did in Cairo, remember?' Charles had the grace to flush; he hated anything which seemed like a reminder of his bad behaviour in Cairo, and Marie soothed him by saying he was 'all dressed up' himself.

Charles was looking well. He wore the scarlet and white sash of an ADC to General Bonaparte and the Cross of the Legion of Honour, which the latter had bestowed, and these adornments were worn on an unfamiliar green tunic, from one pocket of which protruded a copy of the *Moniteur*.

'Oh, you good boy, you brought me a copy of the paper!' exulted Marie.

'I knew you wanted to read about the future Viceroy of Italy,' said Charles, and he looked on smiling while Marie read the three columns on page one which extolled the merits of Eugène de Beauharnais, 'the Son of France'.

'I must say you take it more quietly than the Bonaparte girls do,' said Charles.

'Do they know about it?'

'They heard about it last night. When I reached the Tuileries, the Emperor's loving sisters followed him at dinner time, prepared to eat a sumptuous meal and start a row.'

'Caroline Murat has a vicious tongue.'

'She has indeed, and I didn't like the way she was using it on you.'

'On me? What have I done to offend *la grande Caroline*?'

'I don't know, unless she's jealous because Joséphine means to give you a present.'

'A present? What present?'

'I think she'd like to tell you that herself. But when Caroline heard of it she sniffed and said, "How pleased Napoleon will be!" as if there was some secret understanding between you and him – but there isn't, is there, darling?'

It was such a change from his usual manner, which would have been to accuse her of any form of complicity with Napoleon, that Marie boldly replied, 'Of course there isn't!' and kissed him. She said, 'If you approve of this mysterious present, it's all right. I don't give a fig for Caroline Murat.'

But she did; she cared a great deal. The other woman's malice had opened her eyes to the fact that – close as her friendship with Napoleon had been in Egypt – now was the first time it could have been made a subject for gossip, and in spite of the rumours which linked Napoleon's name with various actresses she minded the gossip much more for his sake than she did for her own.

She had not heard footsteps on the stairs, and though she

244

had been alert enough to the business of the day to pull on yesterday's warm black dress, and then the white overall of her work, she started when she heard a heavy knock on the door.

'I bet you that's Berthollet,' Charles said.

It was certainly Dr Berthollet, cheerful and bluff, looking much better than when Marie said goodbye to him in Corsica, and he had shown all the strain of service in Egypt. He told her she was looking well too and answered her questions about the health of Monsieur Boissy d'Anglas.

'I've had another patient since then,' he said. 'I've just come from the Tuileries.'

'Not Joséphine?'

'Thank you, Marie! I can call Napoleon "sire" but I can't get my tongue round "Her Majesty"! No, not Joséphine, although she called us in. The patient was her daughter, Madame Louis Bonaparte.'

'Oh dear, she wasn't well yesterday. Has her husband come?'

'No, and I've forbidden all visitors except her mother and her brother until she's had a week's bed rest. Now then, my dear, we must get on. We've a lot to get through if you're to revise all you were taught and get quite up-to-date.'

'I'll see you downstairs, then,' said Charles. 'Your friend promised me some coffee, dear, and I haven't had any breakfast.'

He doesn't mean to whine, thought Marie. He called me 'dear' because he's still trying to be nice. But as her husband started downstairs she heard the doctor mutter, 'Same old Charles!' and was not reassured.

Marie, Dr Berthollet and, later, Professor Guiart worked all day on Marie's plans to revise and up-date her knowledge in the eventual hope of bringing health care to the people of Vesle.

Towards the end of the afternoon a message came from Joséphine entreating Marie to return to the Tuileries.

'You have to go,' Berthollet told Marie. 'You'll be back in forty-eight hours, if that's what you want. But your place is at the palace now. You are a true friend of her – um – of Madame Bonaparte.'

'Is the Emperor going to the Channel coast after all?' said Marie.

'La Tour can tell you more about his plans than I can.'

'Charles has had no time to tell me anything yet.' And by the doctor's silence she gathered that he thought this was no bad thing, and wondered if Napoleon's command of the force he had meant to use against England, how called the *Grande Armée*, meant that the resumption of war in Europe would be included in his plans. She thought of the days of Marengo, and she shivered. Then she remembered the coronation, and relaxed. There was that much of breathing space – Napoleon would not risk any new military adventure until the crown was safely on his head.

Eugène de Beauharnais was sitting with his sister. Eugène and Marie had served together in Egypt, and before that they had shared his mother's home in Paris. She knew congratulations were in order and, dropping a formal curtsy, said with a smile, 'Sir, may I congratulate the future Viceroy of Italy on his latest and well-deserved honour?'

'Thank you, dear Marie,' said the young man. 'Hortense, don't you wish any of Maman's ladies could turn a compliment as gracefully as that?'

'They couldn't,' his sister asserted, putting her hot little hands in Marie's.

'Well, goodbye, girls, don't talk too much,' said Eugène, kissing his sister's cheek and Marie's hand. 'Here comes Agathe to show me out.'

'And to tell you not to talk so loud,' said Agathe sharply. 'I've just been in to dress my lady and found she had dropped off to sleep –'

'Then don't wake her,' said Marie. 'She needs rest as much as Hortense does. I'm sure the doctor would say –'

'She was agitated this morning and she was counting on a long talk with you,' said her daughter.

'What "agitated" her?'

'It was a letter from Joseph Bonaparte.'

'Who always irritates her. What had Joseph to say?'

'Oh – oh Marie – it's so monstrous I don't know how to tell you. He claims to have heard from a – a correspondent – that there's a rumour going about in Rome that the Pope may refuse to proceed with the coronation.'

'But *why*, Hortense? Why?'

'Because Bonaparte didn't marry my mother in the Church.'

'But they were married during the Revolution, when nobody could be married in the Church! It was Napoleon himself who brought France back to the Church when he signed the Concordat with this very Pope who now wants to punish him!'

'That's what he told my mother – he was shouting so loud I couldn't help hearing, while they were having coffee this morning. He was in a rage, he said he wouldn't go through the farce of a religious ceremony, as she wanted, with the woman who was his lawful wife before God and man, and then my mother began to cry.'

But she'll wheedle him through it, she always does, Marie thought, and set herself to make Hortense believe that all would be well, that either the Pope would relent or Napoleon would do as his wife and common sense dictated – so that Hortense, lulled by her voice, was nearly asleep when Agathe came in, and Marie could step out with nothing more melo-dramatic than, '*Bonne nuit, ma chérie.*'

She ascended the staircase mechanically. She wanted to avoid an encounter with any of the denizens of the Tuileries, although there was a sound of knives and forks from the grand dining room and she could picture the sumptuous repast being served therein. She looked over the baluster, down the expanse of the grand hall. The greatest soldier of his era had filled it with the paintings and statuary of a conti-nent, but then artifacts meant nothing to him in a home degraded by rancour and jealousy, where his own secret police spied on him and his own brothers and sisters regarded him merely as the purveyor of lands and titles, jewels and incomes, without any return of affection on their side. Although she had told Hortense to stop crying, Marie herself was in tears before she reached the top of the stairs.

Matters looked a little better in the morning. Napoleon's mother, Madame Mère, had paid an early visit to the Tuileries, and had expressed a wish to see Marie in the library. Wondering greatly, Marie set out for the room where nobody ever went except the master of the house, and where she half expected to find him. But the book-lined room was empty except for his mother who swooped on Marie before she had time to curtsy, and embraced her.

'Dear child!' she exclaimed in her impulsive fashion. 'I was determined to see you before I went away!'

'Where are you going, *chère madame*?' said Marie, astounded.

'To Rome, to visit my son Lucien.'

To visit the Pope. To make sure the Pope would not go back on his promise to crown Napoleon, Marie thought.

'I have always felt it my duty to be with whichever one of my children needs me most,' Napoleon's mother continued. 'At present I think it is Lucien. You have probably heard that he is out of favour with Napoleon?'

Lucien Bonaparte had been his brother's chief support throughout the *coup d'état* and his departure, when he became a widower, to live in Italy and study agriculture, had sent a babble of speculation through the Tuileries. Marie did not hesitate to blame the chief of the rumour-mongers. 'I've heard Madame Murat mention it,' she said, and heard what sounded like a muttered, 'Of course!' corrected to: 'The Emperor has a hasty temper, he gets it from me. He was displeased when Lucien declined to pay his addresses to the Queen of Württemberg and declared he would marry to please himself as Napoleon had done. As you did too, Marie; how is your dear Charles?'

Marie welcomed the change of subject, for she disliked the involvement in Bonaparte gossip. And a few minutes later 'dear Charles' appeared himself with a message from the Emperor: would it inconvenience the Emperor's mother to come downstairs and bid the Court goodbye?

25

'Did Madame Hortense have a good night, Agathe? Dr Berthollet says I may see her if she did.' Marie smiled, forcing the grave-faced maid to smile in return.

'Yes you may, you'll do her good. Monsieur Eugène was here and he excited her, they were laughing and crying and I don't know what all . . .' Agathe's complaints tailed off into silence as Marie slipped into the bedroom and embraced Hortense.

'How are you today, my poor dear?'

'Better – much better, thank you. The doctor is very pleased. And oh, Marie, I've had such wonderful news!'

'About what?'

'Eugène's marriage.'

'To someone he knows, I hope?'

'Not yet; they've never met. But the Emperor says she's beautiful and perfectly charming; it's the Elector of Bavaria's daughter, the Princess Augusta Amelia.'

'How does Eugène feel about it?'

'He wants to please the Emperor, of course – and he has heard so many good things of the young lady that he feels sure they will be happy. But Maman is vexed because she wasn't consulted. They had another row about it last night. Oh, Marie, I do wish they were getting on better!'

The appearance of two footmen with breakfast on a wheeled table permitted Marie to say she must go to look for Charles, with whom she had promised to have breakfast, and would come back to the palace when the morning's work at the pharmacy was complete.

Halfway to the dining room Marie's mind, usually so vigorous, arrested itself, and she realized that she was heading in the wrong direction. She had been disorientated by Eugène's news, not so much by the news itself as by his calm acceptance of Bonaparte's right to arbitrate in what should be a man's most private concern, and to decide Eugène's fate as he had already decided his sister's. That sister, whose sweet acceptance of the situation had been touching, had revealed the truth of the saying that every man had his price. Was the viceroyalty of Italy Eugène's price? Hortense had implied as much when she said that Eugène 'wanted to please the Emperor'.

A kind of chill was creeping over Marie, imaginary but so realistic that she almost cried aloud when her cold cheeks were warmed by two strong hands laid across her eyes, but she suppressed the cry, for there was something familiar in the touch of those hands, some harmony of the flesh not felt since the early days of her marriage, so that all she said was, 'Charles! Where have you been?' She let her body relax as she felt his arms go round her, and looked up into his laughing face.

'Where have *I* been? I like that! Where have *you* been, madame? I come back from a long exhausting ride on duty, all eagerness to find my wife, and that pompous majordomo tells me you are closeted with Madame Hortense. So of course a mere male knows better than to interrupt the pretty feminine gossip, so I hang about and wait, and then there you come charging along with your eyes set on something I can't see – '

'Oh, Charles, don't tease me! I was looking for you, looking everywhere, because I want so much to have a talk with you. A serious talk, I mean, and now you only want to tease me and make fun of me – '

'That's not true,' said Charles. 'I'm not making fun of you, but I do think you need to calm down. Why didn't you wait for me up in our room? That's where I went to look for you! It's private, just the right place for a serious talk.'

'I'm sick of waiting up in our room when I don't know what's going to happen – '

Charles heard the catch in her breath and realized that Marie was on the verge of tears. He said hastily, 'Let's sit down here for a few minutes and you can tell me what the trouble is.'

With his hand on her elbow, he guided Marie into one of the 'intimate corners' with which Joséphine had attempted to soften the harsh outlines of the Tuileries. A pair of grey velvet sofas had been placed at right angles to each other, enclosing a low table on which a crystal bowl of scented violets stood between two lighted candles. It was a place for courtship or for confidences, so evocative of the woman who had devised it.

'Charles dear, it was about Napoleon I wanted to consult you. I wanted you to explain something I overheard him say last night and didn't understand.'

In his teasing mood he might have tried to be funny, but he was sensible enough to ask seriously what she wanted to know, and was amazed when Marie answered, 'What is a plebiscite?'

'When did you hear him talking about the plebiscite?' said Charles sharply.

'To Monsieur Cambacérès, when we were all coming down the stairs last night. "You'll have to organize the plebiscite," he said. What did he mean?'

'In plain, or if you prefer it, in vulgar language, he means "Organize the vote!" Our great general, like every parvenu, doesn't want to miss his promotion. He wants every man in France to vote yes to the proposition that France should be ruled by an emperor, who shall be Napoleon Bonaparte.'

This began the most serious quarrel they had ever had. Not even at the time of his flagrant infidelity in Cairo, when Marie had ordered him out of her rooms and out of her life, had she and her husband exchanged so many bitter words. She was furious at his dismissal of Napoleon's concern for the plebiscite vote as the attitude of a paranoid, a parvenu who wished to be invested with the powers of a dictator, and said whatever the system of voting was called she believed that every man in France would vote for him. To this Charles retorted that such a landslide vote was quite unlikely, because 'everyone is not so infatuated with Bonaparte as you are!'

The vicious little scene ended when Charles escorted his wife to their room, bowed her in and slammed the door upon her. She went to the pharmacy alone and did not see him again that day. She had no idea where he spent the night, nor did she care.

She was amazed, next morning, when she answered *'Entrez!'* to a knock on the door, supposing it to announce the maid, and behold!, it was Charles again.

'I don't wish to continue kicking my heels around the palace,' he said, 'so I am going to join Murat in marching with the *Grande Armée* and serving in the training scheme he has devised for them on their journey to the east.'

'Towards Austria?' said Marie.

'Who knows. What are your plans, madame?'

She had lain awake half the night wondering where to go and what to do. There was no trace of those irresolute hours in the steady voice which said, 'That will depend on the doctors. If they agree, I should like to continue my work at the Pharmacie Fontaine.'

'I'm sure the doctors will approve of such a noble resolution. Speaking as a mere husband, might I ask you to consider a change of venue?'

'What do you mean?'

'I know all the advantages of the Pharmacie. A well-equipped labo, a promising colleague-cum-housekeeper ... but you could have the labo *and* Marie-Josèphe if you would live in our own home and make sure it doesn't collapse from sheer neglect.'

'Live at the Quai Voltaire? If that's what you would like, I'm sure I could arrange to do it,' said Marie. 'After all, it's only a few minutes' walk from the pharmacy.'

'Thank you, Marie.' He was smiling and she knew that she was smiling too. They had arrived at a compromise: one of the string of compromises which their marriage had been, and they sealed it, not with a kiss but with a handshake before the Marquis de la Tour, ADC to His Majesty, went off to war again.

After that bleak beginning to the day Marie's attempts to go back to sleep were in vain. She wrapped the quilt around her in a pretence of comfort and lay still, listening to the familiar sounds of the awakening palace until she heard a sound which was not familiar. It came from Napoleon's study, but it was not the voice of Napoleon. It was the voice of a woman, and it was calling for help.

'*Au secours! Au secours!*' The cries were so imperative that Marie got up and put on her dressing gown and slippers before it occurred to her that Bonaparte was involved in one of the adventures which were often whispered about in the Tuileries. Madame Grassini or Mademoiselle Georges had often shared his bed. The latter had on one occasion called for help when she had been terrified by her august lover's fainting-fit, and Marie decided that this was another such episode in which she must not interfere . . . until the imperative cry rang out again. It was the voice of the Empress, wailing, 'I can't get out!'

In a few minutes Marie was standing outside the door of Napoleon's study, from which the mameluke bodyguard had disappeared. Inside, the voice of Joséphine was still wailing, 'I can't get out.' Had Constant, the Emperor's valet, gone mad to constrain the Empress? Or had they all gone mad together? At any rate there was a sane explanation for that cry of, 'I can't get out!' The study door, left unguarded, was locked on the outside.

'Joséphine! What's the matter? Are you all right?' Marie was aware that something was terribly wrong, and that her questions, while no more foolish than anyone would have asked, were singularly unhelpful. Except that the mere sound of her voice was an encouragement to Joséphine.

'Marie, is it *you*? Help me, for heaven's sake! Call the guard – call the servants. Tell them their Empress is a prisoner – and in danger of her life . . .'

She heard the note of hysteria in Joséphine's voice, as she turned the handle of the door and flung it open with such force that she almost overset Joséphine, who was standing close behind it, utterly unlike herself, dressed in an assortment of grey chiffon scarves which gave her the impression of being in disguise. Her face was red and swollen and so were her upper arms, the right held in the tight clasp of Constant.

'Marie, tell this man to let me go!' she panted.

And he exclaimed: 'Madame had better tell me to send for the police! Do you know where I found this woman? Rummaging in the Emperor's desk and reading his private letters! And not the first time, either!'

'He's lying, Marie! I can explain everything!' sobbed the hysterical woman.

'Then come with me and calm yourself,' said Marie. She was horrified, but she put an arm round her friend and led her away.

Back in Marie's room the maid stared round-eyed to see the Empress, bathed in tears, clinging to the arm of the young marchioness, but she was prompt to obey when Marie sent her into the bathroom to heat a cup of milk on a little spirit stove, and gratified when she saw Joséphine sipping the hot drink as daintily as a Persian cat. When she was finally dismissed Marie asked the all-important question, how much truth was there in the valet's accusation that he had caught her rummaging in his master's desk? When the Empress replied, as before, that it was all a pack of lies, she replied coldly, 'Then you had better tell the truth, my dear, for Constant will get in first with his story, and the Emperor may prefer *his* version!'

To which Joséphine replied, 'The Emperor will dismiss that man from his service when he sees this –' and she drew the rags of grey chiffon from her arm, which the marks of Constant's fingers had made an angry red. She burst into wails of justification. She had only wanted to read Joseph's letter, addressed to herself as well as to Napoleon, from the French Embassy at Rome, and stating firmly that Pope Pius VII had again said he could not perform the coronation ceremony unless the Emperor and his 'concubine' were married in church. To which Napoleon had replied, 'Tell the Pope that if he's not here by 2 December, ready to crown me Emperor of the French, we'll go ahead and have the coronation without him!'

'So unreasonable of my husband,' said Joséphine, 'when his Uncle Fesch, whom he made a cardinal, is here in the Tuileries ready to perform a simple ceremony!'

'But the Emperor thinks your 1796 marriage was perfectly legal, and I appreciate his point of view,' said Marie, to which Joséphine rejoined, with a touch of malice in her voice, 'Oh yes, you always do, don't you? Marie, why don't *you* reason with him? You promised to do anything I asked you – why don't you tell him my point of view?'

'This is a very delicate matter. I feel I ought not to interfere in it . . .'

But Joséphine insisted on her promise, and Marie finally gave in. At three in the afternoon she was ushered into Napoleon's study by his secretary, curtsied and felt his cold lips on her hand.

'How are you, Marie? You had a disagreeable experience this morning, I was sorry to hear . . .'

'Not I, but Joséphine, on whose behalf I have come now.'

'To ask me to dismiss Constant from my service?'

'No. I didn't think you would do that, even if you saw her arm.'

'Oh, I have seen it – very regrettable, of course, but Constant is a valuable man. I've sent him to St Cloud to take full charge of my private apartments there. I hope that will satisfy my wife.'

'Forgive me, sire, but that was not my errand. Her Majesty thought herself quite entitled to examine Monsieur Joseph Bonaparte's letter, since it was addressed to herself. She feels you should yield to the Pope's wish for a religious wedding before the coronation, and – oh sire, I think she's right!'

'You know nothing about it,' the hard voice said. 'How can

256

a girl like you understand a man's feelings of resentment at being coerced into a second marriage, revoking the first, which was perfectly legal according to the laws of the Revolution – '

'Which you yourself revoked when you insisted on the Concordat.'

'You argue well, Marie,' said Napoleon. 'And I think you're very kind to Joséphine. Kinder than she sometimes is to you.'

'I love Joséphine,' said Marie. 'I told you why when you and I met in Corsica. It's still true and worth repeating. We were in prison together and when we were released she gave me a home when I was homeless and was a friend when I was friendless . . . isn't that enough?'

'Very good,' said Napoleon, 'and have I no share in your boundless charity?'

'You know you have,' said Marie. 'I have agonized over your plebiscite, and hoped it would turn out well . . .'

'You haven't seen today's *Moniteur*,' said Napoleon. 'The voters expressed their wish to see me crowned Emperor of the French by a majority of three million to two thousand votes. Convincing?'

He had known she would be pleased, he had not been prepared for the intensity of joy which made Marie clap her hands before she threw them round his neck and pressed her lips to his. 'Wonderful!' she cried. 'Now no one can possibly call himself "the new Napoleon".'

'Who would dare?'

'Some of the men who are jealous of you – Moreau, or Bernadotte, or that vile man in Ghent, Laguerre or whatever his name is, who poor d'Enghien got out of your way before he died . . .'

'I have already expressed my regrets for d'Enghien's death,' said Bonaparte coldly. 'It was a misunderstanding – a sad miscarriage of justice. But, Marie my dear, if you feel so strongly about me, why don't you give me some proof? Why don't you let me love you, in the flesh as in the spirit? Please?'

'It isn't possible,' she said, with the emphasis he knew too well. 'In my heart you will always be my love. But you are my friend's husband and I am Charles de la Tour's wife. We are going back to Vesle the day after we have seen you crowned Emperor of the French.'

When Napoleon and Joséphine appeared in the courtyard of the Tuileries in the morning of the second day of December 1804 there was no sign of the argument and dissension which had long marked their relationship. They were attended by his brother Joseph, who had arrived from Rome on the previous day together with the Pope, now housed in the palace of Fontainebleau with Joséphine as his hostess, immensely gratified when Pius VII called her 'my daughter' though surprised that he believed her name to be Victoria. She told Marie that His Holiness had approved the certificate of legality of her religious marriage, which she had obtained from Cardinal Fesch. There were now no barriers to the Pope's officiating at the coronation, though several important points were still unresolved.

The first of these was the succession to the imperial title and dignities. Napoleon's landslide victory in the plebiscite had confirmed his control of the succession, and Joseph Bonaparte, as the eldest of the family, believed it should be conferred upon himself. But the man who was about to be crowned emperor believed Joseph should feel sufficiently honoured with the title of 'Prince' and the glory of bearing his own imperial mantle along with Prince Louis, while Joséphine was fuming because her grandson, little Napoleon-Charles, was banned from the succession because his mother, Hortense, had refused to give him up to his uncle's adoption.

Marie, who was driving to the Cathedral of Notre-Dame along with her husband, rejoiced that Hortense had refused to consider such an adoption. If it had taken place, she thought, there would have been no end to the slander that Napoleon was really the child's father – and perhaps the next child's too. Poor Prince Louis, in spite of his wrecked health, had lost no time in making Hortense pregnant again, and now his own ambitions, and Joseph's, were unlikely to be satisfied without a royal litter, for Napoleon had promised to create him King of Holland. At the thought of her friend Hortense as a queen, a beautiful smile lit up Marie's face, so that Charles, who had been watching her, told her she was as lovely as she had been on their wedding day.

Marie blushed with pleasure. Her wedding dress of white satin had been cleaned and pressed for the present occasion, and she wore her grandmother's parure of seed pearls. Excitement had heightened her colour, and she told Charles that Madame Murat had been very gracious, and had even said she looked 'quite nice'.

'Impossible woman!' was Charles's verdict on Napoleon's sister. 'She's got above herself since he was made a Marshal of France and will carry the imperial crown today. No, but I thought you looked tired when I came back, and I can't wait to get you home to Vesle tomorrow. And I'm so glad your friend is coming with us – I told her so.'

'That was nice of you, Charles. I was afraid she'd want to go to Madame de La Fayette, but Vesle won out . . . and we'll make it the healthiest village in the Department, won't we, dear?'

'Whatever you say, madame.'

At Napoleon's orders all the area round the cathedral, one of the oldest parts of Paris, had been cleaned and refurbished for the coronation. Years of soot had been washed from the stonework, streets and cobblestones had been swept and sanded, tumbledown tenements had been shored up. Statues of Charlemagne and St Denis had been added to the outside, and high over all was the oriflamme, the banner which the Capetian kings had borne in battle, along with the Tricolore, the national flag for ever associated with the victories of Bonaparte. The Pope had already passed that way, and the man he was to crown looked out with satisfaction on the immaculate streets. 'We won't hear so much about the dirt on his white satin slippers,' he remarked to Joséphine. He had been irked by the Pontiff's complaints about the mud he stepped into in the forest of Fontainebleau.

This was almost the only remark he addressed to his wife in the last stage of their journey, before he gave her his hand and led her into the cathedral. Joséphine was less assertive than usual, as if the sight of her husband in his regal dress had given her a new idea of his personality. Napoleon wore a golden circlet of laurel leaves on his head and a tunic and short cloak in what was known as *le style troubadour*, and he had encumbered himself with the massive sword of Charlemagne. It was the only relic of the great man which he had been able to borrow ... the other essentials of a coronation service had been bought from other churches and museums and paid for by himself. The cathedral, filled with his own officers, and military and civilian representatives of foreign powers, buzzed with interest as he and his wife took their places on two thrones – not side by side, but hers on a lower elevation than his own – from which his keen gaze swept the brilliant company as he was accustomed to survey a battlefield.

Only one other man was as intent upon the scene as he was, and that was the artist Jacques Louis David who had been commissioned to record the coronation for posterity and who was planning to falsify the facts by including a portrait of Napoleon's mother, who was not present.

General Bonaparte had planned his coronation as carefully as he planned his victories. He intended to win a great victory over the Austrians and their allies in a matter of days, and he had ordered Marshal Murat to meet him at a place called Austerlitz with this in view, but meantime he was in Notre-Dame, and he had ordered Isabey, the artist, to prepare a number of sketches of the interior of the cathedral so that he might know where everybody would be at any given moment. Isabey had done better: he had procured, and dressed, a number of tiny dolls and arranged them in a series of stage scenes which had been exhibited in Napoleon's study at the Tuileries. Marie had been privileged to see them there without any idea that she herself was the cause of all this trouble; that Isabey's work had been carried out so that Napoleon should be kept informed of her exact whereabouts.

A place had been reserved for her in one of the lighted galleries above the nave, where a chandelier holding twenty wax candles illuminated her golden hair and her shimmering white satin dress. On her wedding day she had worn a coronet of white roses; Napoleon on the day of his coronation wished that she wore these still. Then, looking towards his wife, he saw the diadem which the court jewellers had made as the crown matrimonial, and as the voices of the choristers swelled in yet another anthem, his eyes travelled to Joséphine's lovely face. He thought of their early days, when that face had been transfigured by the passion which flattered him. He had loved her then, and now he was mastered by this later passion for the girl he still thought of as Marie Fontaine. He remembered her, his true love, in her first-aid post beside the Seine, and again when her skill was at the service of his soldiers in their hospitals beside the Nile – always led by the quixotic impulse, which was now taking her away from him to go with her jackanapes of a husband to serve a bunch of peasants at Vesle . . .

He saw that Joséphine had risen from her chair of state and was walking, attended by two pages, towards the centre of the aisle. He made as to accompany her. They were to kneel together before the altar.

Now came the moment which had been the cause of so much bickering, the carrying of Joséphine's train. He risked turning his head slightly and saw that his three sisters were smiling at his wife – at least they had condescended so far! And then they clustered together to make way for Marie. She approached from the side, curtsied to Joséphine and picked up a corner of the imperial robe which had been placed around her shoulders. Hortense took the other corner and Joseph's wife, Julie, laid a hand on the hem. Thus apparelled and attended, Joséphine returned to kneel beside Napoleon in front of the Pope.

They were now the centre of an important group both kneeling and standing: Murat holding the imperial crown on a velvet cushion; Joseph, Louis, the brothers; Cambacérès and Lebrun, the tribunes; while the women attendants slipped away, Napoleon's robe was placed on the altar with the various items of the regalia. While the litany was sung the Pope anointed the Emperor and his wife with the triple unction on head and hands. Then Napoleon took the imperial crown and placed it on his own head. While Joséphine kneeled before him with clasped hands he placed the crown matrimonial upon her head.

He had not expected to be pursued by images from his past. He had intended to enjoy every moment of his present, every triumphant moment of his coronation. That a penniless boy from Corsica should ascend the throne of Charlemagne was a miracle in itself, and he longed for the one person who could have savoured it with him – his mother – to be present in the cathedral. He remembered sitting by her fireside while she told him stories – legends from the past which inspired him. He remembered telling Marie Fontaine – who was shocked but sympathetic – that he found the crown of France in the gutter and picked it up on the point of his sword.

He remembered what he had once said was the proudest moment of his life, when he was gazetted a lieutenant of artillery and commanded troops.

That day, too, he had lacked someone to share the moment and to praise him. And he had felt the same absence today as he stood with Joseph, both arrayed in finery and pride, and said to his brother: 'Oh Joseph, if only Father could see us now! I think he would have been proud of me.'

Carlo Bonaparte had never paid much attention to his younger children, but, thought his son, he was a good father to me, he took pains with me, he took me to school at Brienne to learn French, and now I'm Emperor of the French. I would have tried to be as good a father, but I have no child.

Then the pair proceeded down the nave and ascended the twenty-four steps leading to the great throne set on a dais.

There the Pope blessed them with the words: 'May God confirm you upon this throne, and may Christ cause you to reign with him in his eternal Kingdom.' He kissed Napoleon upon the cheek and added the words used at the coronation of Charlemagne: '*Vivat Imperator in aeternum*. May the Emperor live for ever.'

Napoleon's eyes sought out Marie. He was nearer to her than before and by candlelight he could see tears on her cheeks. He remembered the story she had told at Vesle of 'one candle burning' and prayed that light might shine upon all her days. He knew that she was praying for himself, for he remembered what she had said at the Tuileries and he saw her lips moving in the same words.

'May the Emperor live for ever – in my heart.'